TOUCH OF FROST

WINTER'S QUEEN BOOK 1

JENNIFER ALLIS PROVOST

CONTENTS

WINTER IS COMING

I lead an interesting life, and I am by far the least interesting part about it. Let me explain.

I'm a run-of-the-mill white guy with a Ph.D. in Shakespeare. My sister, the geologist, loves to point out how impractical my degree is. Because of said impractical degree, I work as an English professor at Carson University, and I do some writing on the side. My third novel, *Bones of the Bard,* was about none other than Shakespeare himself. That book became a worldwide bestseller, and now I'm putting the finishing touches on my fourth book. It's all about Shakespeare's wife, and the working title is *Second Best Bed.*

There. You now know the most remarkable facts about me. Everything I tell you from here on out is about other people.

When I was in my early thirties, I found myself in a relationship with one of my students. Her name was Olivia, and she had gorgeous dark hair and eyes, and was one of the most brilliant people I've ever encountered. Yes, dating a student was a bad idea, but we were in love; well, I was in love. Her, not so much. A few months after we got engaged, she left me. That worldwide bestseller I mentioned earlier? She claimed she had written it and sued me for plagiarism.

Like I said, dating a student was a bad idea.

As it turned out, Olivia wasn't just witty, beautiful, and evil. She was a *leanan sith,* a type of fairy that latched onto creative people and sucked their inspiration dry, much like a vampire drains its victims of blood. I learned this when my sister, Rina—her name is actually Karina, but I've called her Rina since she was a baby—and I went to Scotland to avoid the inevitable scandal brought on by the plagiarism lawsuit. While we were in Scotland, I fell under the spell of Nicnevin, the Seelie Queen, while Rina got involved with Robert Kirk, a legendary fairy assassin called the gallowglass.

That was not what either of us had expected to happen on our vacation.

Rina ended up rescuing Rob and me from Nicnevin's influence, and the three of us went back to New York. After a few wonderfully uneventful months, we ran afoul of a few Greek deities, Rina and Rob announced they were expecting, and I met one of Rina's students and fell for her, head over heels. That student was also a supernatural creature, because of course she was.

Her name was Anya, and she was perfect.

Embarking on a second relationship with a student had to be an even worse idea, right? But Anya and Olivia were as different as night and day. Anya was fierce, and loyal, with a sharp mind and, when she got angry, even sharper claws. Anya wasn't a fairy per se, though she did have pointed ears and slanted, iridescent gray eyes. She was the daughter of Beira, the Queen of Winter, and a giant called the Bodach, which made Anya a power in her own right. Also, she wasn't evil like Olivia, and that was a definite plus.

The two of us shared a few more supernatural adventures that ended up with Beira being exiled, and Anya was declared the new Queen of Winter. Her reign was slated to begin in a few short weeks.

In Scotland, winter ruled for half the year, from October thirty-first until May first, Samhain to Beltane. In the old days the Queen of Winter would battle the Summer King on the aforementioned holidays for the right to rule, but Anya claimed that it wasn't done that way any longer, mostly because the Summer King had gone missing long ago. Now Anya and the Seelie King, Fionnlagh, would turn the wheel of the year together, which was one less thing to worry about.

Even though Anya wouldn't need to engage in battle with the Seelie, her anxiety over coming into her power was plain. Worse, I had no idea how to help her; no one did, since Beira had reigned over the cold season for longer than anyone could remember. With her mother's continued exile, Anya had only her memories to guide her. I worried the coming tasks would overwhelm her—but I had a memory of my own to guide me.

My mother had suffered from recurring bouts of anxiety. I remembered incidents from when I was very young; the smallest details could spark an attack, and sometimes she'd get so low she wouldn't leave her bed for days at a time. Then Rina came along, and Dad formulated a plan to beat Mom's demons. He started us all on a rigorous daily schedule that ran from breakfast to a post-dinner walk. Dad's theory had been simple: if Mom kept busy, she wouldn't have time to worry. His plan worked, and it wasn't long before Mom was laughing again.

I'm going to use the same plan with Anya. We're going to eat at fine restaurants, explore museums and antique markets, and use up every moment of time we can. Winter's coming, and we couldn't stop it even if we wanted to. No use worrying over it.

ANTIQUING

I adored Glasgow in the summer.

In truth, I adored Glasgow all the year 'round, but summer was different. The heat imbued a new vibrancy into the already bustling city, and the people responded in kind. There were outdoor concerts, and markets, and a myriad of other ways to soak up the sunlight. We still had our fair share of rain, but this was Scotland. Anyone who went out without an umbrella deserved whatever drenching they got.

Not that I'd been taking advantage of summer's lazy days. Even as the season warmed, my new affinity for the cold made itself known, loudly and often. At first I only experienced the odd chill, but before long my food cooled as soon as it was set before me, and the ice in my drink never melted. Last week Christopher and I went to our favorite coffee shop, and I froze a cup of tea with my breath. I hadn't set foot outside the flat since. Instead, I sat on the sofa, or sometimes on one of the many window seats, and watched others live their lives. If I endured much more of this frigid isolation, I'd be as mad as my mother.

"Hey." Christopher sat beside me and kissed my cheek. Today I was on the front window seat watching the birds fly past our building. "It's a beautiful day. Want to go antiquing?"

"Antiquing?" He'd noticed I'd been inside for a week, and had graciously refrained from mentioning it. Until now, that is.

"You know, shopping for vintage furniture and artwork."

"Don't we already have enough things in our flat?"

"It's not about buying so much as browsing," he replied. I didn't see the point of going shopping without intending at least one purchase, but Christopher so loved the local markets. He was also trying to help me in his own kind, gentle way.

"Perhaps we could take a stroll past the university," I said. I'd been encouraging him to seek employment in his chosen field of teaching, and utterly failing. "Do you think they've looked over your credentials?"

"Whether they have or not, I doubt they do much hiring on the weekend," Christopher replied. "That's one of the reasons antiquing is the ideal Saturday activity. Afterward, we can stop by that coffee shop you like."

"Will you buy me a sweet?" I asked. "As long as it's not ice cream."

He laughed. "You got it, beautiful. No ice cream."

"Anya, what are you doing?"

"Hmm?"

I glanced up from the rime of ice I'd created on a warped glass cabinet front. We were at yet another antique market, the third we'd found that day, and Christopher was hunting for treasures amid others' cast-offs. Antiquing was his favorite weekend hobby. As for me, I preferred sleeping late, followed by a hearty breakfast.

I also preferred having control of my abilities. I hadn't meant to freeze the cabinet door, just as I hadn't meant to frost the crystal pitcher one aisle back, or ice over the lovely reclaimed stained glass window depicting Saint Mungo and the robin. The cold was flowing out of me unchecked, rolling across everything I touched and leaving scars in its wake. Here I was on the hottest day of summer, freezing all I touched.

I heard a ping. The glass window was cracking. I had to leave this place before something horrible happened.

Christopher peeked over my shoulder at the design I'd created. "Pretty," he said. I wonder what he would say if he knew about the rest of my handiwork, scattered among the market stalls. "Have you seen anything that might be a good present for the baby?"

The babe in question was the one his sister, Karina, was due to have within a month or so. He'd already purchased many gifts for the bairn, yet he was always on the lookout for more.

"Really, Christopher, what could be suitable for a bairn here?" I gestured to encompass the lot of dusty furniture and moldering books and fabrics.

"I thought we might find a rock specimen, or maybe a fossil," he replied.

"Those sound like presents for your sister," I said, and he didn't disagree. Karina was a geologist, and her home was filled with odd rocks and stones she found in and around Crail. "I don't think you'll find anything like that in this poor excuse for a market. These aren't even proper antiques."

"How so?"

"I'm the oldest thing here."

A crooked smile that went straight to my heart. "You're bored, aren't you?"

"A wee bit," I admitted, though I was far more terrified than bored. I heard the cracks deepen in the glass behind me, and shifted so my body blocked his view of the cabinet.

"All right." He tucked my hand into his elbow, and we walked toward the exit. "What would you like to do for the rest of the day?"

"Perhaps we can take a walk?" I glanced over my shoulder, and saw rows and rows of merchants finding shattered, frozen glass. One yelled something about youths vandalizing their wares, but it hadn't been a youth. It had been me.

"What's going on back there?" Christopher wondered, craning his neck for a better look.

"I'm sure it's nothing," I said, steering him away from the destruction. "I'm in the mood for a hot cup of tea. You?"

"Sounds wonderful."

I pushed the door open, ignoring the frozen handprint I left behind. I needn't have worried about Christopher noticing the handprint since there was something far more interesting in front of us. Across the street from where we stood was a flower seller. Next to the flower seller's cart were three men far out of time, easily a millennia or more. They were armed with spears and shields, wore long hair and beards, and the cloaks and short battle tunics and trews that had been common many centuries ago. I was staring at a group of Picts smack in the middle of modern Glasgow.

I turned my back to them; I didn't know if they could see through the glamour that made me appear human, and wasn't of a mind to find out. "Christopher." I glanced toward the Picts. "Can you see them?"

"I can," he replied. "Are they... Saxons?"

"Picts, I believe."

"Picts. Of course." We approached a shop opposite from the Picts, and studied their reflection in the window. "What should we do?"

"I don't know," I said. "They don't appear to be bothering anyone. Perhaps we leave them be?"

"They're carrying spears."

"Aye, they surely are. Knives, too."

"Aren't you curious as to how they got here?"

"I am curious, but I would rather observe than engage," I replied. "For now."

"What if they do something?"

Before I could answer, ten additional men easily as far out of time as the Picts appeared out of the ether. Eight of the men surrounded the Picts, while the other two stood guard on either side. Based on the oblivious people moving around these newcomers, only Christopher and I were aware of their arrival.

"Odd." I leaned closer to the window glass, scrutinizing the newcomers' appearance. They wore metal helmets with face guards that tied underneath their chins, bronze armor, and red cloaks pinned at their shoulders. In addition to spears, they carried short swords, and curved, rectangular shields. "Where do you suppose these new ones are from?"

"Oh, those guys are Roman. No doubt about it."

I glanced at Christopher. He elaborated, "See those?" He indicated the shields in the reflection. "They're called scutums. They were carried by Roman legionaries."

I blinked at the reflected men. "When were legionaries last about?"

"They were replaced by mounted cavalry in the third, fourth century." Christopher rubbed his chin. "And I don't think any legions ever made it this far north, though there is a legend about an entire company getting lost in Scotland. As you said, odd. Maybe we—"

"Wait." I touched Christopher's arm and angled myself so I was watching the thirteen strangers over his shoulder. The legionary, who I assumed was their chief, nodded to the Picts, then he called to his men. They formed up and marched up the hill, disappearing from view after ten measured paces. The Picts, who appeared content with whatever had been decided, ambled off in the opposite direction. I lost sight of them when they turned a corner.

"Let's grab some lunch," Christopher said a bit too loudly. Lunch was the last thing I wanted. What I did want was to know who these men were, why ancient Picts and Romans were wandering about in modern Glasgow, what their appearance foretold. I was the future Queen of Winter. I needed to know what was afoot on my island!

I turned to Christopher to say as much, and saw his bright blue eyes, his strained smile... and I capitulated. Again.

"Lunch sounds wonderful," I said. "What about that Vietnamese spot we went to a few weeks ago?"

Christopher's smile deepened. He'd been telling everyone he encountered about the summer rolls we'd had as if they'd been imbued with magic. I'd preferred the lemongrass chicken. "I like the way you think."

"Of course you do." I glanced at the flower seller, and added, "Will you go on ahead and reserve us a table? I'd like to pick up some flowers for the flat." His brow tensed, so I added, "Order me an ale?"

He brought my hand to his lips and kissed my knuckles. "Ale it is."

I watched him walk away for a moment, then I crossed the street and examined the bouquets for sale. As soon as Christopher was out of sight, I followed the Picts. When I turned the corner I found them leaning against a brick wall as if they belonged in this city and in this time.

"Why are you here?" I demanded.

"The gods will it so," answered one wearing a heavy gold torque. "Is that not why we're all here?"

"Why are you in Glasgow? Bit out of the way for your lot," I added, nodding to their garb.

"Why do you care?" he countered.

"Glasgow is my city, and I'll not have anyone causing trouble."

He laughed. "My lady, a more powerful man than you sent us to this very place."

"More powerful than me?" Ice skated across the pavement, licked at their boots. "Are you certain of that?"

"In a few months you may be his match, but not in the height of summer."

He nodded to the other two, and they went on their way. I debated following them, but I didn't want to keep Christopher waiting too long. I went back to the flower seller, purchased a bouquet of daisies, and continued on toward the restaurant where he waited. While I walked, two thoughts kept me occupied: the Picts were sent here by someone powerful, and that individual could be a threat.

I slipped on the icy street. As I regained my footing, I glanced back, and saw ice spreading across the cobbled pavement. Perhaps I was the threat to Glasgow, and the Picts were here to stop me.

Let them try.

LUNCH AND LANTERNS

I'd just been seated when Anya arrived at the restaurant. She blew into the dining room like a hurricane, her buttercup yellow hair streaming behind her and her gray eyes wide and searching. One hand clutched a bouquet of daisies that were just browning at the edges, while her other hand was a tight fist. Even so, snowflakes dripped between her fingers.

Anya saw me and smiled. "Have you ordered yet?" she asked, after she sat across from me.

"I have not," I said. "That was quick."

"How long does it take one to purchase flowers?"

"I meant your confrontation with the Picts."

She tossed the daisies onto the table. "Are you accusing me of lying?"

I glanced at the bouquet. The frost-burned bits were already drying out and flaking away. "I can see you bought flowers."

The poor, ignorant server approached our table. "Can I get your drinks?"

"Two of whatever ale you have on tap," I said.

"And a pot of tea, as hot as you can make it," Anya added.

The server's brow pinched as she scribbled away on her pad. "Two ales and some tea, hot as a volcano, coming up."

"Are there volcanoes in Scotland?" I mused. "I'll have to ask Rina." I watched Anya, the way her throat worked as she worried the edge of the placemat. "So, what did you learn about them?"

She glanced at me and visibly relaxed. Had she really thought I'd be angry about her speaking with the Picts? "Not much, other than they're an arrogant and unfriendly lot," she replied. "How did you so easily recognize the Romans?"

"I studied Latin for years," I began. "Most American schools have a language requirement, and learning Latin dovetailed nicely with my studies of Elizabethan literature. It gave me the ability to read primary sources in their original language without any translator's bias."

"Did Shakespeare write in Latin?"

"His plays were always performed in English, which was the language of the people."

"Has Maisie found a home for your newest book?"

Apparently, we were going to talk all about me and ignore the elephant in the room. "She's working on it. Anyway, back to the Romans. One of my professors was obsessed with Roman Britain, and his lesson plans were all about military campaigns from the first and second centuries. He even dressed up as a legionnaire on weekends and participated in reenactments."

Anya nodded. "How did those Romans look to you?"

I shrugged. "Like Romans. I've never actually seen a real legionnaire, you know."

She smiled. "No, I suppose you haven't."

The server delivered our beers and a scalding hot pot of tea, and took our order. Not surprisingly, Anya ordered the hot pot. As I watched her pour her tea, a light from above us caught my eye. The ceiling was decorated with paper lanterns in various shades of orange and red. Usually they just hung there, but today they sparkled as if lit from within, but I couldn't see any cords. Then I saw a large wet spot on one of the lanterns.

The sparkling wasn't from a string of lights. Anya had frosted them.

"Do you think being near heat kicks your powers into overdrive?" I asked.

"The chill comes and goes as it sees fit," she replied. "The Picts claimed to be working for someone. Someone more powerful than me."

"Who in the—"

"Here we are," the server announced as she returned with our food. "Hot pot for the lady, and our special spring roll platter for you, sir. Anything else I can get you?"

Before I could reply a cold, wet chunk of paper hit the server's shoulder. Similar wads were falling throughout the restaurant, with customers getting up from the seats and shouting as the wet blobs fell onto their heads and splattered on their food.

Anya's gaze moved around the room, then she looked up at the lanterns and gasped.

"Maybe a box," I replied to the server. "A to-go box would be great."

HAPPINESS AND REGRETS

Things hadn't been going well in the weeks since the Picts and Romans had appeared in Glasgow, and disrupted Christopher's precious market day.

The bad news began with news reports of vandalism at the antique market; it seemed that every piece of glass and crystal I'd walked by had frozen, and subsequently shattered. I only remembered frosting a few items, but the images of glass shards littering the market floor told a different tale. The reporters had wanted to brand it a hate crime, only they couldn't agree on who the perpetrator hated, nor the intended victims.

I'd watched Christopher's jaw tense as he read the reports, his only indication that he knew I was responsible. Then he came across photographs of icy Glaswegian streets and drifts of snow sparkling in the August sunshine; perhaps it had been a pocket blizzard, wondered the weather forecasters. So far, no news reports had linked the unseasonal ice on the debacle that happened at the Vietnamese restaurant, but I was sure that was coming. I blamed everything on the arrival of the Picts, insisting that their movement through time must have affected my abilities. Even though Christopher smiled and let the matter drop, I know he hadn't quite believed me. How could he, being that those interlopers were long gone and I still couldn't control the cold?

Perhaps the Picts and Romans had every right to be here, and I was the one who didn't belong.

Now, I stood in front of the picture window at the fore of our flat, gazing down at the busy streets. My mother never understood why I'd gravitated to the city, being that we were country folk through and through. To her, the city was little more than a tomb for the living, packed to the brim with overworked and under-entertained individuals, the lot of them going about their daily slogs until the end of their short lives.

I'd never shared her opinions about Glasgow, or New York, or any of the other cities I'd spent time in. For me, the cities teemed with life, so much so that I could lose myself in the crush of bodies. Among my own kind I'd always been an outsider, but when I was surrounded by mortals I felt as if I had a purpose. I once thought my calling was to be their protector. Now, as winter loomed closer every day, I didn't know what to think.

Blue sparks shocked then chilled my fingers. I clenched my hand, willing my body to chase the cold away. The cold snaps had started shortly after the gallowglass had ruined the scheme my mother, the prior Queen of Winter, had wrought against his lover. Once she was helpless, Fionnlagh, the Seelie King, punished my mother by stripping her of her title, then saw fit to further humiliate her and he transferred her dominance over winter to me. A logical choice, being that of all my mother's children, I'd been the only one present, as well as the only one not currently imprisoned in stone. Then the king exiled my mother to the Winter Palace, and I was truly alone.

I remember how winter's power had washed over me, the cold coursing through my veins and settling into my bones. I'd wondered how long it would take for my body to freeze solid, what would happen to the seasons if I couldn't control the cold...

Within a few hours the power steadied itself within me, and the coldness receded. My pride got the better of me, and I assumed I could wield the chill as well as Mum ever did.

Then the cold snaps started.

The first snaps had been few and far between, and only occurred when I was already a bit cool, such as when I was out of doors, or already had a hand in the icebox. Now, the chills came whenever they pleased, and they weren't limiting themselves to my hands. Frost ran up my arms and down my spine, coursed down my legs to form icy pools 'round my feet. I suspected that these chills would only intensify as the days wore on; it was already September, and I would don my icy crown soon enough. Come sundown on Samhain—the beginning of winter's reign over Scotland—my body and soul would likely be little more than cold, hard ice.

I glanced at the calendar on the wall. It was September fourteenth, which meant that I could be human for another forty-eight days. Forty-eight short, short days, during which I could walk with Christopher, laugh with him, wake in his arms. On the forty-ninth morning I might end up freezing him to death.

Gods, why was the first day of winter October thirty-first? Why couldn't I have my life until December first, or the winter solstice? Even as I lamented that my time as Winter Queen would begin long before the actual season, I knew the answer; I'd grown up with Mum telling me stories of the old days, back when the land was still young. Then, she had ruled over half the year, from Samhain straight on to May Day. On May first, she relinquished her crown to the Summer King, and he wore it as he ruled the warm half of the year.

Of course, that wasn't the way things were done now. In a fit of jealousy, my father had dethroned the Summer King, thus allowing the Seelie Court to rise to power. In time, the Unseelie Court was formed, and in that refuge of the darker side of Elphame had grown alongside their bright cousins. So things have been ever since.

What no one seemed to know—at least, Mum hadn't admitted to having the knowledge, and she knew almost everything—was where the Unseelie had come from. Some suspected they were Seelie gone bad, but the flaw in that theory was that the Seelie had never been good to begin with. What she had known was that the Seelie and Unseelie Courts were locked in a perpetual battle with neither showing signs of defeat, or triumph. Even amongst all the gods and monsters in Elphame, the dark and light fae were an enigma unto themselves.

Another mystery was why the current Seelie King now wore the antlered crown for the entirety of the year, rather than only in summer. When my father had dethroned the Summer King, he'd also inadvertently given the Seelie an extra bit of influence over the land. Mum had always claimed it didn't bother her, but I hadn't believed that, not for a moment. If she was satisfied with the state of things, why had she never attended functions at the Seelie Court? And why had she tried reestablishing the Wild Court?

I'd wondered often where and why Mum had gotten the idea of her presiding over the Wild Court. For one, that court was the home of the cast-off fae, the boggarts and phookas and other solitary fairies who were either too ugly for the high and mighty Seelie, or had already been sent away from the Unseelie Court. It had been a haven for Elphame's cast-offs, and had been disbanded long ago; for all Fionnlagh's supposed might, he was wary of those he'd censured gathering behind his back. Mum, who' been a queen long before Fionnlagh was born, had no place associating with that lot.

Then again, Fionnlagh had censured her. He was the one who'd punished my father and brothers, and thus took them away from her. Mum often said that losing most of her family nearly drove her mad, and the true purpose of the Wild Court had been for her to gain enough power to bring Da and the rest back to her.

If only it had worked. I missed them too.

My fingers thawed, albeit slowly, and I forced the rest of my body to relax. My deepest fear was that my newfound powers would somehow harm Christopher, but I had already taken precautions. While we'd spent the last few months together at the flat, he still had a room at his sister's house in Crail. I'd been prepared to beg Karina to take him in for the winter months, even grovel at her feet, but I needn't have worried. When I'd finally gotten up the courage to ask her, Karina's goodness shone true.

"Of course Chris can stay with us for a few months," Karina had said. "He's always welcome here. You are, too," she added, with a gentle hand on my forearm. She'd been more than six months into her pregnancy at the time, and her other hand rested on the curve of her belly.

"Thank you," I'd said. "How are you feeling? Is the lass behaving herself?"

"Faith is behaving as much as you would expect Robert's child to," she'd replied with a rueful smile. "She likes to do her gymnastics while I'm trying to sleep."

"Och, she's a sense of humor, then," I'd said. "I believe that aspect may be from her mum's side."

Karina had laughed at that, and soon enough Christopher and Robert joined us, the former all smiles while the latter was more concerned with Karina and the bairn's well-being than any sort of levity. Those who knew Robert only as the gallowglass, the most feared warrior in all of Elphame, would be hard pressed to recognize him as a doting father to be. And Christopher, he'd just been happy that his sister was happy. I shared in their happiness, too, though for me it was bittersweet. Soon enough they would all be lost to me, and who knew if they'd want to take up with me again in the spring.

Who knew, indeed.

The cold snap returned, this time in my other hand. I made a fist, strangling the chills before they could travel up my arms and into my heart. I felt a surge of triumph as the chills died, but it was a hollow victory. The chills were getting stronger, and more frequent. No matter how much I pretended otherwise, my days of happiness with Christopher were numbered.

Not a Baby Shower

I yawned, stretched, and rolled over in bed. Anya wasn't beside me, which wasn't unusual of late; the shorter, and colder, the days got, the less she slept. It was enough to make me wonder if she'd stay awake from the end of October clear through to Beltane.

My phone beeped. I grabbed it and silenced the alarm, then I scrolled through whatever emails had appeared overnight. There were a few from my agent, Maisie, keeping me updated on her efforts to sell my latest book to a new publisher. My last book had been a great success, but my former publisher decided to hop on some negative press I'd received concerning my former fiancée as a way to increase sales, a tactic known in the business as a dick move. Of all the things I didn't need, my own publisher running a smear campaign against me was near the top of the list. I could screw up my life perfectly well without their involvement.

I closed down my email and checked my calendar. There was exactly one thing on it: be at Rina and Rob's place for eleven. Anya was also invited, but the way her abilities had been acting up made me wonder if she still wanted to attend, or if she even should attend. The last thing Anya needed was to accidentally cover Crail in snow and have someone connect it to Glasgow getting iced over last August.

I got out of bed and went in search of Anya. Our flat was on the top floor of an old stone building, and the front had these tall bay windows that gave us a bird's eye view of the city below. It was Anya's favorite spot in the flat. My favorite spot was next to her, no matter where she was.

I found Anya standing in front of the bay windows, but she wasn't watching the city streets come to life. Instead, she was clenching her fists and staring at the sky.

"Morning." I reached for her but stopped myself just short of her skin. Once we'd been so affectionate, we practically lived in each other's arms. Now, she only liked to be touched when she wasn't feeling the cold growing inside her. Since I couldn't tell by looking at her whether or not her power was making itself known, I'd learned to let her initiate any and all contact.

She cocked her head toward me and smiled. "And a good morning to you. Slept well, did you?"

"I did." She hadn't even twitched from the neck down. "Did you rest at all?"

"Aye. I did."

"Are you still up for heading down to Crail today?"

"Of course. It would break Karina's heart if we didn't attend her luncheon."

I turned toward the clock on the wall, and did a bit of travel math in my head. "Okay. We're supposed to be there by eleven, and since the drive takes almost two hours, we'll need to leave soon."

"Christopher, you do know that I can have us there in the blink of an eye."

She was referring to her teleportation ability, but I liked driving. While I'm secure enough in my masculinity to be in a relationship with a woman much more powerful and intelligent than I will ever be, I do like being in control every so often. Driving was one of the few things I could do better than Anya, and I wanted to hold onto it.

An even bigger but was that Anya's teleportation skill didn't seem to be affected by the increasing coldness in her, at least not yet. Denying her from using her ability would be cruel, and I'd do anything to keep her from hurting.

"All right, then. We'll go your way."

A few hours later, Anya teleported us to Rina and Rob's house, and we arrived at eleven on the nose. In the States, this little get together would have been called a baby shower, but Rina was adamant that this was nothing more than Sunday brunch with friends; the fact that her due date was drawing near was just a coincidence. I made sure to bring a gift, just in case.

Anya teleported us to the garden rather than inside the cottage as a precaution. If Anya and I had appeared in Rina's kitchen smack dab in the middle of her guests, there might be more chaos than my pregnant sister could handle. Besides, this way we got to say hello to the wights.

"Master Stewart, Mistress Darach," Wyatt called as he flew toward us. The wights were tiny sprites that tended gardens, and at least a dozen of them lived at Rina's place. I don't know if wights had a formal hierarchy, but Wyatt, a blue sprite with wings reminiscent of a dragonfly and fluffy hair like a dandelion gone to seed, was definitely the man in charge. "How wonderful to see you both."

"Thank you. The garden looks great," I added, just to see Wyatt blush beneath his bright blue skin. "I'm sure Rina's quite pleased with it."

Wyatt chirped something in his native language. It must have been a joke, because Anya laughed and chirped a reply. Wyatt alighted on her shoulder for a moment and rubbed his head against her throat, then he flew off and resumed tending the roses.

"Flirting with the wights?" I teased.

Anya raised an eyebrow. "Careful, or I'll flirt with taller men, too."

We laughed, linking hands as we walked from the garden to the front of the house. I saw the massive black truck that belonged to the cottage's caretaker, Dougal MacKay, parked out front, with his equally massive red toolbox sitting in the bed. That toolbox had produced every item we'd asked of it, from enchanted maps to tools to engage in magical combat. I'd considered asking it for one of those fancy espresso machines, but Anya had shot down that idea. According to her, if magical objects thought they were being used for personal gain, things went south fast.

The cottage's front door was ajar, so we let ourselves in. The main rooms of the cottage were packed with people, and every flat surface was covered with trays of food and stacks of wrapped presents for Rina and the baby. Rina's not-a-baby shower was tuning out to be rather shower-like, after all.

I was casually acquainted with most of those in attendance at the not-shower. Almost all of them were neighbors and friends of Rina's from the village; I didn't know if Rob had any friends either here or in Elphame. It certainly wasn't in his nature to make nice with people. Standing near the makeshift bar was my friend, Ethan Jacobsen, but I was more interested in the lady standing at his elbow: Rina's best friend, Colleen Worley.

"Ethan, good to see you." I reached out to shake his hand, and he pulled me into a hug. "How's St. Andrews treating you?"

"I'm surrounded by brilliance," he replied, then he caught sight of Anya and winked at her. "Still hanging around with this boring old writer? Say the word, and I'll show you some real excitement."

Anya looked down her nose at Ethan, but there was laughter in her voice. "Doubtful, that, you old fool."

"The lady speaks true," Ethan said, and I turned toward Colleen.

"I can't believe you got on a plane," I said as I hugged her. I held her at arm's length, and asked, "You did fly, didn't you? Tell me you didn't take a ship."

"Actually, I swam," she said with a smirk. "As if anything could make me miss Rina's baby shower."

"Brunch with friends," Rina yelled from somewhere near the sofa.

Colleen rolled her eyes. "Anyway." She noticed Anya standing beside me. "Hello—it's Anya, correct? I remember you from Carson University. It's good to see you again."

Anya shook Colleen's hand. "A pleasure for me, as well. Are you still employed at the school?"

"Technically, but only for online classes. The campus itself won't be ready for students until the spring semester, at least."

Anya laughed softly. "Warring gods do tend to leave a mess in their wake."

"Oh, you should have seen what those *drakaina* did to the cafeteria!"

Since they were getting on well, I left Anya with Colleen and Ethan and made my way toward Rina. She was seated on the couch, and surrounded by people offering her advice on everything from labor and delivery to preschool options. I supposed they meant well, but Rina looked more like a prisoner than the guest of honor. As the elder brother, it was my duty to intercede.

"Chris," Rina called when she saw me. She tried to leap up, but she was too round for those types of movements. I grabbed her hands and hauled her upright, then I draped my arm across her shoulders.

"Everyone, this is my brother, Chris," Rina announced.

"Hello," I said. Rina named her guests, and we waved at and greeted each other in turn.

"Now if you'll excuse us I need to introduce him to a few other people." She smiled, and we turned toward the kitchen area. "Thank you so much for rescuing me," she whispered. "That was horrifying."

"You looked like a deer facing down a semi." She led me toward the counter, which was laden with all types of cakes and pastries. "Did Rob make these?"

"I made them," said a red-headed woman. "I wouldn't be surprised if Robert was scared of the oven."

A most amusing image of Rob wearing a frilly apron and oven mitts flashed behind my eyes. My gaze darted around the room until I found him, wearing his usual outfit of jeans and a flannel shirt. He was standing between Anya and Ethan, and looked baffled about something the latter had said.

"Chris, this is my friend, Nancy," Rina said, slowly and a bit too loud. I assumed Nancy had a hearing impairment. "Nancy, Chris is my older brother."

"Nice to meet you," I said. "And these desserts look wonderful. May I take a few for my girlfriend?"

The redhead, Nancy, smiled sweetly. "Of course you may. Please, do."

"Come say hi to Anya," I said to Rina, then I grabbed a plate and filled it with tiny cakes for Anya. She adored sweets. "We brought gifts."

"I told you not to," Rina said, but before she could protest further, we were standing in front of Rob and Anya.

"Are those for me?" Anya asked, eyeing the cakes.

"They surely are," I replied. After we'd all said our hellos, Anya withdrew a very old bottle of Glenfiddich from her bag and presented it to Rob. He smiled at the bottle as if it were a long-lost lover.

"To help the bairn sleep," Anya said with a wink. "Her parents, too."

"Thank ye for the fine gift, though I admit it may not last until Faith's arrival," Rob said.

"We've something for her, as well," Anya said. She handed Rina a gift bag. Inside it was a mobile meant to be hung over the cradle, decorated with smiling plush dinosaurs.

"Aww, guys." Rina dashed a hand across her eyes. "It's so sweet."

"Wait, there's more," I said. "We got an entire dinosaur nursery set, and get this—it came with a stuffed trilobite!"

"What the devil is a trilling bite?" Rob asked.

"Trilobites are extinct marine arthropods," Rina replied. "They're super cute."

Rob's forehead wrinkled. "Ah. More o' the cute."

I nodded toward the stacks of presents, all of them wrapped in bright patterned paper and bedecked with bows and ribbons. "I'd wager those boxes are filled with adorable pink dresses and stuffed effigies of smiling woodland creatures. Soon enough, my friend, you will be drowning in cute."

Rob regarded the bottle of whiskey in his hand. "This may be needed much sooner than anticipated."

I clapped him on the shoulder. "I'd be glad to help with that."

It wasn't long until Rina was sitting on the sofa again, this time opening the scores of gifts. Since neither me nor Anya, nor Colleen or Ethan, had any children, we could only feign interest in baby clothes and toys for a short amount of time. The four of us ended up sitting at the kitchen table making our own entertainment with a bottle of Scotch. It wasn't as old or as smooth as the whisky we'd given to Rob, but it did the job nicely.

After we'd all had more Scotch than was proper that early in the day, Ethan glanced to his right, then his left. "I've just had a revelation," he drawled.

"Has the spirit of the Scotch bestowed its knowledge upon you?" I asked.

"No. Well, yes, but that's something else entirely." He leaned closer, and said, "You, my friend, have had relations with every person at this table."

"Relations?" I spluttered through the haze of whisky. "I'm not related to anyone here, except Rina."

"Not related," Ethan said. "Relations."

"Oh," I said as Ethan laughed. A moment later, Colleen and I joined him. We were all laughing, except for Anya. She stared at the three of us like we were monsters, then she got up and walked out of the cottage.

"Anya, wait," I called after her.

"Cripes, Chris, I didn't mean to upset her," Ethan said. "You two are so close, I figured she already knew."

"I know you didn't." I clapped his shoulder, then I followed Anya outside. She was gone, along with my way of getting home.

"And this is another reason why I prefer driving to teleportation," I muttered to myself.

I stayed outside for the next hour, at first waiting for Anya to return, then waving to the shower guests as they left. Eventually Rina stood beside me on the front stoop. "Colleen told me what happened. She's gone?"

"So it would appear."

"I take it she's mad?"

"Oh, most definitely."

"Will she hurt you?"

I weighed the possibility. "Physically, no. But she scares me when she pulls these disappearing acts. Every time I'm left wondering if I'll ever see her again."

"Has Anya been doing this a lot? Taking off without a word?"

"Lately she has. She's worried about winter."

"You mean about her ruling winter?" Rina asked. "I thought she'd know a few things already, being that she grew up with Beira."

"I thought so too, but apparently whatever Beira did, she kept to herself," I replied. "And for all that Anya does remember, we don't know if things will be the same for her, or if we're wading into new territory." I leaned back against the cottage's wall. "She has no idea what to expect, and it's driving her crazy. When she gets herself too worked up, she blinks out."

"That's got to be hard, for both of you." Rina looped her arm with mine and laid her head on my shoulder. "I never knew about you and Colleen."

"It was only once, right after I started at Carson. We were pretty drunk."

"Obviously. You are not her type."

"Yes, she has since made that abundantly clear on many, many occasions." Even though I loved my life with Anya—emerging goddess powers, disappearing acts, and all—I missed these quiet times with Rina. Ever since our parents died, it had only been the two of us, me and my kid sister against the world. Since we first came to Scotland, our worlds had gotten a lot bigger but Rina's calm presence was the one constant in my life.

"Other than my girlfriend's vanishing act, how is everything going?" I asked.

"Pretty awesome. Something about Scotland brings out the best in us Stewarts."

"You are right about that."

The baby shower wound down soon after Rina's and my talk on the front stoop, which made sense; women in their ninth month of pregnancy weren't known as party animals. While everyone said their goodbyes to Rina and Rob, I checked train schedules on my phone. Initially, I'd wanted to ask if I could stay the night, but Colleen had already claimed my old room, and after Ethan's gaff I was not suggesting she and I be roommates. Depending on what time the trains were running, I'd either return home tonight, or stay at Ethan's and catch a train in the morning.

Rina came up behind me and tried peeking at my phone, but her belly wouldn't let her get close enough. "Tough to be sneaky when you're the size of a Sherman tank," I said.

"I am nowhere near that big," she replied. "I can get you home, if you want."

I set down my phone. "Really? How?"

"With a portal." She patted her belly as she continued, "Either I'm getting the hang of this whole walker thing, or something about being pregnant helps me tap into my ability. Hey, maybe if you get Anya knocked up, all this winter stuff will work itself out."

"Very funny." I didn't mention that Anya had been scared to touch me for fear of turning me into a block of ice, and that adding a baby into the mix might be more than she could handle. A baby would definitely be more than I could handle. "Are you sure you can send me that far? Glasgow isn't exactly close."

"Distance doesn't seem to be an issue with these portals," she said. "As long as I want to send you someplace one of us has been to before, off you go. I bet I could send you all the way to New York."

"Let's save that experiment for another time," I said. "I'm ready if you are."

"Okay." Rina closed her eyes for a moment, then she touched the center of my chest. "I'm sending you to your living room. Sorry in advance if you end up half in the sofa."

"What?"

A second later, I was standing in my living room, as promised, with no part of me stuck in the sofa or any other pieces of furniture. I could still hear Rina's laughter, making me wonder if sound could travel through a portal, or if she'd figured out a new way to torment me. It was probably the latter. I shucked off my shoes and left them by the front door, then I entered the bedroom. The Scotch was wearing off, and I was craving a nap. I found Anya was lying on our bed, her back toward the entrance.

"Hey," I said. "I didn't know you were here."

"Where else would I be but in our home?" she countered. "Is the party over?"

"It's winding down. Rina portaled me here."

"Ah."

I sat next to her, and stroked her long, buttercup yellow hair. "I'm sorry about what Ethan said. It wasn't fair for you to be caught off guard like that. I should have told you."

"Why didn't you?"

"Honestly? I never thought about it." I fluffed the pillows and repositioned myself against the headboard, stretching out my legs next to Anya. "All of that happened so long ago, it's like it was in another lifetime. If Ethan hadn't brought it up, I might never have thought about it again."

"I fear that's the difference between you and I," she said. "You can let the past go as easily as a leaf floats downstream. I've never been able to do that. I think about mine all the time."

She left off that our romantic pasts were very different, and while mine hadn't been a bed of roses, hers was a constant source of pain and guilt. "His name was Liam, right?"

"Aye. Liam."

"Do you regret being with him?"

"Being with him? No, I don't. When we were together, he was the sweetest, most loving man. Those memories, I cherish." Anya cleared her throat. "Then I showed him my true self, and he ran from me, making the sign of the cross and shouting that a devil had bewitched him. That was the moment I cursed him to speak only gibberish. My ears couldn't take any more of his squawking."

I watched Anya as she lay next to me, her back rising and falling with her breath. The human guise she often wore was beautiful, but her true form was stunning. Beyond her physical appearance, she had a kind and selfless heart. For Liam to wound her so deeply he must not have been the sweet man he presented to Anya, but then I'm biased. Either way, he got what he deserved.

"Are you planning on cursing Ethan?" I asked. I didn't want her to dwell on Liam more than necessary. "Because frankly, him speaking less might be for the best."

Her shoulders shook, and I hoped I'd made her laugh. Anya rolled over and looked up at me. "Is Rina cross with me?"

"She is not. She just missed you."

"I missed her, too. And you."

"You didn't have to leave," I said. "Ethan was ready to apologize."

She shook her head. "Leaving was the only option. I was mad, and when I get mad, I get cold. Since I didn't want to turn your sister's home into an iceberg, I left."

I tucked a bit of hair behind her ear. "Were you mad at me, or mad at everyone?"

"I was mostly mad at Ethan," she replied. "What a crass man he is, to be going about revealing others' past lovers. It's indecent."

"That's Ethan, indecent to the core." I slithered down so I was lying next to her, then I took a chance and gathered her against me. She nestled against my chest, and placed one hand over my heart.

"I was a bit angry with you, as well," she whispered. "I wish you'd told me, but I understand why you didn't."

"I'm sorry. If I could go back in time and warn you, I would."

Anya drew back and fixed me in her iridescent gray gaze. "If you somehow gain the power of time travel, I hope you put it to better use than that."

We smiled at each other, then I tucked her head beneath my chin. "All right. If I learn how to rewind time you make the travel plans. Deal?"

"Deal." She settled into my arms. "I will miss this so much."

"Miss what? Me?" I kissed her forehead. "I'm not going anywhere."

"Not you. Warmth."

HIS TO CARE FOR

We were still in bed hours later, Anya sleeping against me while I wracked my brain trying to figure out how I could help her. There was an air of grim inevitability about Anya; winter was getting closer every day, and her powers, and therefore the cold, were getting progressively stronger. What's more, even if we could hold off winter, I don't think Anya would want to. I wasn't sure what the lack of seasons would do to Scotland as a whole, but I was willing to bet it wouldn't be anything good.

Eventually, I decided to dust off my research skills and learn about winter deities. Graduate school, and all the research the required essays my studies had entailed, had prepared me for my later life in rather unexpected ways.

Anya had resigned herself to a future as a living yet frozen corpse. The problem was that she only had her fears guiding her; her mother had never prepared Anya to take over as the Queen of Winter, because Beira had never planned on passing on her mantle to Anya or anyone. Now Beira was exiled to an ice palace in a different dimension, and Anya was stuck figuring this out on her own.

No, she was not on her own. She had me, for all the good that would do her.

I opened my laptop and typed "Scottish Winter Folklore" into the search field. Not surprisingly, most of the articles were about the Cailleach Bheur—Beira herself—and detailed the many legends associated with her. I wondered if all of these stories were about the same Beira. If so, Anya's mother was hundreds, or possibly thousands, of years old.

Perhaps age and experience had lent Beira the necessary skills to control winter, since she'd never seemed overwhelmed by the cold. In addition to her having found ways to cope with winter's chill, she'd always presented as a human woman. Thanks to Beira's fight with Rob and the giants back at Glen Lyon, I knew she bled like a human, too. All of these facts begged the question, if Beira had remained flesh and blood, why was Anya on track to freeze solid?

I looked at Anya as she slept peacefully on our bed, and swallowed the lump in my throat. Anya's new abilities weren't just freezing her body, but her empathy, too. Every day brought her deeper into the cold, and we both knew it was only a matter of time before she was a figurative and literal ice queen. Once that happened, I wasn't certain me or these lukewarm Scottish summers could bring her back.

"Then let's make sure she doesn't get lost in the first place," I muttered as I searched for winter deities from other cultures; since Beira wasn't available, there had to be someone or something else that could help ease Anya's transition. I soon learned that this area of the world didn't want for supernatural beings who affected the cold. I grabbed a pencil and notebook, and soon enough I had my list winnowed down to two candidates: Skadi and Boreas.

Skadi was a Norse deity of winter, mountains, and skiing. More importantly, her father was a giant, and I thought that might lend some common ground between her and Anya. I also liked Skadi because my mother had been Scandinavian; I liked to think Mom was sending me a sign from beyond the grave. My other candidate, Boreas, was the Greek god of the cold north wind. Since Rina still kept in contact with Persephone, I was hoping I could fact check some of my research with her.

Look at me, sending off my essays to be edited by a goddess. Arrogance, thy name is Stewart.

Since me connecting with any gods was obviously never going to happen, I opened a new search window and entered "winter stories". That search generated thousands of examples of hard winters, each more dreadful than the last. And these weren't all folk tales; there were news articles about planes crashing onto snow-covered mountains, people abandoning cars on the roads during blizzards and freezing to death as they walked home, and farm animals dying of thirst because their water froze over. Winter wasn't just cold, it was fricken' terrifying.

Throughout it all, warmth was the solution; heating coils to thaw water troughs, keeping yourself bundled in extra layers, drinking hot beverages. Being that I'd grown up in the northeastern United States I'd already known that staying warm was the best defense against frostbite and hypothermia, but maybe warmth, as mundane an idea as it was, had been Beira's secret. Maybe she'd learned to keep her body warm enough to keep the chill under control.

I wasn't a Seelie or any other sort of magical creature, but I had a few tricks up my sleeve. I headed into the kitchen and found the tea Anya liked, a custom blend she purchased regularly from a nearby coffee shop. I had no idea what was in it, but as soon as the boiling water hit the herbs, the scent of a flower garden wafted upward.

I waited for the tea to steep. After three minutes I gauged it done, poured Anya a cup, and entered the bedroom. The scent woke her.

"Hey, beautiful," I said. "I made you something."

"You made me tea?" she asked as she accepted the mug. "Whatever for?"

I shrugged. "Just because."

She smiled as she sipped her tea, and in that moment, I resolved to do anything and everything to help her control her power. Anya was mine to care for, and I wouldn't let the cold claim her.

FROSTY MORNING

After my sudden departure from Karina's luncheon, and Christopher's discovery that I was sulking at home, he had gone out of his way to pamper me. His attentions had been a bit suffocating at first, but I did love feeling loved. The night began with him making me tea, then he ordered my favorite takeaway and we spent the night on our sofa eating far too much rich food and watching black and white movies. It was one of the most peaceful, romantic nights I'd ever had, and I drifted off to sleep so warm and content I'd forgotten all about winter's chill.

The next morning I woke up frozen in place.

It took me some minutes to reach that conclusion. For the past few weeks, I'd woken up chilled to my core, no matter how many blankets were piled atop me; feeling like a block of ice was fast becoming my new normal. I only noticed something amiss when I attempted to roll over. My limbs were like boulders, resisting all movement.

"Christopher," I whispered. I don't know why I whispered his name. I should have cried it at the top of my lungs. He heard me all the same, and his eyes snapped open.

"What's wrong?" He propped himself up on an elbow. "Are you sick?"

"I can't move."

He flung the blankets aside and scrutinized my naked form. Despite the many months we'd been sleeping together, I was still shy around him, and Christopher had always respected my modesty. Now he inspected me as his sister would a rock specimen.

"Wiggle your fingers," he ordered, and I did. "Toes." After those digits complied, he sat back on his heels and rubbed his chin. "I don't think you're paralyzed."

"Is that good?"

"I guess it's better than actually being paralyzed. Try to move your arm a bit more." He drew a blanket across my torso, but stopped halfway. "Hang on."

Christopher laid down flat beside me, his face close to my upper arm. "The sheet is stuck to you. That's why you can't move." He prodded the sheet, and I could feel my skin pulling along with it. "But how did you get stuck in the first place?"

"I-I don't know." I threw my weight forward and sat up, pulling the bedding loose as I did so. Christopher moved behind me and peeled the sheet from the back of my neck.

"There are ice crystals on your skin," he said. "Anya, you froze to the bed."

"But only me?" I demanded. "You weren't cold at all?"

"I wasn't, which is another oddity. I'm going to get some warm water."

I lay half-upright, swathed in frozen fabric, wondering how this had happened. I didn't remember Mum ever freezing to anything, not even when she molded ice with her bare hands. What's more, my skin wasn't frozen. It was cold as death, yes, but still soft and pliable.

Christopher returned with a bowl of water and a tea towel. "Should we start at the top or the bottom?" he asked.

"Bottom," I replied, because I wanted to watch him work. My fascination with how I'd frozen to the bed was overriding my terror, and I wanted that terror overridden for as long as possible.

Christopher dipped the towel in the water and wrung it out, then he gently swabbed my ankles. The ice melted almost instantly, and soon enough I was standing next to the bed and pulling on my robe.

"This is strange. Stranger." He peeled back the sheet and revealed evidence of ice down to the mattress. "It's as if the cold dripped off you." He got down on his knees and felt under the bed. "There's ice on the rug, too."

I covered my mouth with my hands and turned away. "I could have killed you."

"But you didn't." Warm arms encircled me from behind as he kissed my neck. "Even when you're sleeping, you never chill me."

"For now." I pulled free of him and entered the bathroom. "I'm going to take a bath. A very, very hot bath."

"Want me to—"

I shut the door before he could finish speaking. As much as I enjoyed bathing with Christopher, I had no assurances that I wouldn't freeze the bathwater solid, possibly with him in it.

I sat on the edge of the tub and turned the hot tap fully open, then I dropped my robe and stood in the tub. The hot water scalded my feet, but I squeezed my eyes shut against the pain, accepting my penance. After a moment, the pain was gone.

I looked down and grabbed the wall for support. The scalding hot water had turned to ice.

BABIES CAN'T READ CALENDARS

I stared at the closed door, wondering if Anya was shutting me out of just the bathroom, or her life entirely. I understood that as Queen of Winter, Anya would go many places where I couldn't follow, and I'd come to accept that. Now I wondered if she needed someone who was capable of crossing glaciers with her.

Someone who wasn't a mortal.

Someone who wasn't me.

"Don't get paranoid," I muttered. I tore the bed apart and threw the sheets into the laundry. Maybe the fabric had caused some kind of reaction against her skin, and her coldness had gone into overdrive as a defense mechanism. Maybe I should get some unbleached, undyed, organic cotton or linen bedding. Maybe one hundred percent wool blankets would help, too.

Maybe I could make Anya an entirely new bed out of love and good intentions.

I sat on the bare mattress, my head in my hands. This situation couldn't be fixed with new bedding. In fact, there wasn't anything to be fixed. Anya wasn't broken. She was becoming something new. And whatever she was becoming, she was amazing.

No one had known how she would react to the transition from her usual self to Winter's Queen, not even the Seelie King, and now her mounting anxiety was ranging out of control. It was like she was drowning and I was watching her slip under while I remained safe on the shore. I couldn't even toss her a life preserver.

I will find a life preserver, and drag her back to dry land.

The sound of running water ceased. I knocked on the bathroom door.

"May I come in?"

"Aye."

I opened the door, and saw Anya sitting in the tub. The water reached the rim of the basin, but her skin still had that bluish cast. I knelt next to it and reached for her hands. She moved to the side of the tub and pressed her forehead against mine.

"You're warm," I said.

"For now. I fear it took far too many liters of scalding water to thaw me this small bit."

Worried she might burn herself, I dipped my fingers in the water. It was lukewarm. Instead of asking if we'd run out of hot water, I kissed her. "Warm or cold, I love you either way."

Her fingers tensed on my arm, but she remained silent. Before I could say anything else, my phone chimed.

"It can wait," I said when she drew back.

"What if it's an emergency?"

"You're more important."

"Answer it. I'm fine."

I gave her a look that told her she was very much not fine. She smiled, and settled back in the tub. I returned to the bedroom and grabbed my phone. The caller was Rina, so I accepted.

"Favorite sister," I greeted.

"Only sister," she responded. Rina's voice was weak, and her labored breathing made her sound like she'd run a mile. "The proper greeting is best sister in the history of sisters."

"Are you okay?" A thousand images of Rina being hurt flashed behind my eyes. "Where's Rob?"

"He's right here. He's great. I'm great, and Faith's here, too. We're all doing great."

"You had her? When? You're not due yet!"

"Funny thing about babies, they can't read calendars, so they show up whenever they feel like it."

I leaned again the doorframe, so happy I thought I might weep. "How is she? How are you?"

"She's perfect. Come meet your niece."

I glanced toward the bathroom. "I have a situation here. When will you be home?"

"What kind of situation?" she demanded.

"Nothing that involves you, and nothing I can't handle," I replied. "What if we come by the cottage tomorrow?"

"You better," she said. I could almost hear her pouting. "Faith is excited to meet you and Anya."

"Not as excited as we are to meet her." I paused. "Love you, favorite sister."

"Love you too, best brother."

I ended the call and set my phone down. My baby sister just had a baby. I'd never felt so many emotions concurrently; pride, love, protectiveness. I glanced at the bathroom door and felt another: determination.

I reentered the bathroom and sat on the edge of the tub. "Can I come in?"

"I fear it's not very warm."

"It's fine." I stepped into the tub and settled opposite from Anya as tepid water sloshed onto the tiled floor. Our legs fit together like puzzle pieces. "That was Rina. She had Faith."

"Och, already?" Anya said. "I've no idea yet how to be an aunt."

"The uncle business is new to me, too."

"How is Karina? Did she sound well? How is the bairn?"

I smiled, only partly because of my brand new niece. For Anya to be so concerned with my sister and her baby I knew the cold hadn't reached her heart, and if I had things my way it never would. Anya may be the Queen of Winter but she won't be defeated by it, not if I had to chip her out of ice every morning and boil her back to life. One life preserver, coming up.

ICE AND NIGHTMARES

"In all my days, I have never seen a man so excited to meet a child that wasn't his." I said, looking on as Christopher changed his clothes again. It was his fourth outfit of the morning, and it wasn't yet nine. "Actually, from what I've heard, most men aren't that interested in meeting their own bairns."

"What kind of awful men do you know?" he asked as his blond head emerged from the neck of his woolen jumper. This latest one was blue, and the bright shade made his eyes the color of a clear summer sky. It was by far my favorite jumper of the morning. "On second thought, don't answer that."

Christopher turned toward the mirror and ran his hands through his hair. While he was excited to meet his niece, he was also glad we were driving to Crail rather than teleporting. He hadn't mentioned me leaving him stranded at his sister's house, and me not protesting us taking the two-hour journey by car—two hours each way, mind you—was a small apology on my part. Ever since I'd agreed to travel via the roads, he'd been so excited he was walking on air.

Truth be told, I was feeling happier than I'd been in weeks. I hadn't frosted over once since my long soak in the tub the day prior, and I'd felt hardly any chills. It was enough to make me hope my new abilities were settling into my bones, and that soon I'd soon have an iron control over the cold, just as my mother had.

Christopher turned toward me and asked, "Well? How do I look?"

The fourth outfit did the trick, then. "You look like a man about to meet his niece for the first time."

He grinned. "Let's get going, beautiful."

Soon enough, we were zipping up the M80 toward Crail. As much as I loved the speed and convenience teleporting, I also loved driving with Christopher. The sheer joy on his face when he sped across the countryside warmed my heart, and coming from me, that's saying something.

"Do you want to have children?" he asked out of the blue.

"We've talked about this before," I replied. "Have you forgotten?"

"I remember every word you've ever said to me, but things are different now." He was right about that, and I owed him my honesty.

"I used to want children, many of them," I began. "One of my dreams was to have a huge house filled with family, the way things were when I was young. Now, I don't know."

Christopher's jaw tightened. I reached over and laced my fingers with his. "Has your niece's birth affected you so strongly?"

"Yes, but it's not just that." He released my hand so he could shift gears, then reclaimed it. "I've told you that I once had a fiancée."

I ignored the cold lump in my gut. Usually it didn't bother me that Christopher had had many relationships before he met me, but the intermittent chills I'd been living with had frayed my nerves down to the quick. "You have."

"When Olivia and I were a couple we made all sorts of plans, but we never once talked about children. In all the years we were together, kids just never came up. I didn't imagine what I'd be like as a father, and I never, ever thought of Olivia as a future mother."

"Perhaps that's because she was actually a *leanan sìth*, and Nicnevin's lackey," I suggested.

He laughed. "You have a point."

"I can see you as a father," I said. "Giving rides on your shoulders, helping them with their lessons."

"Them?"

"You can't have just one!"

"How many, then?"

"At least three, or four. No, four is better; don't want an odd one out."

He glanced at me, the corner of his mouth curled up. It was enough to make me forget I'd ever been cold. "That's a lot of kids. We're going to need to get working soon."

"Christopher, winter is nigh, and—"

"Winter is still over a month away." When I remained silent and frowning, he continued, "Spring, then?"

"Spring, what?"

"Then we can start."

Those four words uncoiled a rope of fear that had been wound around me since the Seelie King bestowed the chill upon me. Christopher believed in me. He was confident that I could reign over this and every winter thereafter, so confident that he was already planning what we'd do in the spring. He was planning his life with me. With him by my side, I could make plans, too.

"Spring it is."

When we arrived at the cottage, it wasn't the gallowglass but Karina's friend Colleen who opened the door.

"Well, hello," she said. "Fancy seeing you here."

"Hey, Col," Christopher said as we stepped inside. "I figured you'd be on a plane home by now."

"I had little choice in the matter," she replied. "No sooner had I gotten Ethan's drunk ass out of here and Rina started making faces and complaining about her back. Then Rob jumped into action and started shouting orders. No way was I going home when the baby was almost here."

"Faith came in a hurry, then?" he asked.

"Quick as a bunny, she was here." Colleen faced me, and took a deep breath. "Anya, about what Ethan said. I am so sorry you had to hear that."

"No apologies are needed," I said with a wave of my hand. "Ethan, now he's the one what should be apologizing. Boorish man. I only left so I wouldn't yell at him myself and upset Karina."

She smiled. "You, I like. Come on, now. The happy family is in the upstairs bedroom."

We followed Colleen upstairs and found mother, bairn, and gallowglass nestled together in the family bed. Pretty as a picture they were, with Karina propped up against the headboard with the bairn in her arms, and Robert leaning on his elbow next to her. They were so absorbed in staring at their child they didn't notice our arrival.

Christopher knocked on the doorframe. "Congratulations."

"Chris," Karina said, her face lighting up. "You're here! Hey, Anya."

"Of course we're here." Christopher sat beside Karina, and she handed him the bairn. He held her as naturally as if he'd cradled a thousand such babes. "Hello, baby. I'm your Uncle Chris." He glanced at Karina. "Faith Elizabeth?"

She nodded. "Elizabeth was Robert's mother's name, just like our mom."

"She's beautiful," Christopher said. "She looks exactly like you did when you were a baby."

"There is no way you could remember that."

Christopher smiled. "I've got pictures to prove it." He glanced at Robert. "Celebratory Scotch?" he suggested.

Robert nodded. "A fine thought."

Christopher handed the baby to Karina. Robert kissed Karina's and then Faith's forehead, then he and Christopher left in search of the promised whisky. Colleen took Robert's place next to Karina and gazed at the bairn.

"Have a seat, Anya," Karina said, and I did. "Would you like to hold her?"

Before I could reply, Karina lifted the bairn toward me. I had no choice but to accept the tiny, warm bundle, and I was so glad I did. Faith was a bonnie wee lass, with round pink cheeks and a shiny mouth the color and shape of rose petals. Fine black down covered her head, and I wondered if it would stay that color, or if it would all fall out and grow back blonde or red. With a magical child such as she, anything was possible.

"She's perfect," I cooed, holding Faith's face close to mine. "Oh, Karina, what a special lass you have here."

"Yeah, she is pretty awesome. You know, Robert's already hinting at wanting a few more."

"I can see why, what with this beauty you've given him."

Karina beamed at that, and went on about how she'd never wanted a large family, being that it had just been she and Christopher growing up, but now that Faith was here she thought a few siblings wouldn't hurt. I squeezed my eyes shut, remembering my father and brothers and how they'd all been taken from me, and while I'd had the burden of growing up as an only child the loss of them had driven my mother mad...

"Anya!" Colleen snapped.

I opened my eyes and saw Colleen and Karina staring at me, their eyes wide and terrified. "What, now? Has something happened?"

Karina swallowed, and said, "There is ice on Faith's blanket. Anya, I don't know why you're doing that, but you need to stop."

I looked down at the babe, and saw the frosty rime on her swaddling. I thrust her into Karina's arms, then I scuttled off the bed and backed away, terrified and ashamed of what I'd done.

"I'm so sorry," I said, my tears freezing to my cheeks. "Karina, I don't know what came over me! I would never harm Faith in any way!"

"I know you wouldn't." Karina had stripped off the icy blanket and placed Faith against her breast. "Only the blanket got cold. Faith didn't even wake up." She stroked the bairn's head, then she fixed me in her gaze. "Anya, are you all right?"

At that moment, my heart grew so full it burst. Here she was, a woman who'd given birth not two days prior and who'd almost had her infant frozen solid, and yet Karina was concerned for me. I did not deserve her, or Christopher, or even the basest comfort. I was a monster made of ice and nightmares, destined to freeze anyone foolish enough to come near me. I blinked out.

MEETING FAITH

I followed Rob downstairs and toward the kitchen. Stacks of gifts in varying stages of unwrap were clustered on the coffee table and counters; from what Colleen had said, Rina went into labor one minute and the next minute Faith was here, leaving them no time to properly clean up after the shower. That was to be expected, and far be it from me to critique anyone's housekeeping skills, but a small group of packages near the front door caught my eye.

"Are those more presents from the shower?" I asked. These packages weren't just wrapped, they were decorated with fresh flowers, seashells, and polished stones. When I got closer, I realized that they were wrapped in fabric rather than paper. It was expensive fabric at that, all heavy damasks and jewel-toned silks.

"They are meant for Karina," Rob replied, as he hunted for glasses in the cabinets.

"Is this how royalty wraps gifts?" I wondered, fingering a length of ribbon.

"Ye are not far from wrong." Having found the glasses, he set about washing them. "Those items are from our *other* friends."

"Other... Wait, are these gifts from gods?"

"Aye, that they are," he replied. "And no' just from ones we've met. It seems that Persephone has relayed the tale o' how Karina outwitted Demeter to her entire pantheon. Ye see that one with the shells? That's from Poseidon himself."

"Wow." I took a closer look at the packages, trying to match the decorations to the gods. "So the one with the pomegranate is from Persephone, the one with roses must be from Aphrodite, Artemis obviously sent the one with the antler… Who sent the one covered with thistles?"

"Nicnevin. We shall open that one outside." Rob set two sparkling clean glasses on the counter and opened the bottle of Glenfiddich. "Now, about that celebration."

I picked up my glass. "To Faith."

"To Faith."

We clinked glasses and drank. "How does it feel to be a father?"

"Faith is no' me firstborn." My face must have betrayed my thoughts, and he continued, "Afore I was taken I was married. I had two sons, though the younger was no' born until after Nicnevin had me."

"Wow. That's… wow." I drained my glass, and Rob refilled it. "I'm sorry."

"Don't be. Me boys had good, long lives, and now Karina and I have the chance to watch Faith grow. Children are always a blessing, ye ken."

I heard a sound behind me. I turned and saw Rina wobble down the stairs, baby Faith sleeping in her arms and Colleen hovering behind her.

"Hey, should you be up and about?" I asked. Rob was at her side in an instant, helping her navigate the steps and settling her on the couch.

"I'm fine, you overprotective men," Rina said as Rob tucked a blanket across her lap. "You know, in the old days, women had babies and went right back to working in the fields."

"Bah," Rob said. "In my youth, when a woman bore a child she stayed abed for a month or more to ensure both her and the bairn's recovery. Birth is a most harrowing experience for all involved," he added as he scooped Faith into his arms.

Rina smiled ruefully. "I did feel harrowed. Wicked harrowed, in fact."

I looked at the stairs, which remained empty. "Rina, is Anya still upstairs?"

"She left, right after she almost turned Faith into a Popsicle," Colleen said.

I dropped my glass as Rob asked, "What manner of things is a Popsicle?"

Rina's gaze slid toward him. "Frozen fruit juice."

"What d'ye mean, frozen?" Rob demanded. He set Faith on his lap and felt her cheeks, then her hands and her tiny, tiny feet. "She does no' feel cold."

"She's fine. Anya just got some frost on her blanket." Rina bit her lip, then she turned to me. "She's not handling her transformation into the Queen of Winter very well, is she?"

I ran a hand through my hair. "No, she's not, and it's getting worse." I picked up my glass—luckily it hadn't shattered—then I grabbed a kitchen towel and cleaned up the spilled whisky. "Is this how her powers are supposed to manifest? Is she supposed to be randomly freezing things and people? Maybe this is how it's meant to be."

"What does Anya say about all of it?" Rob asked.

"Well, now, that's part of the problem." I tossed the towel into the sink and refilled my glass. "She doesn't say much about it, other than she's terrified. And while it's great to know where her mind's at, I don't know how she's feeling physically, if she's in pain or even if she's feeling better than ever. Even when she does share things with me, it's still a mystery."

"Interesting," Rina said. "Is she behaving any differently?"

"She hardly sleeps anymore. At first I thought it was something like an adrenalin surge from her new powers, and she was too wound up to relax."

"But that was no' the case, was it?" Rob prompted.

I wiped my hand over my face. "She's afraid she'll freeze me in her sleep."

"That couldn't really happen," Colleen said. "Could it?"

"When she woke up yesterday morning, she was frozen to the bed."

Rina gasped and covered her mouth. Faith squeaked, and Rob adjusted her against his chest. "Ye were aware that she has scant control over winter's chill, and yet ye brought her here, to me home? Ye let her hold me bairn?"

"I handed Faith to Anya," Rina said, ever ready to defend me from whatever mess I'd gotten myself into. "And in case you've forgotten, Anya defied her mother to help save me and Faith. Both of us owe her our lives."

Rob grunted. "Aye, I have no' forgotten. I also have a bride and daughter dependin' on me to keep them safe." Robert kissed Faith's head, then he handed her off to Rina.

"Anya remains welcome here, but she must keep her distance from Faith," he said. "At least until she can control the cold. Beira once froze me solid, and I'll no' have that happen to me bairn."

"What about me?" Rina asked.

Rob brought her hand to his mouth, and kissed her knuckles. "Or you."

Rina smiled. "What are we going to do about Anya?" When we all stared at her, she continued, "We can't turn our backs on her. Anya needs us. What with her mother exiled to the Winter Palace, and her father and brothers still a bunch of stones in a field, we're all she has."

"I agree that she is in need o' help," Rob began, "and while I will do whatever I can for the lass, we are no' the ideal ones to be assisting her."

"Then who is?" I asked.

Rob shrugged. "I admit that I do no' ken the answer. What we must do is find one who similarly had an elemental gift thrust upon them, and ascertain how they dealt with their new gifts."

Colleen leaned forward and regarded Rob. "Exactly how are we going to do that? Are these elemental gifts common around here?"

Rob frowned. "I suppose no'."

"I appreciate that you want to help Anya," I began. "Truly, I do... But these theories aren't helping her right now. She's alone and freaking out, and I need to find her."

"Do you have any idea of where she might be?" Rina asked.

I set down my glass and approached the couch. "May I?"

"Of course," Rina said, lifting the baby toward me. I picked up Faith and held her close, enjoying that irresistible newborn scent as I thought about Anya. She wouldn't have gone back to our apartment, not so soon after freezing to the bed. When Anya was scared she behaved like a wild animal, and retreated to some place safe to rest and lick her wounds; I'd once called her my feral cat, and she flashed me her claws in response. I took to calling her kitten, instead.

But where would she retreat to? If our apartment was off-limits for the time being, it would have to be a place she felt safe, and she's always said she felt safest with family. She couldn't go home to Beira, but I knew exactly where to find Anya's other parent.

"Yeah. I do."

THE OLD MAN'S HOUSE

After fleeing the walker's cottage in Crail, I did what I've always done what I was confused and hurt: I went straight to my father's house in Glen Lyon. Nothing had ever calmed me so much as a long conversation with Da. Since he, along with all of my brothers, had been imprisoned in stone over two centuries ago, our conversations were rather one-sided, but they remained a comfort like none other.

The story of how he'd gotten himself into such a state was an interesting one, and the details of it changed depending on who was telling it at the time. The version I understood to be closest to the truth was that my father, an older and supposedly more powerful being than either my mother or the Seelie, was tired of Fionnlagh and Nicnevin ruling the warm half of the year and sought to extend winter first by a few weeks, and then a few months. Da's plan was doomed to fail from the start; aside from the land needing the warmer months for obvious reasons, he'd previously tried taking over the warm season before when he dethroned the Summer King. With the Summer King gone, the Seelie had risen in their place, and my parents' rule remained confined to the winter months alone. But Da was determined to take control of the entire wheel of the year, even if his goals were a bit too grandiose—and poorly planned—to come to fruition.

When Da's plans came to light Mum had feared the Seelie King's wrath would extend to her, but she needn't have worried. If she'd been imprisoned along with Da we wouldn't have a winter, arguably as disastrous a situation as the land losing its summer. That meant that Da and my brothers were sentenced to spend half a millennia in stone, the exact length of time they had been working to eradicate summer—at least, that was the length of time they owned up to—while Mum remained free. Their sentence was already half over, and I couldn't wait to see them again.

As to why I also remained free, Mum claimed it was because I'd been too young to be part of the scheme, but that explanation had never sat well with me. Most of my brothers hadn't been involved either, but they'd all received the same punishment. The Seelie King had wanted to make an example out of them, and so he did. Why I wasn't worthy of such a fate remains in question. I was grateful to have been overlooked by the vindictive madman, but the inequity has always befuddled me.

Our varied punishments had never seemed odd to Mum. Whenever I questioned her, she admonished me to accept the boon fate had given me, lest she stick me in stone herself.

I purposefully arrived a kilometer or so from Da's house, an ancient stone hut called a shieling just north of Loch Lyon. The locals called the shieling *Tigh na Bodach*, which meant Old Man's House. Times past there would be bonfires constructed on the peaks in the Cailleach Bheur's honor on the high holy days, and offerings left in her name. There was even a boulder at the shieling representing Mum, though to my knowledge she'd never been imprisoned in it. With her, you never could be sure.

I'd arrived at such a distance in order to take the traditional path downhill toward the shieling. My da had always said keeping to the old ways was a sign of respect, and it was the least I could do for him. Imagine my anger and astonishment when I found three men standing in front of my father and brothers, and they weren't just any men. They were the Picts Christopher and I had encountered in Glasgow last month.

Sir Walter Scott, bless his poet's heart, had once referred to Glen Lyon as the longest, loneliest, and loveliest glen in Scotland. All of his words were true, which made the men's appearance even more unusual. I could accept an odd person or two turning up in a city, but at the far end of a remote glen? Da used to say that when the coincidences began outnumbering the facts, what you were left with was never a coincidence.

I strode toward the shieling and the men; I didn't know if they'd seen me teleport in, and in case they hadn't, I wanted to keep my ability under wraps. The way their leader had spoken in Glasgow they were aware that I am the Queen of Winter, but he may have been posturing for the benefit of his men. If that was the case, I didn't want to reveal more than they already knew.

I also carefully put on my human guise, strengthening the magics that stretched across my eyes and ears. Whoever these individuals were, hopefully they couldn't penetrate my glamour.

"Can I be helping you?" I called when I was within their earshot.

"Hello there," replied the leader. Once again, he was bedecked with a heavy gold torque and gauntlets. "Lost your way, have ye now?"

"I could ask the same of you." I stood before the three of them, confirming that they were indeed the men I'd met in Glasgow. I felt my claws press against the inside of my fingertips, and taut bands of cold twining around my wrists. "This spot isn't on the way to anywhere."

"We're just on our way to Atholl, and stopped to pay our respects to the lady," the leader replied, sweeping his arm toward the shieling. He was watching me like a hawk, no doubt trying to gauge my reaction.

"Good of you, to keep the old ways," I said. "Too many have forgotten."

"Aye, 'tis the truth ye speak."

"Were you also keeping the old ways in Glasgow?"

"Always do, my lady."

These forced pleasantries were turning my stomach. "Interesting that I've never once seen or heard of you before August, yet now your path keeps crossing with mine."

"'Tis a small island. We were bound to meet, eventually."

He smiled. I didn't. We regarded each other for a moment, then he tipped his head toward me. "We'll leave ye to your business, then. Good day to ye."

I watched them amble away and down the glen, holding them in my gaze until they were out of sight. Why had they been here? Where had they been hiding in the month since I'd seen them in Glasgow? Had they been spying on me?

Could anyone spy on me, an elemental queen able to come and go in the blink of an eye?

I should have gone after them. I should have demanded their names, the names of those they served, and an explanation as to why three men who should have lived and died hundreds of years ago kept appearing in my path. I should have done all those things and more, but I didn't budge. What if I went after them, and instead of asking any of those questions, I froze them instead?

I shook my head, clearing away those thoughts. The only people who knew why those men had been here were the three who'd just left, unless they'd shared their plans with my father and brothers. Since the former were gone and the latter still in stone, I wouldn't get my answers today.

It was long before Samhain, which meant the stones remained on the meadow in front of the thatched roof hut. What with Mum in exile, they were all the family I had left in this world. The shieling's tradition was thousands of years old; on Beltane, the stones were brought outside to enjoy the sunshine, and on Samhain they are returned to the warmth and safety of their hut. No one, least of all me, ever thought every male in my family would end up imprisoned in these sacred rocks.

I knelt in front of the largest stone and touched the surface. Frost bloomed underneath my fingertips. "Da, can you hear me?" I asked, desperately. "Do you know what's happening to me? Can you help me?"

Silence. I hadn't expected a response, but I had wanted one. I so, so wanted one. I needed his counsel, his kind words. I shifted so I was laying on my back beside the stone, the glen stretched out below me. Maybe I would freeze to Da's stone, and my family and I would all be forgotten relics, far removed from the world and anyone we could harm.

CAN'T GIVE UP

"You're sure you want to drive?" Rina asked. Again. "I can send you there. It's no problem."

"Thanks, but I've had enough teleporting for now." Even as the words left my mouth, I wondered if I should recant and accept her offer. I was fairly certain Anya had gone to the shieling in Glen Lyon; we'd gone there several times this past summer, and she'd mentioned that whenever she was upset or confused, she would talk to her father. A one-sided conversation, that, but I've had many such conversation with my parents. Sometimes those conversations were the only things that kept me sane.

"It's a two-hour drive," Rina said. Also again.

"Yeah, well, I already drove two hours to get here. Might as well keep up that tradition." I sent the directions to my phone. "Why is everything two hours away? Scotland's such a small country. You'd think stuff would be close together."

"Chris."

I glanced up. Rina's mouth was pressed in a thin line, her arms tense at her sides. I put my phone in my pocket and gave Rina my full attention. "It's all right. I like driving."

"And at the end of the drive is an eight-mile hike."

"I know. Remember, I've gone that way before."

"You have to cross three rivers!"

"I know!"

"It would seem that Christopher knows the way, and that Karina is concerned for his safety," Rob said. He was sitting on the sofa with Faith. "Perhaps we should next investigate why Christopher prefers to undertake such a difficult journey when he could easily avoid such."

Well, that was concise. "I can't just appear next to Anya," I said. "Who knows how much that would shock her? She needs to settle down, not have me fall out of the sky when she isn't expecting me."

"I can send you somewhere up the glen," Rina began, but I shook my head.

"I need some time, too. I need to think about what happened, decide what I'm going to say to her... Figure out how I can help. So yeah, I am going to drive for two hours and walk for eight miles, and hopefully, at the end of all that, I'll have some answers."

"What if she doesn't want to see you?" Rina pressed.

That was a gut punch. "You're right. Maybe she doesn't, but she does need help. If, when she's better, she wants me to go, I'll go."

Rina frowned, but she didn't argue. "Is your phone charged?"

"I can charge it in the car."

"Make sure you do, and call me as soon as you get there."

"I will."

The drive was pleasant enough, and I had plenty of time to do some thinking about me and Anya. At first, the image I couldn't get out of my mind was Anya holding a frozen, blue baby. I knew that was just my worst fears talking; I hadn't seen Anya hold Faith, and by Rina and Colleen's own accounts Faith wasn't harmed. Still, the thought of my newborn niece being frozen solid rattled me.

But she hadn't frozen her. What's more, since I hadn't witnessed what happened—not that I doubted Rina or Colleen—I couldn't pass judgement without hearing Anya's side of the story. I owed her that. No, I owed her far, far more.

After everything that had happened with Olivia, and then Nicnevin, I'd resigned myself to spending the rest of my life alone. I felt betrayed and humiliated, used and discarded like so much garbage. I couldn't imagine ever being intimate with anyone again, and had resolved to remain solitary, perhaps forever.

Then I'd walked into Rina's Geology 101 class, and I saw Anya.

I'd been able to see through fae glamour ever since Nicnevin took me to Elphame, so I knew right away she wasn't human. Somehow, Anya also knew I could see her for what she was, and she relentlessly pursued me. Okay, maybe relentless isn't the right word, but she refused to give up on me. She brought me out of my shell and back to myself at a time when I couldn't find my way back on a map. That meant I couldn't give up on her.

I reached the end of the road. I parked near the hydroelectric dam—such a modern structure in the midst of this ancient landscape—and began my eight mile hike. First, I sent Rina a text.

Chris: Just parked. Starting the hike now.

Rina: Be safe.

Chris: Always.

I pocketed my phone, nodded a hello to the local sheep, and started walking. Hang on, beautiful. I'm coming.

COLD COLD HEART

"Anya?"

I blinked, dragging myself upward from sleep. The shadows had moved far across the meadow, yet I hadn't moved at all. I remained on the ground in front of the shieling, my head next to Da's stone. With any luck, I'd remain here with my father and brothers, and never move again.

"Anya!"

Hearing my name said twice with such alacrity convinced me I wasn't hallucinating. I got to my feet, steadying myself against Da's stone, as Christopher appeared at the end of the trail. I stood and gaped at him, hardly believing my eyes.

"Christopher?"

He paused, then he ran forward and pulled me into his arms.

"Anya, Anya, I was so scared." He held me at arm's length. "Don't ever disappear on me again."

"You came looking for me?" I asked, stunned. Glen Lyon was one of the most remote places in Scotland, and very far from Crail. Fionnlagh had been careful to leave Da where those who would seek to help him would have a tough time reaching him, never mind offering aid. Yet here was Christopher. He had come for me. "How did you know where to look?"

"After what happened, I figured you'd need someplace familiar," he replied. "What better place than with your family?"

After what happened... "Is the bairn well?"

"She is." Christopher tilted up my chin and flicked my frozen tears away. "You didn't hurt Faith, not one bit. No one is mad at you."

"Not even the gallowglass?"

"Rob doesn't count. He's always mad."

I placed my hands on his chest and closed my eyes. "I did not mean to frost her."

"Anya, you're frosting me now."

My eyes snapped open, and I saw the ice crystals spreading across his jumper. "No, no no no," I said as I backed away.

"Anya," he began, but I turned away.

I clenched my fists and screamed at the heavens. Why was this happening to me? Why was I being punished, slowly becoming a frozen corpse when I had done nothing wrong? My father and brothers had been turned to stone, my mother was imprisoned in a destroyed palace, but they had all earned their punishments. Me, I had always been the good daughter, the calm, respectful child who had always done what was asked of her. My life was nothing but centuries of good behavior, and my reward for all that goodness was suffering.

"It's not fair," I yelled.

"It isn't," Christopher said. Gods, why was he still here? Anyone with the common sense of a sheep would have fled long ago. But by my side he remained, even though my mother had deceived us both and nearly cost his sister and unborn niece their lives. Even though I'd nearly frozen his niece to death.

"Why aren't you running from this madness?" I demanded. "Can't you see that I'll be the death of you?"

"If anything, you'll be the death of yourself," he said. "Why are you pushing all of us away? We only want to help you."

I crossed my arms over my stomach. "No one has ever helped me," I said, and that was the truth. As much as my mum had gone on about how she'd waited eons for a lass in the house, after I'd been weaned she paid little attention to me. In the beginning she was so wrapped up in her love for my father she could barely see her nose in front of her face. Later, after he and my brothers had received their punishments, she'd been consumed first by grief, and then vengeance. Plotting revenge against one's enemies leave little time for raising a daughter.

Christopher laid a hand on my shoulder. "I'll help you."

Those three words unraveled me as if he'd tugged on my heartstrings and pulled apart the skein of my being. I grabbed his face and kissed him hard, so hard that for a moment I feared I'd hurt him; he was only mortal, far too fragile for the likes of me. If I had caused any pain, he enjoyed it, since he grabbed handfuls of my hair and returned my passions tenfold.

I glanced behind him, saw the shieling. I wrapped my arms around Christopher and blinked to our flat.

"Whoa," he said, steadying himself against me. "Why did you bring us here?"

My answer was to kiss him again. In the next breath we were on the floor, he on his back and me astride him. We tore at one another's clothes, then I turned my face upward and screamed again, this time in pleasure. I felt the cold creeping up my spine, its feathered tendrils seeking out my heart and freezing the veins in my neck, but I didn't care. The cold was power and I craved it, craved that which meant I was no longer a helpless child...

"Anya."

Christopher said my name so softly I almost didn't hear him. I looked down and to my horror the cold had invaded his body, leaving a rime of bluish ice spreading outward from his navel. Another moment and it would freeze his heart.

I acted without thinking, and teleported us to the nearest hospital. The staff stopped what they were doing and stared at the two of us, half-naked and iced over as we were.

"This man is freezing to death," I said. "Can you help him?"

"Of course." A woman dressed in medical attire approached us and set her hand on Christopher's forehead. She saw the ice covering his chest and gasped.

"Good God, fetch a gurney," she cried. Christopher was whisked away from me as she shouted instructions. "What happened? Did he fall into a loch? Miss? Miss!"

I didn't answer. Instead, I teleported as far north as I could, beyond the Arctic Circle and to land as cold and barren as my heart. Once there, I threw myself into the snow, and wept.

FROSTBITTEN

I woke up in a hospital room, alone and attached to a dozen beeping monitors. Everything about the room was cold and sterile, from the walls to the
over-bleached sheets and blankets swaddled around me. What the hell was I
doing here?

I remembered kissing Anya, then she teleported us to our flat. That had been
a great idea on her part, as the next moment found us tumbling to the floor and
making love. It was amazing, watching her let go and lose herself in the moment
like she'd done when we were first together in New York, before gods and destiny
tried ruining us. The moment she slid down onto me, I knew we'd never be
ruined.

Anya tossed her head back in pleasure, then blue and white lines snaked out
from between her breasts and crawled over her skin. In a heartbeat's time she
was blue up to her chin, her breasts like icy orbs topped with crystal peaks. She'd
been beautiful, a true winter queen. Then her white hand had touched my chest,
and the cold invaded my body. I remembered calling her name, but before she
acknowledged me, everything went black.

One of Anya's worst fears had nearly come true: she'd almost frozen me to
death.

But I'm not dead. I'm still here, and Anya still needs me.

I tried moving to a more comfortable position in the hospital bed, but the
skin across my chest was tight and hard and my joints were stiff. I lifted the

blankets and saw bandages wrapped around my torso. Whatever my official diagnosis was, it wasn't looking good.

A woman wearing scrubs and a lab coat entered the room and started checking the monitors. I assumed she was a doctor, but you know what happens when you assume.

"Hello," I said, startling her. "I don't suppose you know how I ended up here?"

"I most certainly do," she replied. "Mr. Stewart, is that right?"

"It is. Call me Chris." I glanced around the room, searching for my clothing. "I take it you gleaned my name from my wallet?"

"We did." She retrieved a bin that had been out of my line of sight below the bed, and set it on the tray table. In it I saw my shoes, socks, phone, car keys, and wallet, and nothing else.

"Did I show up naked?" I asked. I was naked under the blankets, and the rest of my clothing seemed to have vanished.

"Mostly so. We cut off what clothes were left in order to treat your frostbite." She sat in the chair next to me. "I'm Dr. Todd."

"Thank you," I said. She demurred, and I wiggled my fingers and toes. They felt fine. "Frostbite, you said?"

"Aye, but interestingly enough, your extremities weren't affected." Great. Being the interesting patient in a hospital was never a good sign. "The damaged area was localized to your torso, which was covered in a layer of ice. The frost ranged from your solar plexus all the way to your groin."

"Groin?" I surreptitiously moved my hand lower and grasped my penis. I found it and my testicles present and accounted for.

Dr. Todd noticed my movements, and frowned. "Yes, your bits and pieces are all intact. Your heart and lungs were what was in imminent danger from the hypothermia, but we warmed you up in time. It was touch and go for a while, since your core temperature had dipped below twenty-eight degrees."

"Twenty-eight degrees," I repeated, then I remembered we were in Scotland. "That's what, eighty degrees Fahrenheit?"

"It's bloody cold for a living body, no matter how you slice it," Dr. Todd snapped. "The woman that brought you here, what do know about her?"

Anya had brought me to the hospital. I guess that was the least she could have done, being that she'd been the one who'd frozen me. "Dr. Todd, I can truthfully say that I don't know nearly as much about her as I'd like. Has anyone else been by for me?"

"Not yet. Is there someone you can call?"

"Yeah. My sister."

Dr. Todd located a charging cord for my phone. While my phone powered up, I found out what hospital I was in, then the doctor gave me some privacy and I called Rina.

"Hey," she greeted. "Did you find Anya? Is she okay?"

"I did find her. How's Faith?"

"Best baby in the history of babies. What happened? Was Anya upset?"

I pinched the bridge of my nose. I'd intended to give Rina an edited-down version of what had happened, but I couldn't imagine her letting me get away with that. Besides, the last time I was less than forthcoming with my sister, I ended up enthralled to the Seelie Queen. "She gave me frostbite. I'm in a hospital now."

"What? Are you all right? Which hospital?"

"I'm fine. Well, I'm healing. Anya brought me here after, ah, you know. Can I talk to Rob?"

"Sure. And you're going to tell him exactly where you are and I'm sending him to get you."

"Can, ah, he bring me some clothes, too?"

Rina made a wordless noise of frustration, then she handed the phone to Rob. Once he was on the line I told him a more detailed version of what had happened, and where I was. He grunted and hung up.

"I guess that went well," I muttered.

I set my phone on the tray table and lay back. It's not like I could do much else, bandaged and hooked up to an intravenous drip like I was. The bandages on my chest were itchy, but I had a feeling that scratching would make everything worse. Dr. Todd had explained that after raising my core temperature they'd spread an ointment across the frostbitten areas, and that I would likely develop rather intense blisters as my skin repaired itself. She further explained that keeping my recently frozen skin covered and dry was essential. I assured her that I would follow any and all instructions. I was just glad my heart hadn't frozen solid.

All of that forced immobility meant my imagination kicked into overdrive. Every time I closed my eyes I saw Anya above me, frozen solid and more beautiful than ever. Had that been a glimpse of her future, one where she exists only in ice and snow? One without me?

I shook my head. I didn't think that was the case. Anya had been resisting the cold for weeks, but the pull was getting too strong. Maybe the key was for her to give in to her new abilities and find a way to exist in harmony with the cold.

Harmony. We can manage a little harmony, can't we?

About twenty minutes after he hung up on me, my brother-in-law, the gallowglass, appeared in the doorway of my room; or rather, he filled it. I was six feet tall, but Rob towered over me, his broad shoulders and barrel chest adding to his supersized appearance. Rina, who was much shorter than I was, looked like a Munchkin when she stood next to him.

Rob surveyed my room for a moment before he entered. His size, coupled with his quiet, determined nature, made it plain why Nicnevin had chosen him to be her personal assassin. Back when he'd been a preacher, he must have scared the devil out of his parishioners, literally.

"Rina sent you?" I asked, meaning that he'd arrived via portal.

"Aye, she surely did," he replied. "Are the doctors treatin' ye well, then?"

"They saved my life," I replied. Rob nodded, then he dragged the chair around so he could watch both me and the doorway, and sat. "You didn't happen to bring any clothes, did you?"

Rob loosed a knapsack from his shoulder and tossed it onto the bed. I looked inside, and saw an assortment of shirts and pants that I'd left in my old room at the cottage. "Thanks," I said. "How's Rina doing?"

"Do ye mean before or after ye called and told her that Anya fair near killed ye?" Rob countered.

"She didn't mean to," I said. "Things just got out of hand, and she lost control."

Rob raised an eyebrow but didn't ask me what had gotten out of hand, which was great. I really did not want to explain how having sex with my girlfriend had almost transformed me into an ice cube. Based on the look on his face, and the fact that I'd needed him to bring me clothes, he'd already figured out what had happened between us.

"That's twice in one day that Anya has lost control." He paused, and added, "That I am aware of."

The question hung in the air between us, and I saw no reason not to tell him everything. "The closer it gets to winter, the worse it gets. At first it was just random chills. Now she can't hold a teacup without the tea freezing solid."

"Mmm." Rob rubbed his chin and settled lower in his chair.

"What are you thinking?" I demanded, suddenly terrified that the Seelie had sent the gallowglass to dispatch a rogue snow queen.

"Calm yourself," Rob says with a glance toward the door. "I do no' need the doctor's lecturin' me on agitatin' a patient."

I leaned back against the pillows. "So you're not going to kill her?"

"No, lad. Karina and I wish to help her." Rob stood and walked toward the window, which had a spectacular view of the hospital's car park.

"Karina and I have been speakin' about Anya, and what may come o' her new abilities, e'er since the Seelie King bestowed them upon her," he began. "At first we made a joke of it, wonderin' if you'd end up the Winter King to her Queen."

My hand gravitated toward my bandaged chest. "Do you think that's a possibility?"

"Anything is possible. What we are more interested in is what's likely." Rob faced me, and continued, "Therefore, I ask ye this. Why is Anya unable to control a power that has been within her, in one form or another, since the day she was born? She is no stranger to power, or abilities beyond the mundane."

"I... don't know." He was right in that Anya had always been powerful. I'd watched her battle gods and monsters, and win. Since she was Beira's daughter a measure of control over the elements must have been passed down from her, and who knew what other abilities she inherited from her father, the giant.

"I also don't know much about her father, The Bodach, or what Anya may have inherited from him."

Rob smiled. "Seems to me ye need to learn a bit more about this lass ye so adore."

I gave him a look. "And exactly how much does Rina know about you?"

"She is well aware of everything that matters. What has Anya told ye about her da, Old Bod?"

"All I really know is that he's a giant that liked to pick a fight." I watched Rob for a moment, remembering that despite that he looked to be in his forties, he was almost four hundred years old. "Have you ever met him?"

"Met? No, I ne'er did meet him, but I was aware o' him. Everyone knew who Old Bod was, or knew someone who'd suffered a thrashin' at his hand. For all that he was a fighter, he was a kindly man, and would give ye the shirt off his back if ye were in need o' one. Your Anya comes from noble stock, she does."

"Maybe it's his influence that's causing her power to go awry."

"Perhaps. Or perhaps there is something more sinister at play. We have no' seen that bastard Damian since the incident that caused Beira to be exiled."

"You really think he's involved?"

"That one is trouble, and unchecked trouble at that. I do regret that he slipped through me fingers at Glen Lyon."

Rob was referring to my uncle, John Damian, who'd kidnapped Rina and tried to offer her up to Beira. Their goal had been to force Rina to open portals at their command and create a third fae court that Beira could rule over. Beira had also tricked Anya and me into freeing thirteen giants, whom she then employed as her guard. She had felt secure behind the line of giants, confident that she and Rina were untouchable.

Rob had shown up, defeated all thirteen giants and then Beira herself without breaking a sweat. But John had gotten away.

"I haven't seen or heard of him since then," I said. "I don't think Anya has, either. She would have told me."

"Aye. I've no doubt she would have." Rob withdrew a compass from his pocket. "Do ye recall Dougal's toolbox, and the box's ability to produce that which is needed?"

"I do."

Rob opened the compass's case, and turned the instrument toward me. The needle was pointing due south.

"Help me out. What is this compass telling me?"

"The needle always points toward Damian. I have been tryin' to track him this way, but a direction only tells ye so much. However, south o' this hospital is Glasgow."

Where Anya and I lived. "There are quite a few places south of here," I said, but Rob shook his head.

"When I'm at home in Crail, the needle points southwest. What's southwest o' Crail? Glasgow." Rob snapped the case shut and pocketed the compass. "I believe Damian is somehow meddlin' with both you and Anya."

"Why would he do that?" I asked. "He must know that we'd figure it out eventually, and tell you. Wouldn't it have been smarter for him to stay far away from us?"

"That man left sense behind when he kidnapped Karina. He kens well that I shall find him, and make him pay for what he did to her. He's just hoping to cause a bit o' mischief to distract me and stave off the inevitable."

"I wouldn't call making Anya's powers run wild a 'bit of mischief'."

"I suppose not. Now, it seems to me that we have two tasks that we can execute in concert: find Anya, and find Damian. We can help her best by ending whatever he's done to her."

"We?"

"Aye. I am no' letting you approach the Queen o' Winter alone, ne'er mind that she loves ye, and I do have a score to settle with Damian."

"You really think he's involved?"

"Aye. Me gut tells me so." He paused, and added, "There is also the matter of your sister."

"What about Rina?" I demanded, half sick with fear that something had happened to her or the baby.

"She has told me in no uncertain terms that I am to protect ye from Anya, Damian, and anything else that looks at ye askance. If ye wind up in hospital again, I fear she may no' let me in the door."

"Are all gallowglasses as altruistic as you?"

"I have no notion." He rubbed his chin, and I didn't know if he was considering my question or how to best make me pay for that sarcastic comment. "Every gallowglass that came afore me is dead, the last having been killed by me own hand, so we can no' ask them. However, I do know that they all acted in their own interest. Perhaps me actin' a bit selflessly now and again is what's kept me alive all these years."

"Perhaps." I stared at the compass in my hand, turning it this way and that while the needle remained pointing south. Could it really be that easy? We just had to find my uncle, get him to undo what he'd done, and Anya would be all right?

No. Of course it wouldn't. But it would be a start.

"Starting with Damian is a good plan, but it's only a beginning," I said. "He's wily, but I have a feeling this goes far beyond what he's capable of."

"Agreed," Rob said. "'Tis only a start, but we do need to begin somewhere. After ye've had your rest, we shall begin our quest."

"Quest for what?"

"To find Damian, and save the queen."

Help from a Friend

I emerged from the Arctic sea and strode onto the icy beach. The sun was cold and clean and bright, reflecting off ice floes and the impossibly blue water. I now understood the cold: it refined sensations, magnified them, and made me able to fully understand my surroundings. Cold was life and knowledge.

That knowledge extended to the ground beneath me. The sand against my bare feet was the only sensation I felt, each and every grain in sharp contrast to its neighbor. Frozen sand sliced and scraped my skin, but I didn't bleed. My blood was frozen in my veins, a river of rubies that nevertheless coursed throughout my body.

I'd fully embraced the chill and frozen myself solid, from my skin all the way through to my bones. But freezing hadn't made me weak; like a tree, I'd learned to move with the wind and it had made me all the stronger. No, I wouldn't shatter if you hit me, but if you managed to break off a piece of me, I'd use the sharp edge to slit your throat.

The last shreds of my clothing had long since washed away. I couldn't remember how they'd gotten shredded, or much of anything before I'd plunged into the sea. The clothes were of no matter, since layers of ice had hardened against my skin like so many plates of armor. I remembered my mother's own plate ice armor, how the bright winter sun had reflected off of it and tossed rainbows about her throne room. Now it was my turn to wear the armor, and the icy crown of shards. Soon enough, I will drag a blanket of snow across Scotland and lull the land to sleep.

I will be the Queen of Winter.

But first, I needed to make that crown.

I spent hours sitting on the beach trying to form a proper crown, but none of them came out right. Either they were lopsided, or too small, or tiny cracks appeared in the ice and ruined the shine. I decided that was just as well, for what I deserved was the Queen of Winter's true crown, the one forged of millennia old ice that was still held in the Winter Palace's vault. The Winter Palace had long since been nudged out of this dimension, and I was unable to reach it on my own, but I knew just the person who could send me there.

I teleported to Crail and knocked on the walker's front door. Karina, the walker herself, opened it a moment later. She was barefoot, clad in plaid pajama bottoms and a long sleeved knit shirt, her long brown hair secured in a bun atop her head.

"Anya," she began, then she looked up and down my body. "Are you wearing ice?"

"I am. May I enter?"

"Of course." Karina stepped aside and allowed me entry. I glanced about, at once relieved the gallowglass wasn't present, and disappointed that Christopher wasn't there either. "How is the bairn?"

"She's sleeping," Karina said too quickly. I glanced toward the stairs, and saw her friend Colleen standing sentry before the bedroom door. Memories pulled at my senses, but try as I might, I didn't know why they were keeping the bairn from me. Even so, I felt a prick of shame. "Can I help you with something?"

"Aye, lass, that you can. I need you to send me to the Winter Palace."

Karina took a step back from me. "Is that really a good idea? Fionnlagh made it seem like Beira was supposed to stay there alone. You know, in exile and all."

"Being that I am now the Queen of Winter, there are items housed within the Palace I must retrieve in order to properly commence my reign."

"And you can't teleport there on your own?" She took another step back. I looked behind Karina and saw her phone lying on the kitchen counter. "I thought you could go anywhere."

"Who do you want to call?" I asked.

"Chris," she replied, and my heart clenched. "Thank you, for bringing him to the hospital."

"Hospital," I repeated, then the memory of what I'd done smashed to the forefront of my mind. Christopher, my lover, dying beneath me, his skin freezing and his heart unable to bear winter's true chill. Unable to bear me. I clenched my fists so hard my nails cut into my palms, while frozen tears rolled down my cheeks and shattered on the floor.

"Anya."

I raised my head, and saw Karina crouching in front of me, her hand on my forearm. The weight of my despair had driven me to my knees.

"Chris is going to be okay," she said. "They warmed him up at the hospital. Robert is there with him now."

Two pieces of good news then: Christopher was alive, and the gallowglass was occupied for the time being.

"That you, for letting me know." I stood, and Karina did as well. "If I don't have access to artifacts contained at the Palace, I might freeze the next person I touch. I don't want to hurt anyone, Karina." I grasped her hands. "Will you help me?"

Karina looked at our interlaced hands. "Why aren't you freezing me now?"

"I-I don't know." Perhaps Karina had a sort of immunity to my abilities. I recalled that when I'd frosted the bairn, Karina's command had reversed the chill. "Send me to the Palace. It's the only place I will find answers I need." When she didn't move, I said, "Please."

She pursed her lips. "You do realize I'm going to tell Robert and Chris that you're going there. I might tell the Seelie, too."

"I ken that." I touched her cheek. "They are all welcome to follow me."

Karina nodded. "All right. Imagine the Winter Palace."

I closed my eyes and recalled the vast white halls, the vaulted ceilings made of clear blue ice that never melted under the harshest sunlight. Of course, the palace didn't look like any longer, being that the Seelie had destroyed it after my father's treachery came to light, but I liked to remember it as it was. "I am."

Instantly I appeared in the Winter Palace's grand foyer; I hadn't even had the opportunity to thank Karina for her kind assistance. I looked around but didn't see the tumbled walls and caved in ceilings I'd expected. The palace was as lovely as it had ever been, perfect ice and snow sculpted to my mother's exacting standards. The floor was solid blue ice harvested from ancient glaciers, and it shone like a mirror. In front of me rose a curving staircase made from packed snow, and frozen crystals sparkled on the banister. At the top of the stairs was my mother, the Cailleach Bheur of legend, seated on a throne of ice.

"About time you got here," she said.

THE COFFEE SHOP

R *ina: Your girlfriend just swung by.*

    Chris: Is she still there?

Rina: Nope. I sent her to the winter palace.

I stared at the screen for a heartbeat. "Rob, Anya was just at your house."

Rob's phone was in his hand and he was talking to Rina before I realized he'd moved. After a short, heated conversation, during which he spoke mostly Gaelic, he ended the call.

"Faith and Karina are unharmed," he said, as he pocketed his phone. "Colleen, as well."

"Of course they are," I began, then I recalled that I was lying in a hospital bed because Anya had almost killed me. She hadn't meant to hurt me, but she had done so all the same. "Rina understands Gaelic?"

"She understands me," he replied. "Get dressed. We have work to do."

I indicated the hospital bed I was lying on and plethora of machines monitoring my every function. "I'm still hooked up to an IV."

"Then unhook yourself." Rob stood and made for the door. "I'll see about settlin' your bill."

I stared after him for a moment, then I hit the call button. Arguing with him would only give one or both of us a stroke, probably me. Within a few minutes, a nurse arrived, and nearly had a fit when I told her I was ready to check out. While I was trying to calm her down, Dr. Todd appeared in the doorway.

"Do no' fash now, Laura," Dr. Todd said to the nurse. "Mr. Stewart is fine to be discharged."

That shocked both me and the nurse, but at least I had my leaving credentials. With the nurse's help, I got disconnected from the various monitors and tubes. Soon enough, I was dressed and as ready to go as I'd ever be. When I left my room, I found Rob and Dr. Todd standing near the nurse's station, speaking softly with their heads bent toward each other. Dr. Todd saw me first.

"I'll advise Himself as to what's happened," she said to Rob. "Fare well, both of you."

Dr. Todd turned on her heel and walked down the corridor. Rob walked toward the stairs, and I fell into step beside him. "What was she talking about? Who is Himself?"

Rob gave me a look, and kept walking. "Shit, she means the Seelie King, doesn't she? My doctor was a fairy!"

"Yes, and no' exactly." Rob pushed the stairwell door open, and we descended toward the ground level. "Margaret is like meself, a human who got entangled in the Good People's affairs."

I stopped moving. "Is she an assassin?"

Rob laughed. "No' hardly. She has, on occasion, offered her services to the Seelie as a midwife."

We reached the ground floor, and navigated the corridors toward the car park. "Is Rina going to send us a portal?" I asked, since we weren't close to Glasgow or Crail.

Rob handed me a set of keys. "No. Karina and Faith are resting."

"I thought she sent you here."

"She did." We exited the building, and I saw a massive, shiny black pickup truck parked in the closest spot. "She also sent Dougal's truck."

I'd driven Dougal's magic truck before. While it wasn't as much fun as taking my BMW out for a spin, the truck had an otherworldly cruise control that ensured we always got where we were going, whether we knew the way or not. It also tended to shave hours off of standard travel times. All in all, not a bad ride.

We got in the truck and headed toward the flat I shared with Anya in Glasgow. Rob was certain John Damian was somehow affecting Anya's abilities, and that he must be doing it close to where we lived.

"How would I have never noticed him?" I wondered out loud. "He must know that I would recognize him. Maybe he disguised himself?"

"That, or he goes where Anya does, and you do no'."

"But, we're never apart."

Rob glanced at me and cocked an eyebrow. It was enough to make me replay our last few months together.

"Well, we used to be always together," I continued. "We were inseparable for those few weeks we spent in New York. Then we moved to Crail and things were weird for a bit, but we were back together soon enough."

"And what about in Glasgow?" Rob prompted. "Surely ye both keep some time for yourselves."

I recalled all the days I'd gone down to the coffee shop alone to get some writing done, all times I'd stopped in bookstores looking for my next great read. Anya liked coffee and books too, but it was awfully boring watching someone else write, and since she was far older than I was, she was considerably better read than I'd ever be. I'd never once wondered what she was doing while I was plugging away at the keyboard or browsing bookshelves, since I trusted her completely. "Yeah. We each keep some time for ourselves."

"Do ye recall when she began unintentionally freezing things?"

"I'm not really sure when that started," I replied. "She hid it from me for a while. Or maybe I'm a terrible person for not noticing it sooner. I should have done more to help her."

"Ye can no' blame yourself," Rob said. "'Tis no' as if ye ever expected to love a woman what can turn ye into solid ice. Ye had no idea o' what signs to watch for."

"I guess I didn't." I remembered an incident that had happened a few months ago. "There's a coffee shop we like, not far from our place. I remember one day last summer when Anya's tea kept going cold. She asked the server for a new cup, and we watched him pour it, but as soon as she tried to drink it had already cooled off."

Rob nodded. "That may have been the beginnin' of it, then. What changed after she realized she was the one chillin' her drink?"

"She stopped going with me to the coffee shop, for one," I replied. "Said she was too embarrassed to sit at one of the tables again. Now she just orders breakfast to go and brings everything home. Come to think of it, we stopped going out to eat, too. By the end of August, she hardly left our apartment."

I recalled the last time we ate out; it was at the Vietnamese restaurant. We'd gone there after we'd been to the antique market, and after we'd seen a group of Picts and the Roman legionaries. I didn't see a connection between legionaries and Anya's abilities, but I remembered the news reports of the market vendors' frozen and shattered wares.

The restaurant's ceiling had been decorated with dozens of paper lanterns in shades of orange and red and yellow. The effect was of a perpetual sunset, especially when they were lit up at night. Anya had frozen them all, then the soaked paper dripped to the tables and floor in colorful globs. Even though no one in the restaurant had known she was responsible, save me, Anya was mortified.

"There was an antique market, too, and an incident at a restaurant," I said. "Anya froze, well, everything."

Rob nodded. "Were those incidents before or after the time in the coffee shop?"

"Both were a few weeks after."

"'Tis decided, then. We shall go to the coffee shop first."

I parked Dougal's truck in the spot near my flat where I normally left my BMW, then Rob and I walked to the coffee shop. It was about a block from my building, and it definitely catered to tourists. Anya had loved spending an afternoon sipping a hot cup of tea while she watched the world go by outside the front window. It had been one of the first paces she'd shown me after I'd moved in with her. The shop was one of her favorite places in Glasgow, and she'd been avoiding it for weeks.

"Are ye all right, lad?" Rob asked.

I realized I'd been staring at the shop's sign. "Yeah. It just really hit me how much Anya must have been suffering in silence."

He clapped me on the shoulder. "I am certain she was only attemptin' to keep ye safe. Onward, now."

We entered the shop. I inhaled the sweet, coffee-scented air, and relaxed. It was warm and dark inside, the interior comprised of a slate floor and dark wood corbels with highly detailed trim, along with a scattering of upholstered booths and small round tables. Honestly, the establishment looked more like a bar than a coffee shop, and the first time Anya had taken me there I'd been disappointed there wasn't any whisky on the menu. The rich atmosphere more than made up for the lack of alcohol.

"Want something to drink?" I asked Rob. "On me."

Rob frowned at the chalkboard menu. "Have they any tea?"

"They specialize in coffee. They even roast their own beans, and grind them fresh throughout the day."

Rob nodded, then he strode up to the barista. "I'll have a pot o' black tea, if you please."

Soon enough, Rob had his tea, and I had a mug of dark roast coffee. We claimed Anya's favorite booth, the one near the front picture window.

"The two o' ye came here often?" Rob asked.

"Almost every day," I replied. "Anya used to come by in the morning and bring coffee and breakfast back to the apartment. Some days we'd stop by in the afternoon, too, and I'd do some writing."

Rob grunted, and gazed out the window. I wondered how Rina ever had conversations with this man. After he'd spent some time contemplating the afternoon's foot traffic, he asked, "Is there any other place she went regularly?"

"There's the market," I said. "She loved to stop by and pick up a few things for dinner. Not that she had any idea of what to do with those ingredients," I added.

"Karina can no' cook a meal to save her life," Rob said, and I agreed. "If it weren't for the restaurants in the village, we'd surely starve."

"Anything beyond scrambled eggs is above her skill level," I said, remembering the few occasions Rina had attempted cooking a big meal. The results had always been entertaining, even if we had ended up ordering pizza.

"Anya went to these markets every day?" Rob asked.

"Not really. There are a few big Sunday markets that she likes, but I always went with her to those. We liked the vintage fairs, too. We liked looking for unique things for our apartment." I remembered our last market trip. "Maybe I liked them more than she did."

"Then we're back to this location being the one she came to wi'out ye on a near daily basis."

"Yeah." I glanced around the interior. The shop looked just the same as it had the myriad other times I'd been inside of it. There were even the same two baristas working. "You think someone here did something to her?"

"'Tis a possibility, and one that is easy enough to rule out," he replied. "Tomorrow, ye shall come here first thing in the mornin' and order exactly what Anya is known for purchasin'."

"What will you do?"

"I will be watchin'."

THE WINTER PALACE

I stared up at my mother, who in turned stared down at me from her throne of ice. Only there shouldn't have been a throne, or stairs, or anything beyond heaps of rubble. Here I'd been wracked with guilt imagining my Mum confined to a destroyed palace when actually she'd been in the lap of luxury.

"How is the palace so... whole?" I asked. Even the crystal chandeliers were intact, their drooping swags sparkling in the bright sun.

"Once I returned, the palace righted itself." Mum leaned forward. "You haven't said why it's taken you so long to join me. I've grown quite bored waiting for you to make an appearance."

"You've been waiting for me?" I asked, bewildered.

"Of course I have," she replied. "For it to take you a donkey's year to get here, things must be going well."

"They have not," I said, my voice catching in my throat. Until the moment I saw her, enthroned as the Queen of Winter ought to be, I'd been in denial about how much I'd missed her. How much I needed her. I ran up the stairs, slipping and sliding on the ice and nearly landing flat on my face. When I reached her, I flung myself at her feet and laid my head in her lap.

"There, there," she cooed, smoothing back my hair. "What pains my sweet lass so?"

"Mum, I need your help." Frozen tears rolled off my cheeks and bounced off the icy floor. "I don't know what I'm supposed to do."

"Then help you I shall. Tell me everything, my lamb."

"The c-cold," I began. "I-I can't control it. I nearly froze Karina's bairn. I n-nearly killed Christopher." I whispered the last part, my throat thick with shame.

"The walker's borne her child, then." Mum twirled a strand of my hair around her finger. "Interesting."

"Mum. Can you... Will you help me?"

"Of course I will." She slid off her throne and knelt beside me. Her gaze moved over my body, and she bit her lip. "Anya, why are you iced over as you are?"

I looked down at my body. Plates of ice were all that covered me. "When I emerged from the Arctic Sea, my clothes were gone. The ice has done me well since."

"You swam in the Arctic?" Mum held me at arm's length, then she leaned closer and peered into my eyes. "'Tis a full month and more before the first day of your reign. You should not be this powerful, not yet."

"Mum, I've been this powerful." I crossed my arms over my breast, my hands worrying the ice from my biceps. "When the Seelie King first made me this, I felt the power, but it was no bother. The cold was nothing more than a tickle at the back of my mind, like an old but well-loved memory."

"Was this tickle also beloved by Christopher?"

"He supported me. He did everything he could to help me, and make me happy." I smiled, recalling our first wonderful months in Scotland. "Christopher and I, we didn't know what the future would hold, but we decided to spend every moment together, and we started going around Scotland. I showed him the places I loved. I even brought him back to Glen Lyon, told him which stones were Da and the lads."

"And how did the writer react to meeting our stone family?"

"He greeted each of them by name." I swallowed the lump in my throat. "He treated each and every one of them not as a piece of rock, but as a man stood before him in the flesh."

Mum smiled. "You know, your da would have respected Christopher. He will respect him, once they have a proper meeting. Old Bod has always appreciated a sharp mind as much as a keen blade." She paused. "When did things change for you, and the cold?"

"Christopher and I traveled about the island for almost a month, then I took him home to my flat in Glasgow. Not a week after that, the chill started overtaking me."

Mum let out a string of curses that would have made a giant blush. "Gods below, Anya, I've told you time and again that you should give up that flat. It's too public, too easy for your enemies to find you. Now one of them has, and it might mean the end of us all."

"What enemy?" I searched my memory, but the only enemy I'd ever made who had the power to influence the seasons was Demeter, and she was bound by a *geas* for the next eight years. "I have no enemies."

She placed her hand on my cheek. "You yourself don't. You've always been a good lass, and I daresay that there is no one living or dead that could utter an unkind word against you. But I have enemies, as does your father, and I know of one scoundrel who would make my daughter suffer just to grind salt into my already broken heart."

"Who is that?"

"Udane, the Summer King your father unseated."

THE USUAL

Rob went home to Crail shortly after our visit to the coffee shop, the journey made easy thanks to Dougal's enchanted truck, but not before he promised to return the next day at sunrise. It probably would have been more convenient for all involved if he'd just slept on my couch, but he missed Rina and the baby. As for me, I began my time in the flat by checking public transportation routes between Glasgow and Glen Lyon, and hoped my car would remain where I'd left it until I had time to retrieve it. I could have asked Rina to portal me there, but she had enough on her plate.

After I reviewed the train and bus schedules, I checked my email. Wow, that was a packed inbox. I had emails from my agent, from my former publisher, and offers from a few other publishers trying to pick up my latest work. Between everything that had happened with Rina having the baby and Anya's emerging power, I'd forgotten all about my writing career.

I checked the time, and sent a text to my agent.

Chris: You awake?

Maisie: For my best client? Always.

My phone rang a moment later. "By best client, do you mean most annoying?" I asked, in lieu of a proper greeting.

Maisie laughed her scratchy cigarette smoker laugh. "If you were annoying you wouldn't have this number. Tell me everything."

"Rina had the baby. Hang on, let me send you a picture." I did, and heard Maisie squeal in approval.

"I love her," Maisie declared. "Tell Karina she makes the best babies."

"I will."

Silence stretched between us. When it got to be too much, Masie asked, "What else has been going on?"

"A lot. Um, I have a ton of emails from publishers. I haven't looked at any of them."

"And you know what? You don't have to. They shouldn't be emailing you directly, anyway." I heard papers shuffling; Maisie was always working. Her version of a vacation was filing someone else's paperwork. "Tell you what, I'll sift through these offers, compile a single document listing the pros and cons of each, and we can take it from there. Sound good?"

"Maisie, I don't know what I ever did to deserve you."

"You know exactly what you did. You wrote a great book, and you were smart enough to let me represent you." She paused, and I heard more papers shuffling. "I will have this to you in a few days. In the meantime, don't freak out, don't sign anything, and if you need me please, please call me?"

"I will. Thank you."

"Thank me by writing another bestseller so we can both retire."

She ended the call, and I sat there staring at the ceiling. I didn't have to do any of this otherworldly nonsense. I had an education, and a career, and if I had any sense, I'd go home to New York and leave all this fairy bullshit behind me.

I looked at my phone. The picture of Faith was still on the screen. She was sleeping, nestled in her purple dinosaur blanket. If I went back to New York I'd be an ocean away from Faith, and Rina. I didn't know if I could do that.

I thumbed away Faith's picture. The next was an image of Anya and me, what Rina would call a "lame ass selfie". Our faces were close together, and the background was the suspension bridge over the River Clyde. It had been taken on our first day in Glasgow. I'd asked Anya to bring me someplace she loved, and she teleported us to the river. When I asked why she'd chosen that spot, she replied that with all the changes she'd seen over the centuries, the river was one of the few constants in her life.

I put down the phone and ground the heels of my hands against my eyes. Anya needed me—goddammit, she needed me—and I was contemplating leaving the country. Anya deserved so much better than me.

What Anya needed was a partner that wouldn't shy away when things got rough. She needed someone who would stay the course, and be there for her no matter what. I wanted to be that kind of partner for her, but wanting only gets you so far. I needed to act. My first act as a better man was me doing what I always did when I was down and confused. I called Ethan.

"I assume this is a life or death situation," Ethan said when he picked up.

"I... I just need someone to talk to."

"Hey. Hey. I'm here."

Early the next morning, I received a text from Rina warning me of Rob's imminent arrival. My late night talk with Ethan had centered me, and I knew I was where I was supposed to be: in Glasgow, with Anya. I was her partner, and I would help her through this and any other obstacles we faced. We were in this together. I just hoped the cold hadn't permanently frozen me out.

Since I was already dressed, I went outside, and found Rob leaning against the truck wearing his full gallowglass armor. So much for blending in with the locals.

Despite Rob's armor, no one would mistake him for a knight. Instead of metal plate, he wore a quilted leather jacket and matching pants topped with a long chain mail shirt, and he carried his iron helmet tucked underneath one arm.

Across his back was a massive sword and shield, and I knew he kept various other knives and darts secreted about his body. Instead of traditional leather boots or sandals, Rob wore a pair of contemporary hiking boots, his only allowance for modern culture.

"Morning," I said. "Not going for subtlety, are you?"

"No one will take notice o' me unless I wish it," Rob replied. "We are agreed on the plan?"

"I go to the shop, get Anya's usual order, and we see what comes of it," I recited

"Good." With that, he pushed off the truck, and we set off toward the coffee shop. I doubted that anyone could not notice Rob, and had a feeling he'd end up on Instagram within the hour.

"May I ask you something?"

"Surely."

"Do you actually drive that truck, or is it just going wherever you tell it to bring you?"

"I do no' tell the truck anything. I do no' have conversations with vehicles, as you do with the Beaner."

"Beemer," I corrected. I started to say more, but realized the futility of explaining German luxury vehicles to a man who preferred walking or riding a horse to traveling in anything manmade. It was a wonder he'd done as well as he had while in New York.

"When I drive the truck, I'm actually driving it," I continued. Rob claimed he learned how to drive by watching Rina, but being that she hardly ever got behind the wheel, I wasn't sure I accepted that explanation. "When you drive it, are you even steering?"

Rob shot me a look that said our question and answer time was over.

We arrived at the coffee shop. "You should probably wait outside," I said, indicating his armor and assorted weaponry. Rob drew a vertical line in the air and stepped behind it and out of my sight.

He vanished, right before my eyes.

"Does Rina know you can do that?" I demanded. When his only response was disembodied laughter, I gave up and entered the shop.

The barista working that morning was Nick. He and I got along quite well, mostly because we were both American. He'd come to Scotland to attend university, and dropped out after one semester. That had been more than ten years ago, and he had no plans of going home.

There were a few customers ahead of me, so I bided my time and waited for Nick to help them. Once it was just he and I in the shop, I approached the counter.

"Morning," I said. "Is Anya's order ready?"

It could have been my imagination, but Nick paled when I said Anya's name. "Her order?" he asked.

"Yeah. She gets the same thing every morning, right?"

A bead of sweat rolled down Nick's temple. Not my imagination, then. I leaned on the counter, and said, "Listen, I'm kind of in the doghouse with her. Can you please just put together whatever her usual is? Help a guy out, and all?"

Nick smiled, showing way too many teeth. "Sure, man. Have it ready in a minute."

"Thanks."

I wandered away from the counter, giving Nick some space while he got to work putting together Anya's usual order. His extreme reaction made it plain that whatever Anya had been purchasing—or whatever he'd been adding to it—was something I wasn't supposed to know about. Which begged the question, was Nick one of the evil masterminds, or just an unwilling accomplice?

Scratch that. He'd been doing whatever he'd been doing to Anya for weeks, if not longer. That marked him as guilty in my book.

"Here it is," Nick called. I went back to the counter. Waiting for me was a plain white paper bag, not one of the usual brown ones with the shop's logo printed across the top. I wanted to open the bag right away, but if Nick really was a part of whatever was happening to Anya, I didn't want him to suspect I was on to him, or them.

"Thank you. I appreciate you putting this together for me." I reached for my wallet. "How much do I owe you?"

"Nothing." When I just stared at Nick, he blustered, "I mean, we have that rewards program and all, and Anya hasn't really cashed in on it. It's cool. Really."

I smiled. "Okay. Thanks again."

I picked up the bag and left the shop. As I looked up and down the road for Rob, a hand grabbed me and pulled me out of the street and to Rob's side.

"What the." We were still standing on the cobbled street outside the shop, but we were surrounded by a thick violet haze. Also, I could see Rob again. What's more, those passing by the shop weren't even glancing at the big man with the sword. "Why is everything purple?"

"Ye ken how I cast a bit o' *fath fidh* to hide me sword," he said, and I nodded. I had no idea what he was talking about, but that was beside the point. "This," he gestured to encompass the haze, "is the *fath fidh*."

"Oh." From that inadequate response, I assumed that we were invisible, at least for the moment. "Here's Anya's usual order."

Rob set the bag on one of the shop's outdoor tables and opened it. Inside was a paper packet of loose tea, along with a small cup of black coffee and two sausage rolls. Rob opened the packet of tea and smelled it. He made a face that told me it wasn't a pleasant aroma and set the tea aside. Next, he popped the lid on the coffee and sniffed the steam.

"How me sweet Karina can stomach such bitterness is beyond me," he said as he set the paper cup next to the packet of tea. Lastly, he picked up one of the sausage rolls and ate it in two bites.

"I take it the rolls are safe," I said dryly.

"Aye, as is the coffee." Rob picked up the packet of tea and peered inside. "Whatever they have been givin' her, 'tis in the tea. Fair reeks o' spellcraft."

"Shit." Anya had envelopes of this tea scattered all over the kitchen at home. I had no way of knowing how much of this enchanted brew she'd consumed. "Will she be okay?"

"We can only hope, lad." Rob ate the second sausage roll. "As for ye and I, our next objective is to learn where this Nick fellow obtained the spelled tea."

"How will we learn that?"

"By following him, o' course."

TEMPORARY SOLUTIONS

Rob and I hung out in his violet-tinged pocket dimension for a few hours, watching Glasgow's residents as they went about their morning errands. I'd never thought of myself as a voyeur, but it was fascinating to observe everyone milling about, oblivious to our presence. I finally appreciated why Anya enjoyed people watching, and she wasn't even here to share it with me. It made me realize how much I still had to learn about Anya. I looked forward to each and every bit.

"They really can't see us," I said for what had to be the tenth time. Café patrons had sat near us several times, and no one noticed me or the big guy in chain mail. "Amazing."

""'Twould seem that there really is more to heaven and earth, Christopher, than is dreamt of in your philosophy."

I blinked, as much at Rob's badly quoted Shakespeare as to the fact that he'd actually attempted humor. "Did you just make a joke? This invisibility must be wearing down your shell. Before you know it, you'll be writing poetry."

"Ye forget, before all o' this I was a writer, and scholar of languages. I still feel that the written word was me true calling."

"Think you'll write again?"

"I do hope so." Rob nodded toward the door. "Is that him?"

I turned, and saw Nick leaving the coffee shop. "If we follow him, will this shroud of secrecy come with us?"

"The *fath fith* will hold until I release it."

"Well, then," I said as I stood. "After you, Dr. Kirk."

We followed Nick as he navigated the cobbled streets. He was making good time but didn't seem rushed; then again, he didn't know we were following him. I wondered what other tricks Rob was hiding up his sleeve.

"Ever sneak up on Rina like this?"

Rob laughed out loud. "Never. I fear her wrath more than Nicnevin's."

Nick looked over his shoulder. He must have heard Rob laugh, or the two of us speaking to each other. When he only saw an empty street, he shook his head, then he abruptly turned down an alley and disappeared through a narrow doorway.

"The time for stealth has ended," Rob declared, and the violet tones faded to that of a typical Glasgow morning, grayish and overcast. Rob stalked down the alley, pushed open the door Nick had entered, and ducked underneath the lintel. I followed. The interior was dark, and damp, and smelled like hadn't been cleaned this century.

Something small and furry scuttled along the wall. Hoping it was only a rat, I followed Rob further into the alley.

Rob held up his hand, and we advanced further into the darkness. We found a second entrance, the door of which was flung wide open. We took up positons on either side of the door, and saw Nick standing in the center of a room lit by a single overhead bulb. The floor was packed dirt, and there was a crate repurposed as a desk situated at the edge of the pool of yellow light. I could barely make out the form of a person behind the desk.

"He asked for her order, so I put everything together, he took it and left," Nick said to the person seated behind the desk. "He didn't act like he suspected a thing."

"O' course he acted that way," came a voice from the darkness. "That's how he convinced you to hand o'er the herbs. When was she last in the shop?"

"Only a few days ago," Nick replied. "Even if she didn't drink any of today's concoction, she's dosed up but good."

"Dosed with what?" I whispered to Rob.

"Let us find out." Rob unsheathed his sword and strode into the room. Nick's head whipped around at the sound of Rob's voice.

"Who the hell are you?" Nick demanded as he backed away from Rob.

"That is what's called a gallowglass," said the man behind the desk. "Nasty killers, they are, assassins feared by even the strongest warriors. This one's the worst of the lot of 'em, with more kills to his name than the last ten gallowglasses combined." The man rose and walked around the desk and into the light. I nearly stumbled when I learned his identity.

Rob had been correct. The person responsible for the slow poisoning of Anya was my uncle, John Damian.

"Isn't that right, Robert?" John sneered.

Rob was across the room in a second, his hand around Damian's neck. "I ought to end ye right here and now. Your death would make for a fine notch on me belt."

"We probably shouldn't kill him until we know who he's working for," I said.

Nick stared from Rob to me. "How the hell are you involved with the Queen of Winter and this… this gallowglass?" he demanded.

I shrugged. "Anya's my girlfriend, and Rob's my brother-in-law. I have an interesting family." I stepped up to Damian. At least he had the decency to squirm. "This bastard's my uncle, or so he claims."

Out of the corner of my eye, I saw Nick inching toward the door. Rob must have caught the movement too, since he snatched a dagger from his belt and threw it toward Nick.

"Do. Not. Leave," Rob growled. The dagger had landed in the toe of Nick's boot; either Rob had aimed exceedingly well and missed Nick's foot altogether, or Nick was too terrified to scream.

"I am no' finished with ye," Rob said, then he returned his attention to Damian. "Give me one reason why I should no' kill ye."

"I can share with ye many, many secrets," Damian rasped. "I must tell ye, when me current employer learned o' me' time workin' with Beira, he was quite interested in all I had to tell him. He was especially keen to hear all the details o' Beira's clan, both those in stone and those not."

"Wait," I said. "He—you did say it was a he, didn't you?—has a grudge against Anya's family?"

"Aye, lad," Damian replied.

"I know who's behind this," I said. "We don't need Damian."

"Is that so?" Rob brought Damian's face close to his. "Have ye nothin' more to offer in exchange for your life?"

"I can teach Karina about her ability," Damian said. "I have been acquainted with many walkers. I can help her learn to wield her portals!"

Rob looked at me. I shrugged. "Honestly, I don't care what happens to this guy."

"Christopher, I am your uncle!"

"Are you?" I demanded. "Or are you just some asshole who glommed onto my family?"

Rob grunted, then he struck the top of Damian's head with the hilt of his sword. As he slithered to the ground, I asked, "Is he dead?"

"No. Ye are correct in that we may yet have need o' the scoundrel. We shall keep him alive until Anya is safe," Rob replied. "'Twould be a shame to kill him now only to regret it anon."

Rob turned around and fixed Nick in his stare. "You are to tie him up, stay here, and make sure he does no' leave this room."

"Stay here?" Nick repeated. "For how long?"

"Until I return and allow ye to depart. Understood?"

Nick found a length of rope and began securing Damian's hands. "Understood."

With that, Rob and I walked out of the warehouse and to the street level. Once the door to the hovel was shut behind us, he asked, "Who do ye believe is behind this?"

"There's only one person who hates Beira and the Bodach enough to go after their daughter," I replied. "The Summer King."

We left Nick babysitting an unconscious Damian, returned to Dougal's truck, and headed toward Crail. Someday, I'd find time to get to Glen Lyon and retrieve my car. At least Rob let me drive the truck.

"Think they'll still be there when we get back?" I asked. Nick had not been pleased with Rob's order, but possessed a strong enough sense of self-preservation to not argue with him.

"Truly, I've no notion," Rob replied. "Even if they both flee, I care naught for that coffee seller. As for Damian, I found him today. I can find him again."

"If that comes to pass, I hope I am not present."

"Aye." After a pause, Rob asked, "Ye are certain 'tis the old Summer King who seeks to harm Anya?"

"Not certain, no. But I have a very strong hunch." I flexed my hands on the steering wheel. "Back before the Seelie came about, Beira ruled one half of the year. On May first the Summer King defeated her in battle, took her crown, and he ruled the warm half."

"Aye, 'tis what the old tales say," he said.

"According to Anya, her father didn't like Beira spending time with the Summer King, so one May Day he showed up at the designated spot before Beira and beat the Summer King senseless."

"The land was in chaos afterward," Rob said, and I felt a bit foolish. Of course, he knew the stories, being that he was a folklorist and had lived in Elphame. He probably remembered when all of this had actually happened. "Udane, that was what the Summer King was called. They say the land's ne'er been the same without him."

"So Fionnlagh is a sort of new Summer King?"

"Fionnlagh filled the role Udane left behind, but no' directly. Beira was unfit to rule in summer, and she kent it well, just as Old Bod was no Summer King. The climate was ripe for a newcomer to rise to power, and that is exactly what Fionnlagh did."

"He was the first Seelie?"

"No' the first o' his kind, but he was the first to call himself such. He was too ambitious for his family, being that he hadn't been their first born son. When he learned o' the power vacuum left by Udane, he stepped in. In time, he and his followers took the place o' the Summer Court."

"Then Fionnlagh is something of a usurper," I said. "Did Nicnevin help him?"

"Nicnevin was no' with him when he rose to power," Rob replied. "In the beginning Fionnlagh ruled alone."

"So why didn't the Bodach see Fionnlagh as a threat?" I wondered. "Beira was still associating with a man."

"Aye, but Beira and Fionnlagh ne'er once fought," Rob replied. "'Twas Fionnlagh's idea. They willingly turned the wheel o' seasons together. Because o' his reluctance to engage in battle, Old Bod thought Fionnlagh weak."

"That was a mistake on Bod's part."

"Aye, and he is payin' for it still."

We drove in silence for a time. "If the Seelie began with Fionnlagh, where did the Unseelie come from?"

Rob's expression darkened. "No one really kens," he replied. "The Unseelie King—Maelgwyn, he is called—is a true brute, with tar for blood and a cold, black heart."

"Sounds like Nicnevin."

"Compared to Maelgwyn, Nicnevin is gentle as a spring lamb. Make no mistake, Christopher, the Unseelie Court is made up o' tricksters and thieves, scoundrels who have no honor to speak of. Believe me when I say that those under Maelgwyn's rule are best left alone."

"Why do I have a feeling we'll end up smack in the middle of Unseelie business?"

Rob grunted. "Let us hope you're wrong about that."

Thanks to our magic truck, we reached the cottage in less than an hour. I parked, and Rob and I entered. We found Rina bustling around the kitchen, while Colleen sat on the couch with Faith in her lap, making faces at the baby.

"You're back," Rina said, her face brightening when she saw Rob.

"I am," he replied, bending to kiss her. "Colleen, has she been good?"

"Like an angel." Colleen approached us and handed Faith off to Rob. "Faith behaved quite nicely, too."

Rina smirked at Colleen, then said to me, "You okay?"

"Oh, yeah. Just a little stiff and," I winced, since the aftereffects from the frostbite were still in full effect, "blistered."

"Ugh. Robert, shouldn't you take off your armor before you hold the baby?"

"She likes it. Bairns are attracted to shiny things."

Rina shook her head. "Tell me what you've learned about whoever's after Anya," she said, and Rob and I told her everything we knew. By the time we'd finished, the five of us were spread across the couch and loveseat. Faith had ended up with me, and was contentedly sleeping in the crook of my arm.

"What John said about my ability," Rina began, then she glanced at Colleen. Colleen nodded, and she continued, "We think that me being a walker makes me able to influence Anya's powers."

"Really." I leaned forward. "Why do you say that?"

"When she was icing Faith's blankets I grabbed her arm and told her to stop, and she did, just like that." Rina snapped her fingers for added emphasis. "And when she came here asking me to portal her to the Winter Palace, she was covered in so much ice, she could hardly think. When I touched her, her mind cleared. Colleen saw it happen both times."

My stomach tightened. "She was covered in ice?"

"From head to toe. She was wearing ice instead of clothes."

I swallowed the lump in my throat. Faith squeaked. I adjuster her against my shoulder. "Col, what do you make of it?"

"It's like Rina has a grounding effect on Anya," Colleen replied. "Anya shows up in a frenzy, her thoughts flying around like a hurricane. Then Rina touches her, and it's like she's in the eye of the storm. Calm, and wondering what all the fuss is about."

"Interesting." I looked at Rob. "Do you know anything about walkers being able to do that?"

"I ken verra little about walkers," he replied. "Truly, walkers are a rarity, both in this world and in Elphame, and all are highly sought after. Most are employed by kings, and live like royalty themselves."

"Wait, I could be a queen?" Rina grinned.

"Fionnlagh did give us this fine home, and presented us with a goodly amount of coin," Rob replied. "In time, I am sure he will show his appreciation again."

"But what does this mean for Anya?" I asked. "If Rina can somehow reset her, maybe we won't need to deal with Udane at all."

"I can only affect her when we're in physical contact," Rina said. "It's a temporary solution, but we can do better."

"How?" Colleen asked. "By bottling up some walker-ness? No, what Rina does is a Band Aid at best. We need an actual solution."

"Agreed," Rob said. "We can no' have a rogue winter queen. It's best we deal with this quietly, before the Seelie get wind o' what's happening."

"Why?" I demanded. "What will the Seelie do about it?"

Rob leveled his gaze at me. "If they determine that Anya is a threat to Scotland, they will do whatever it takes to eliminate her."

A CAPE AND A FEW BAUBLES

"Why would Udane be holding a grudge against me?" I asked. Mum and I were still in the Winter Palace's throne room, her in the seat of honor, while I knelt at her feet. "I hadn't even been born when Da unseated him."

"Whether you were alive or not hardly matters," Mum replied. "The fact is that you are my and your father's daughter, and that alone makes you a target not only of Udane's wrath, but of others all across Elphame. What's more, it is known by all and sundry that you're newly feeling your ability, which means you're at your most vulnerable. If someone was of a mind to take you down a peg, they would be smart to do it now, before Samhain."

I stared at my open hands in my lap. The ice had melted away from my palms, and the exposed skin was red and tender, hardly the skin of the all-powerful Queen of Winter I was supposed to be. I wondered if I'd made the skin over Christopher's heart feel much the same. How betrayed he must have felt when I loved him, only to nearly kill him.

"I have felt many things in my life, but I've never felt vulnerable." What with the embodiment of winter for a mother and a giant for a father, even as a bairn I'd been strong. As soon as my legs could hold me up, I was running and romping with my brothers, and let me tell you, none of them ever went easy on me because I was a girl. I took everything they could dole out, and gave it back to them twofold.

Mum put her hand on my knee and squeezed. "Imagine how I feel."

With those words, I was gutted. "Mum, I never meant for you to lose your command of winter."

"I ken that." She patted my knee. "But since that command seemed destined to leave me, at least it went to you, not that Fionnlagh had much choice in the matter. Now, let's see about getting you properly dressed. Even at my coldest I never wore ice day in and day out."

We stood, my frozen armor melting and sliding off my body and shattering on the floor as I did so. I grabbed a cast-off shawl from behind the throne and wrapped it around myself, and followed Mum to her chambers. As we walked, I marveled at the smooth walls and high ceilings.

"Did the Seelie lie about how much damage was done to the palace?" I asked.

"That was one of the few truths they've spoken," Mum replied. "When I was first exiled, the place was in shambles, little more than a heap of rubble." Mum paused, trailing her fingertips across the pristine white wall. "You're wondering why it's not in shambles now."

"The thought had crossed my mind."

"I'm not powerless here. However Fionnlagh stripped my abilities, he only skimmed the surface. I don't think I could accomplish much in the mortal realm, but here I am, as strong as I ever was."

I craned my neck and gazed at the intricate scrollwork that decorating the ceiling. For Mum to repair all of this in so short a time... "Where are Long Meg and the rest? Did the giants help you rebuild?"

"They did, and they're near. Here's my dressing room."

Mum opened an arched doorway and led me into a far more opulent chamber than the one she used to share with Da. She led me toward her wardrobe. Soon enough, my icy armor was gone and, I was clad in one of her white silk gowns, matching leather slippers on my feet.

"There you are," Mum said as she fussed over my hair. "No matter that the power is coming to you in fits and spurts, you are the Queen of Winter, and you shall look the part."

Mum pinned my hair at the nape of my neck, then she rummaged in a drawer and produced a handful of jewelry. "Is all of this really necessary?" I asked as she slid rings onto my fingers.

"To be a queen you must look like a queen, all the more so when you don't feel it," Mum replied. "A cape and a few baubles can mean all the difference between you looking like a fierce ruler, rather than a frightened girl."

I took in Mum's appearance. Her yellow hair hung lank around her shoulders, her dress was wrinkled, her feet bare and dirty. "What sort of look are you aiming for, then?"

"Never you mind about me." With that, Mum settled an ermine cloak on my shoulders. The clasp was silver filigree and set with a blood red ruby. "Let's be off."

"Off where?" I asked as I followed Mum out of her dressing room. "Where are we going?"

"To have a talk with Udane." With that, Mum put on her own white fur cloak and swept out of the room. Having no other option, I followed.

"Why are we going to see him?" I demanded. "What good will come of that? And are you certain he's still alive? They say no one's set eyes on him since Da dethroned him."

"He is well and hale, and I ken just where to find him," Mum replied. "Ever since that day your father left him a bloody mess, I've kept abreast of his whereabouts. When you're in a position of power, it's good to know where your enemies lay their heads. Even better is knowing who their enemies are."

"Has he made many over the years?"

"Oh, yes. So many even I was impressed."

We reached the end of the corridor. Mum straightened the cloak on my shoulders. "Remember, you cannot show weakness, not to him or anyone else we encounter. We are there to ask him what he hopes to gain by all of this meddling with the seasons, nothing more."

"What if he wants to be restored to the Summer Court?"

"That, we cannot do. One, the Summer Court no longer exists and I'm not looking to rebuild a second court, and two, there are the Seelie to contend with. I'll not fight them for Udane's sake, and neither will you."

I nodded, then I faced the door. The edges shimmered, betraying that this was a door between not rooms, but worlds.

"Where will this portal take us? Aren't you trapped in the palace?"

"Actually, I am not. One of my best kept secrets is that while I could not access my home from the mundane world, there are several intact passages here in the Winter Palace that lead straight into Elphame."

"You were never trapped, or helpless. You lied to the Seelie."

"Aye, that I did. Not the first or the last time that happened."

The Anya of a few days ago would have been appalled at her mother's lies. Instead, I merely followed her into the passage.

"What part of Elphame are we going to?" I asked.

"The Unseelie Court."

MORE TO THE STORY

The ladies and I stayed at the cottage while Rob went on a scouting mission in Elphame, seeking information on the Summer King's current whereabouts. Even though Udane had been keeping a low profile since his dethronement, Rob was confident that he was still alive; even Wyatt claimed to have had contact with Udane within the last decade or so.

In fact, Wyatt and the rest of the wights turned out to be an invaluable resource with regards not only to Udane's whereabouts, but also as to what had gone down between him and the Bodach all those years ago. It seemed that the wights had once been fixtures in the Summer Court, and were tasked with looking after the royal gardens.

"The Summer Palace was a true joy to behold," Wyatt said. The rest of the wights clustered around him and nodded in agreement, then they broke formation and settled on Colleen's shoulders and arms, smiling and fawning over Faith nestled on her lap.

"And you remember when the Bodach attacked Udane?" I prompted.

"Oh, yes, Master Stewart," Wyatt replied. "Such a horrible day it was. You see, it was still weeks before summer was due to begin. We weren't thinking at all about the coming battle between our king and the Queen of Winter. Instead, we were organizing our spring planting tasks, as any wight would do at that time of year. All of us were shocked when the Bodach arrived unannounced, more so when he stormed into the great hall."

"He just barreled in and attacked Udane?" Rina asked.

"He grasped my king about the neck, dragged him out of the palace and beat him in the courtyard, flogging him like a common criminal. It was awful." Wyatt wrung his tiny blue hands. "Truly, truly awful."

"That's interesting, that the Bodach got all fired up out of nowhere," Colleen said. "As Wyatt said, Udane and Beira weren't due to meet up for a few weeks. Why was he even thinking about Udane at that time? Something must have happened, something we don't know about."

"Maybe he wanted to catch Udane by surprise," Rina suggested.

I shook my head. "From what I've heard about the Bodach, he didn't need surprise. Anya says he held a grudge against Udane for years; centuries, even," I said. "He didn't like that Beira was spending time with another man, and his solution was beating the crap out of him. A bit ham-fisted, literally, but it removed Udane from the equation."

Rina shuddered. "The Bodach sounds like a giant asshole."

"It also sounds like he was jealous of his wife's power," Colleen added. "Beira was the Queen of Winter, but what was the Bodach, other than a giant?"

"That's similar to how Fionnlagh is a powerful Seelie, but his wife is a human that caught his eye," Rina said.

"Nicnevin's human?" I asked.

"She was," Rina replied. "Now, she's something else entirely."

I remembered the days when I was under Nicnevin's spell, body, mind, and soul. I'd existed only to please her, and would have done anything, no matter how painful or humiliating, to gain her approval. Ever since Rina had freed me from Nicnevin, I'd told myself that she was an otherworldly monster, and that was one of the reasons why I'd fallen so easily and so hard for her.

But she was a human. A regular woman, albeit an evil one. I did not take comfort in the fact that a human was one of the most evil beings I'd ever encountered, or that I'd been so easily duped by one.

"How did she become the Seelie Queen?" I asked.

"I don't know," Rina replied. "Somehow she hooked up with Fionnlagh, and here we are."

"Whatever Nicnevin is or isn't is beside the point," Colleen said. "I'm still curious why the Bodach went after Udane in the first place. Does Anya remember many details?"

"Does that matter anymore?" I asked. "It happened a long time ago. According to her, this all went down before she was born."

"These fairies have long memories," Colleen said. "It may be old news to us, but we're all dealing with the aftereffects of his actions in the here and now. If Udane had never been dethroned, the Seelie would never have come to power. It was the Seelie that made Anya the Queen of Winter, right?"

"Right," I repeated. "And it was the Seelie King that punished the Bodach and his sons by trapping them in stone."

"There's something more here," Rina said. "There are too many coincidences, and they all point to the Seelie wanting Udane and Old Bod out of the picture."

"Agreed." I thought for a moment. "Wyatt, what do you know about Udane's family? Did he have a wife, kids, anything like that?"

"He had many children," Wyatt replied. "The Summer Palace was filled with the sound of their laughter."

"Where are they now?"

"When the Bodach stripped Udane of his might, his children were likewise disempowered," Wyatt replied. "Most have scattered to the four winds by now."

"Have they." I rubbed my chin. "Why would they do that?"

"What are you thinking?" Rina asked.

"I'm not sure," I replied. "But it would seem to me that for a being as powerful as Udane, it would take more than a beating to destroy his power base. And if his children were as powerful as he was, where did they go? Wouldn't they have helped their father?"

"You think he wasn't stripped of power, but rather he went into hiding," Rina said.

I nodded. "It makes the most sense, and I bet his children went with him."

Rob walked through the front door, looking much the worse for wear from his sojourn in Elphame. His armor was streaked with soot, his helmet was missing and his hair wild, and there was a fresh dent in his shield.

Rina's eyes widened. With a word, Rob sent his armor away, and strode up to her clad in modern jeans and a St. Andrews sweatshirt. I wondered if that had been a gift from Ethan.

"Beloved," he greeted, bending to kiss her forehead.

"Sweet words and magicing the evidence away doesn't mean I didn't see it," Rina said. "What happened?"

"Many things." Rob sat between Rina and Colleen; the latter handed over Faith, and we waited impatiently while he said hello to the baby. "It seems that our Anya's put Elphame into a bit of an uproar."

"Elphame could use a nice uproar," Rina said.

"There is nothing nice about this," Rob said. "It seems that with Anya feeling the cold so early, she's drawing a fair amount of power from the Seelie Court."

"She's drawing their power?" I asked. "But how? Anya's not Seelie. Beira came before the Seelie, and the Bodach is a giant."

"'Tis a mystery, for the time being," Rob replied. "Fionnlagh has worked himself into quite a state over it."

"Chris has a theory," Rina began. "He thinks that if we can figure out why the Bodach went after Udane all those years ago, we'll have a clue as to why Anya's powers are going haywire now."

"A sound plan," Rob said. "Alas, I do no' ken what got Old Bod in such a state over Udane. However, I did learn that while Udane was unseated and the Summer Court destroyed, the man himself is alive and well."

"Then let's go talk to him," I said. "Where is he?"

"He has taken refuge in the Unseelie Court."

"I thought that was the one place worse than Nicnevin's lair."

"Oh, it is." He held the baby close. "It surely is."

THE PATH TO THE UNSEELIE

I followed Mum through the doorway in the Winter Palace, only to be shocked at what was on the other side. I'd expected to walk out onto a glacier, or a snow-covered field, but the landscape around the home of the Cailleach Bheur was a warm, wildflower filled meadow.

"This is... warm." I brushed my hand over a stand of yellow flowers. "Won't the palace melt?"

"If it melts, it will be because I wish it to," Mum replied. "Come now. It's not long before the path descends into Elphame."

We proceeded down the wide path, me wondering how many times Mum had snuck out of the palace since her exile began. I sensed the moment we crossed into Elphame; the ether was different, at once welcoming and stifling, as if a too-sweet fragrance had been used to cover the rot beneath. For all that I'm an otherworldly being I'd never once felt at home in Elphame, and I believe those in Elphame would have happily ignored my existence for all eternity.

When Mum's feet touched Elphame's enchanted soil, her appearance changed at once. Her untidy hair became sleek and glossy, her eyes brightened, and her spine went straight as an arrow. Her clothing changed as well, with her drab dress becoming a blood red gown as gilded sandals wrapped themselves onto her feet. Mum was not the Queen of Winter any longer, but her inborn power proved itself no less strong.

One by one, the wolves came to her. They'd been her familiars from the beginning, long before she'd been named Cailleach Bheur by mortal men. She greeted each in turn, burying her long fingers in their ruffs and calling each by name. After everyone had reacquainted themselves, the wolves took up positions along either side of us, and we traveled as one.

"Is it much farther?" I asked. I'd never been to the Unseelie Court, and I didn't know the way.

"No. We're not far at all," Mum replied.

I took in my surroundings. We were walking on a well-trod path, and while such pathways were common in Elphame this one seemed to lead straight from the Winter Palace's door to the Unseelie Court. The Winter Palace was supposed to have been cut off from Elphame centuries ago, and no one in their right mind traveled to the Unseelie Court without due cause.

"You're certain that he—Udane—is at the Unseelie Court?"

"Aye. I am."

I observed my mother's regal gait, her sure footing as she walked the path surrounded by her wolves. "You've walked this road often."

"That I have," Mum replied. "I must confess, after your father unseated Udane, I felt a fair measure of guilt. It wasn't Udane's fault your father was a jealous man, and Udane had only been performing his duties when we met to turn the wheel. Not only that, I missed our tussles, infrequent as they were. So I kept up with him, and visited him whenever I could spare a moment."

Tussles. She said tussles, not battles.

"It must have been difficult for you to meet with him, what with father around," I said.

"Oh, it was," she replied. "But then your father sought to encroach on summer, and Fionnlagh wouldn't have that."

"But the palace was set apart from Elphame shortly after the Seelie rose," I said. "How did you visit Udane after that?"

"I simply walked from the palace into Elphame, much as we are doing now," Mum replied. "Imagine my delight when I was imprisoned in the palace all those months ago, only to find that my old pathways were still intact, including this one we now walk upon. Truly, you becoming the Queen of Winter was a blessing in many ways."

I stopped walking. "You said that you missed Udane. Why? I thought you and he were enemies."

"I never claimed to be his enemy. Adversary, yes, but never his enemy. Winter and Summer were meant to rule the year in harmony, two halves of the greater whole. He was my counterpart, my companion."

"Shouldn't your companion have been Da?"

"Never doubt that I loved your father, and that he still holds my heart. What Udane and I have is something different, something older. We complete one another. We always have."

She was speaking of Udane in the present tense. "You've been seeing him all along," I accused. "And Da knew all about it, didn't he? It's why he hated summer so much, and the Seelie after Udane was dethroned. Da and my brothers are suffering in stone prisons, yet it's all your fault!"

"Anya," Mum snapped. "What your father did was despicable, and you ken that well. He sought to end the summer times altogether on our island, and all over an ancient grudge. Can you not see how the land would have suffered with no summer? How the people would have suffered without the time to grow crops and tend their stock?"

Reluctantly, I agreed. "You are right, of course," I conceded. "Da was in the wrong, and he accepted his punishment with grace."

Mum nodded. "That he did. For all that your father has the temper of a bull, he is a proud and righteous man, and a man I am proud to call my husband."

We resumed walking. As we made progress, I took note of the parts of Elphame we were passing through. We were fast leaving the regions I was familiar with, and entering Unseelie territory.

"Mum, when was the last time you visited Udane?"

"Not since shortly before you were born."

DON'T DIE OVER THERE

After Rob revealed that he'd learned Udane was taking refuge in the Unseelie Court, he and I thought our next steps were clear. Rob and I would go to the Unseelie Court, find Udane, and persuade him to talk to us. Neither Rina nor Colleen thought this was an especially good plan.

"This is not smart," Rina said as she made sandwiches. Rob had come back from Elphame starved, and I figured I should eat something before traveling to another dimension. From what I recalled, Elphame wasn't big on restaurants. "You two are literally walking into the lion's den."

"I do no' believe there's another option to be had," Rob said. "Ye stated yourself that there must be more to what happened between Udane and Old Bod, and since Old Bod's in stone, we can no' talk to him. Therefore, we must speak with Udane. I can no' imagine he will ever come to us, so we must go to him."

"But aren't the Unseelie the evil fairies, the worst of the worst?" Colleen asked.

Rob leveled his gaze at her. "All o' the fae are evil, Seelie, Unseelie, and the rest. They care naught for a mortal's life, nor his soul."

"And yet you serve their king," Colleen said.

Rob sighed. "Aye, but trust me when I say he is the best option o' them all. While I can no' go so far as to say he has a soft spot for mortal beings, he does treat his subjects with a fair measure o' respect."

Colleen shook her head. "Still, should Chris be going over with you? He's not really equipped to handle these creatures."

"Thanks for the emasculation, Col," I said. "I've been to Elphame before, and every night I sleep next to the Queen of Winter. I know what these creatures are like. I'm also smart enough to stay out of their way."

"He does run pretty fast," Rina said. "But Colleen does have a point. Take Wyatt with you?"

Colleen smirked at me. I smirked back. "Why Wyatt?" I asked. "Think we'll come across a garden that needs weeding?"

"The wights can cross into Elphame and return at will," Rina replied. "If something happens and you need to come home, Wyatt can come tell me. Then I can send a portal for you."

Having an extraction plan was a good idea. It also made this foray into evil's home a bit more real. I hoped we were doing the right thing.

"All right. Wyatt will be the third man in our group. When do we leave?"

It had been Rina's idea for Rob and me to get some sleep before we left for Elphame. Her reasoning had been sound; in my case, I was still recovering from nearly being frozen alive and I needed the rest. Rina insisted Rob needed rest, too. In both our cases, we didn't know how long it would take us to find Udane, so it was best to be as alert and prepared as possible.

After a few hours sleep, we all gathered in the walled garden so Rina could ship Rob and me to Elphame. The wights were gathered around us in all their multicolored glory, and not one but two wights would be making the trip to Elphame with us. Wyatt would be staying with me, because he spoke English;

that way if Rob and I got separated I would have Wyatt's assistance. Traveling on Rob's shoulder would be Violet, the lavender wight that had stayed with Rina when she was kidnapped by our uncle. If Violet hadn't acted as bravely as she had we might not have found Rina in time. That made her aces in my book.

These little guys were the best. I'd say they were worth their weight in gold, but wights were so tiny they weighed almost nothing. They were worth at least my weight in gold, maybe double that.

"I don't know," Colleen said, shaking her head. "This plan is full of holes."

"I assure you, Mistress Worley, Violet and I shall care for Masters Kirk and Stewart as if they were our own blossoms," Wyatt said. "We shall keep them safe."

"Yeah, blossom," Rina teased Rob, pulling his head down for a kiss. "Stay safe, and don't let Chris get himself killed."

"Aye, beloved," he said. "Aye to both."

It was sweet, watching Rob say farewell to Rina, and then Faith. My heart clenched as I wondered if I'd ever have a moment like that with Anya.

"Don't get any ideas," Colleen warned; my face must have betrayed my sappy emotions. "But don't die either, okay?"

"I can agree to not dying. Take care of my niece."

Rob and Rina parted, then she propped up Faith against her shoulder. "All right. Robert, think about the Unseelie Court. Hold an image of it in the forefront of your mind. Chris, you need to be in contact with Robert."

I put my hand on Rob's shoulder. Rina nodded, and we were gone.

LAND OF DUST

Mum and I kept on the road to the Unseelie Court, the wolves keeping pace even though the way got rougher the farther we went from the Winter Palace. The road leaving the palace had been paved with stones as smooth as ice, but the surface had long since given way to packed earth. As the pavers crumbled to dust, the low hedge that bordered the road became a tangle of unkempt branches reaching up and over until they resembled a willow run. By the time we crossed into the Unseelie Court, the willows had been taken over by brambles, sharp and tearing at our clothes.

Mum glared at an offending branch that had dared to catch on her cape. The wolves growled, deep in their throats. The branch curled in on itself, the whole of the shrub wilting at her anger. My face must have betrayed my horror, because she asked, "Have you ever been to the Unseelie Court?"

"Never," I replied. "I've hardly ever been to the Seelie."

Mum sniffed. "Just as well. Those Seelie will just as soon betray you as offer you a cup of tea."

"Isn't everyone like that here? Even us?"

"We are of an older and far nobler family than those upstarts, and don't you forget it. The Unseelie Court is just a bit further on."

The brambles fell back, whether of their own accord or by my mother's influence, I did not know. The path let out in a desolate meadow, vast and flat and covered with golden grass ripe for haying. At the other end of the expanse was a castle perched atop a rocky crag. There were or no trees or flowers or even grass in the shadow of the crag, as if the vegetation couldn't survive in the darkness. Instead, there was only bare soil and stone, all of it varying shades of gray.

"All of this gray should be ugly, but it's not," I said. As my eyes adjusted to the scene I saw that the grays had vivid undertones, ranging from purple to blue to red. "It's as if a layer of dust collected on the most beautiful gems. Everything remains as lovely as it ever was, but the lot of it needs a good scrubbing."

"You'll find that there's much more to the Unseelie than meets the eye." Mum straightened her shoulders. A wolf flanked her on either side, her guardians in this feral court. "Come. Let us speak to the king."

I fell into step beside her. A third wolf came up beside me. I rubbed behind his ears, and said, "I thought we were here for Udane."

"Only a fool would venture into the Unseelie Court and not pay their respects to the king," Mum replied. "And make no mistake, Anya, Maelgwyn has eyes and ears everywhere. Like as not, he is already well aware of our presence."

I'd never before heard anyone speak Maelgwyn's name louder than a whisper. Many feared that saying his name was akin to summoning him, and no one with a drop of sense wished to invite Unseelie attention. Then again, no one courted the Queen of Winter's attention, either.

The wolves stayed with us as we ascended the wide, low steps of the castle's entrance. The caste itself was tall and thin, all hard angles cut from black stone. Guards clad in shining black armor with spears in hand stood sentry all along the balustrade, and not one of them challenged our presence. When we reached the top of the stairs a footman pulled open the grand doors and announced our arrival.

"Her majesty, the Queen of Winter, and a guest," he called into the darkness. We hadn't even told him our names.

"You've been here before?" I asked.

"I have," Mum replied. "Come, let us not keep the king waiting."

We followed the footman down the dark, echoing corridor, those echoes magnifying once we entered a large room. It was so dark that we were nearly standing on Maelgwyn's toes before I could make out his throne. His throne was perched atop a tall, narrow dais, matching the crag his castle sat upon. Even though he was seated, his long limbs told me he was a tall man, while his fine features and shock of short, white hair reminded me of a scholar rather than a heartless king. He was dressed as a noble would be in silks and velvets, all in the shades of gray he apparently adored. Thanks to a softly glowing lamp at his elbow—the only light in his hall—I could see the reflection of many rings on his fingers and a heavy necklace at his throat.

The king's jewels weren't the only reflections in the hall. Though there was little light I could sense that the hall was vast, and it was packed with onlookers. Courtiers, perhaps, or maybe the king surrounded himself with mercenaries and assassins. No matter who or what they were, they skulked in the corners and against the walls, with only the occasional glint of burnished metal or polished gems revealing them in the darkness.

"My lord," Mum greeted, bowing her head.

"My lady, the Cailleach Bheur," Maelgwyn said by way of greeting. "What brings you to this land of dust?"

"I bring news," Mum replied. "I no longer rule the dark half of the year. That honor now belongs to my only daughter, Anya."

"Anya?" Maelgwyn leaned forward into the pool of light and peered at me. His eyes were gray and devoid of pupils, much like my own. "When did this happen? Tell me, lass, when did you become winter's queen?"

"At the start of spring," I replied.

"Why did this come about?" Maelgwyn continued. "I'd always thought Beira would need to exit this mortal coil for her power to pass on." Mum moved to respond, but Maelgwyn held up his hand. "I'd like to hear it from Anya, if you don't mind."

"The Seelie King is the one responsible for this change," I replied. "He transferred the power from my mother to me."

"Ah. Fionnlagh. He does love to meddle." Maelgwyn leaned back and steepled his fingers underneath his sharp chin. "Tell me, Anya, are you enjoying your reign?"

"I've yet to begin."

Maelgwyn considered my response, then addressed Mum. "That is all well and good, Beira my dear, but why journey all this way to advise me of such? I have no interest in how the wheel of the year turns. Your man saw to that long ago."

Mum bristled, but her voice was even when she spoke. "I am here to beg for your help. Someone has bespelled Anya and caused her control to run amok, and I am no longer strong enough to find those responsible."

"Beira, begging me for help?" Maelgwyn threw back his head and laughed. "I seem to recall I once begged you for help, yet you turned your back on me. Why should I do anything for you now, save throw you out of my court?"

"You wouldn't be helping me, but Anya," Mum replied.

"And why should I lend help to a lass I've never before met?" he countered.

"Gods below, Udane! Can't you see that she has your eyes?"

At Mum's outburst the whole of the Unseelie Court stilled. Maelgwyn was the first to move, and descended his dais as gracefully as a dancer. He stood before me, peering down into my face with his head cocked like a bird. His gray gaze held me transfixed, and it was another moment before I realized what Mum had said.

"She called you Udane," I said. "You were the Summer King?"

"Why did you never tell me?" Maelgwyn asked. "All these years, Beira. You could have ruled beside me."

"You ken well why that never would work," Mum replied.

"Why would you rule together?" I demanded, backing away from Maelgwyn and my mother. "Why are his eyes like mine?"

"Anya, I always meant to tell you," Mum began. "The Bodach, though he loves you as his own, is not your father."

I felt like I was falling so fast I could hardly breathe. I was Anya, daughter of the Queen of Winter and the Bodach—only I wasn't. I was the Unseelie King's heir.

Or was I the Summer King's child?

I did the only thing my broken, betrayed heart allowed. I turned away from my lying parents, and blinked out.

UDANE, THE SUMMER KING

Rob and I trudged across Elphame toward the Unseelie Court with the two wights flitting around our heads. Since Rob had always served the Seelie, this was the first time he went deep into the Unseelie side of fairyland. Therefore, Rina's portal had only taken us to the edge of the kingdom. My first thought was to wonder how far we'd have to walk to reach the Unseelie King's castle. My second was to wonder what had leached the color out of the landscape.

The farther we went into Unseelie territory, the less vibrant the colors became. Trees still had brown trunks and green leaves, but the hues were washed out and pale. The same held true for the grass, sky, and everything else we passed by. It made Rob and I stand out like Technicolor characters in a black and white movie, and Wyatt and Violet were almost too bright to look at.

"This is odd," I said, indicating the muted landscape. "All the colors are going to gray."

"In Elphame, a land mimics its master," Rob said. "Do ye recall how Nicnevin's palace was dark and rotting?"

I remembered many things about Nicnevin's palace, and wanted to forget them all. "The Unseelie King is like Nicnevin?"

"He may be," Rob replied. "No one truly kens."

"You must know something about him."

"Aye, I've heard a tale or two. He rules alone, and likes it that way. The stories tell that his heart was sorely betrayed some time ago, and he has yet to recover."

"Then the gray is sorrow," I deduced. "But he's not actually evil?"

"Truly, ye ken as much as I regardin' his nature."

"That is not reassuring."

"'Twas no' meant to be."

We rounded a bend, and saw a dark crag ahead. "I take it that's the Unseelie's headquarters?"

"It is, may God have mercy on our souls," Rob replied.

The wights landed on our shoulders and chirped like over-caffeinated spring peepers. "What's up?" I asked.

"He is near," Wyatt said, while Violet chirped in the wights' native language. "Our king is near. May we fly on and locate him?"

"O' course," Rob said. "Do no' stray too far."

"Then can sense Udane?" I asked.

"Evidently so."

"At least we know we're on the right track."

I watched as the wights flew on ahead. We left the packed earth road we'd been following and stepped onto a more formal stone path that led to the Unseelie King's palace. The palace was a tall, dark edifice covered in spires and pointed gables, balanced precariously at the edge of a cliff like a Halloween cartoon. If it hadn't been for the black clad Unseelie warriors armed to the teeth and stationed every few paces, the effect would have been comical.

Rob ignored the warriors as we passed; he'd been to hell, literally, and wasn't impressed by the Unseelie's display of bravado. None of the warriors attempted to stop us, and we ascended the stairs to the palace without incident. At the top of the stairs, a guard wearing obsidian armor glared at us from beneath his helmet.

"Name and business," he demanded.

"I am Robert Kirk, the gallowglass in service to the Seelie King, and I am requesting an audience with His Majesty," Rob replied.

The guard swallowed hard. Apparently even the Unseelie Court's guards had heard about the gallowglass. "Is my lord expecting you?" the guard asked.

"No."

"And you are? His page, I presume?" the guard asked me.

"Ah, sure."

The guard spun on his heel and entered palace. Since no one was stopping us, Rob and I followed.

Whereas the outside of the palace and the surrounding landscape had been washed in gray, the inside was pure darkness. I couldn't see the ceiling of the corridor or the walls, and I only knew where to go because what little light there was reflected off the guard's glasslike armor as he led us through the palace. Luck alone kept me from stumbling or walking into a wall, or worse, Rob.

Eventually the corridor emptied into a large room that had two candles burning in wall niches on either side of the entrance. The floor was polished red tile, and beyond the pool of candle light it receded into blackness along with the walls and ceiling. There was a shard of light emanating from the center of the room, and it revealed the man we were looking for.

Maelgwyn, the Unseelie King, was perched on a dais in the center of the chamber. His hair was white, his skin was pallid, and he was as skinny as a skeleton. A woman with long blonde hair reclined on the dais's steps, her head resting on the king's knee. Her gown was a true red, not the washed-out colors that made up the rest of the Unseelie Court. It branded her as an outsider better than a nametag would have done.

Before the guard could announce us, the woman spoke.

"Gallowglass," she called. "Have you come for what's left of me? I've already lost near everything, thanks to you."

"Beira?" I blurted out. "I thought you were in exile."

"Only a fool would think you powerless," Rob said, then he added with a shallow bow, "Your majesty. Forgive me my outburst."

"I will allow it," Maelgwyn said. "I am well aware of how Beira brings out the worst in men." He caressed her hair. Beira stretched like a cat, pushing her head against his hand. "Has Fionnlagh sent you, gallowglass?"

"He has not," Rob replied. "I am here on me own business."

"Please, then, enlighten the court as to your purpose," Maelgwyn said.

Rob nodded again. "As ye wish, your majesty. I am here on something of a family matter. Surely ye are aware that a new Queen o' Winter will rise this year."

Maelgwyn glanced at Beira. "I have heard tell of that."

"Someone has poisoned the new queen. We mean to find who's done it, and set things to rights."

"We?" Maelgwyn repeated, his gaze settling on me. "Who is this individual? And why are he and the gallowglass interested in the Queen of Winter's health and well-being?"

Beira touched Maelgwyn's hand. "That man is Christopher. Anya would make him her husband."

I almost fell over when Beira said that. Before I could properly process the concept of me being married to Anya, Maelgwyn leaned forward on his throne and scrutinized at me.

"This is the man she chooses?" Maelgwyn's eerily familiar gray eyes took in every aspect of my appearance. I don't think he was impressed. "I wonder why?"

"I have wondered much the same," Beira said. "His sister is the walker I told ye about."

"Who else have you told about Rina?" I demanded.

Beira smirked at my outburst, but Maelgwyn smiled. "He has fire, I'll give him that." He descended the dais and came to stand directly in front of me. He was amazingly tall, at least a head taller than Rob, the effect made more so by his skeletal form. "Smells of Nicnevin, though."

I will never live that down. "She enslaved me for a time. It was before Anya and I met."

"I'm sure." Maelgwyn paced a slow circle around me. "A gallowglass, a walker, and now the Queen of Winter. You are surrounded by remarkable people, Christopher. What is remarkable about you?"

I looked to Rob. He shook his head slightly, the gesture conveying that he didn't know why Maelgwyn was so interested in me, either. "I'm rather intelligent."

"Then how did Nicnevin snare you?"

"Damned if I know."

Maelgwyn's brows lowered; apparently, he didn't like it when his guests cursed. Before he could chastise me—or turn me into a toad—the wights appeared out of the darkness and settled on his shoulders. They chirped at Maelgwyn like a pair of parakeets, and he chirped right back to them. They carried on like long-lost friends catching up over drinks, and then the unthinkable happened: Maelgwyn, the dour Unseelie King, laughed.

I stepped closer to Rob. "What is happening here?"

"I have no notion."

"Gallowglass," Maelgwyn said suddenly. "The little ones tell me they've been tending your garden."

"'Tis true, your majesty," Rob replied. "Because o' the efforts o' the wights, I can rightfully claim the most beautiful garden in all o' Scotland."

"I once claimed that honor." Maelgwyn carefully lifted Wyatt in his hands, then he held him close to his heart and stroked Wyatt's fluffy blue hair. "I once claimed many honors that are now lost to me."

"We can rebuild," Beira said.

Maelgwyn smiled at her. "Yes. We can, and we will." He gazed lovingly at Beira for a moment, then he returned his attention to Rob. "Forgive me. After the events of earlier today my mind is far afield. You said you were here about Anya?"

"We are."

"I'm afraid she's not here."

"We are no' seeking her. We need to speak with Udane, he who was once the Summer King. We have heard tell he resides in your court."

Wyatt launched himself toward Rob. "Master Kirk, you are speaking to the Summer King!"

Rob's gaze flew from the wight hovering in front of him to Maelgwyn. "Udane? My lord, is it so?"

"I am he, though I haven't gone by that name in some time. Ages, even. Now, tell me who poisoned my daughter."

THE COLOR OF SADNESS

After I fled the Unseelie Court, I wandered about Elphame for a time. I let my feet carry me as they wished, and I was soon deep within the gray and depressing Unseelie lands. A fitting place to match my dark thoughts.

How could Mum have kept this hidden all these years? I tipped back my head and wailed at the sky. The sky remained silent, but I realized that my parentage hadn't been a secret; at least, not completely. While Mum apparently never told Maelgwyn, or me, Da had known right along. What's more, Mum and Maelgwyn's relationship had lasted centuries, and Da had been aware of it for a long, long time. I wondered if any of my brothers were Maelgwyn's children, too.

Elphame loves nothing so much as a scandal, which meant that others must have known about Mum's affair with the Summer King. Suddenly, I understood why Mum avoided the Seelie Court. Her lie had been found out, and she'd almost cost the land its summer not once, but twice; if my true parentage were discovered, that would have only added to her crimes. I also finally understood why I hadn't been put in stone with Da. He wasn't my father.

How had Maelgwyn not known about me?

I pulled up a handful of wildflowers and picked off the leaves. Everyone knew that the Unseelie Court was packed full of spies, and Maelgwyn was kept apprised of everything that happened in Elphame. He must have heard tell of Beria's gray-eyed daughter. Then again, he hadn't known Mum was dethroned, or maybe he just hadn't cared. Maybe his vast network of spies was just a myth, a bit of creative rumor mongering he used to keep himself isolated.

One thing I kent to be true—what a short list that was becoming—was that Maelgwyn ruled alone. He had never taken a mate or consort, and even courtesans were barred from his court. Why would a man with such power and influence choose to close off himself and his kingdom?

I stared at the gray flowers in my hand. Gray, the color of sadness. Perhaps Maelgwyn had loved my mother, and the loss of her had wounded him so deeply he couldn't imagine moving on. His heart had been broken, and he built a wall around it so strong even the most powerful mage couldn't break through.

A new image floated past my mind's eye: Christopher. He was as colorful as Maelgwyn was washed out, with his bright blond hair and summer blue eyes, the way he laughed easily and often. Christopher's heart had been broken many times, yet he still loved deeply and without compromise.

Christopher could help me make sense of all this.

I blinked directly to our flat. "Christopher?" I called. I needed to talk to him, seek counsel from him, have him hold me and comfort me as I told him how my entire life was a lie. "Christopher?"

Silence. Of course, he wasn't here. He was in the hospital where I'd left him.

He was in the hospital because I'd almost killed him.

I crumpled to the floor and wept, my frozen tears bouncing across the carpet and making little drifts near the sofa's legs. More than anything, I wanted to go to him, but would he really want to see me, now or ever again? Would he see me as his lover, or as his icy death? Would I end up gray and alone like Maelgwyn?

I feared I already knew the answer.

A GALLOWGLASS FIGHTS TO THE DEATH

"You are Anya's father." My gaze moved from Maelgwyn to Beira. "And the Bodach, therefore, is not."

"I'll no take judgement from the likes of you," Beira huffed. "Warming Nicnevin's arse as you did."

I ignored the insult, and asked, "Does Anya know?"

"Of course she does," Beira snapped.

"The question is, does Old Bod know," Rob muttered.

"I'm told that he does," Maelgwyn said. "I daresay he's known much longer than I have."

Rob's mouth was a slash across his face as he took in the scene; a powered-down Beira, an Unseelie King who was also the long lost Summer King, the wights—who seemed to be the only ones who knew what was going on—and me, a human who was in way over his head.

"This information does change our mission," Rob said at length.

"How so?" Maelgwyn asked. When Rob moved to continue, Maelgwyn gestured for him to be silent. Wow, the Unseelie King just shushed the gallowglass. "Actually, I'd like to hear of this mission from Anya's man. Christopher, is it?"

"Yes. Christopher Stewart." I took a deep breath, and began. "Anya has had some difficulties taking on her duties as Queen of Winter. Rob and I investigated, and we discovered that Anya is being poisoned. John Damian," I paused to glare at Beira, "was the man supplying the poison, but we don't know who supplied him. We couldn't think of anyone with a grudge against Anya, but we thought we identified one individual with a rather large grudge against Beira." Again, I glared at Beira. "But we were wrong, weren't we? Udane—I mean, you, my lord—didn't poison Anya. Did you?"

"Why would you think I was holding a grudge against Beira?" Maelgwyn asked as he rubbed Violet's ears. "Could it be because she allowed that brute of hers to beat me senseless and then raze my court to the ground? Or because she let him raise my daughter as his own?" He met Beira's gaze. "I'd forgiven her for the beating and the loss of my court long ago."

"But no' the loss o' your daughter," Rob said.

"You and the king have something in common, gallowglass," Beira said. "I hear tell the walker has borne your child. Was to be a lass, yes?"

Rob's jaw worked. "Aye. Faith is with us."

Beira's eyes narrowed. "Pray she stays with you."

Rob's sword was out and pointed at Beira's throat faster than my eyes could track. "Speak o' her again and I'll have your head."

"Lower your sword," Maelgwyn boomed. "Have your petty squabbles elsewhere. Indeed, it is past time for you to depart."

"What about Anya?" I demanded.

"What about her?" Maelgwyn countered. "If you cannot protect her, she made a poor choice in you. If you can indeed offer her guidance or defense, then prove it." Maelgwyn returned to his throne, caressing Beira's shoulder as he passed.

"Actually, I care not what either of you do," he continued. "I am more than capable of seeing to my daughter's welfare without your meager assistance. Out, now."

Rob sheathed his sword, offered a half bow, and turned on his heel. I paused, watching Maelgwyn on his dark throne, and Beira reclined on the dais. I couldn't imagine those two caring for a child or even a goldfish, but Maelgwyn was right. If I was worthy of being Anya's partner, I had to help her myself.

Rob and I were silent as we exited the Unseelie Court and left the grayed out territory. Once the colors were at full strength again, I asked, "Now what do we do?"

"We must return to Crail," Rob replied. "I fear this situation has just gotten a great deal more complicated."

I began to reply, then I saw three men standing in the road ahead of us. "Up ahead. It's the Picts."

"There are no Picts in—" Rob saw them and stopped moving. "What do ye ken o' those men?" he asked.

"Not much," I replied. "Anya and I saw them in Glasgow last August. She said they were Picts."

"Aye, that they are. Why did ye no' mention them before?"

"Um. In hindsight, that may have been an error on my part."

Rob shook his head, then he strode forward to the Picts. One hand was raised in greeting while the other rested on the dirk at his waist. "Conall," Rob called. "Greetings to ye and yours."

"And to you," Conall replied. The heavy gold jewelry at his neck and wrists marked him as the leader. The two men flanking him remained silent. "Have ye business with the Unseelie, then?"

"Yes and no," Rob replied. "Were ye sent by the king?"

"O' course we were." Conall nodded toward me. "Who's that, now?"

"Me bride's brother." Rob bared his teeth. "Which means if ye hurt him, ye will have to deal with me."

"What makes ye think we'd harm the man?"

"Why are ye blockin' our path?"

Conall drew his sword. "I can no' let ye leave until I ken why ye both are wanderin' about Unseelie land."

"Then ye shall be reportin' your failure to the king himself." Rob drew his sword and stepped forward. "Christopher. Run."

"Run? And leave you?" I demanded, forgetting that he was Elphame's deadliest assassin and I was an English teacher that played basketball on weekends.

"As ye will." He withdrew the dirk from his belt and handed it to me. "If ye stay, ye fight."

I stared at the knife in my hands. The blade was at least a foot long, and no more than an inch at its widest. The heavy wooden handle shone with decades of use and was worn satin-smooth. Before that moment the biggest knife I'd ever held was a fancy chef's knife I used to chop vegetables.

To be worthy of Anya, I must fight for her.

Conall bellowed a war cry and rushed Rob. Rob deflected Conall's sword with his own as one of the other Picts attacked his left flank. I braced myself for the third man's attack, but it didn't come.

The third man raised a horn to his mouth and blew.

Shit. He'd just called in reinforcements.

"Wyatt," I yelled. The wight appeared in an instant. "Go to Rina! Tell her we need to come home now!"

Wyatt nodded and disappeared.

The Pict lowered his horn and advanced toward me.

I raised my knife—

And I was in Rina's kitchen.

"Where's Robert?" Rina demanded.

"About ten feet to the right of where I was!"

Rina faced the open area in the center of the cottage, and Rob and Conall appeared, their swords locked together. The latter paused, staring at the cottage and Rina. Rob used his distraction to his advantage and kicked Conall's midsection, sending him sprawling on the floor.

"Now," Rob bellowed. Rina extended her arm, and the Pict was gone.

Rina, Rob, and I stood in a loose circle, staring at the empty spot where Conall had been. There were dark footprints on the carpet, but otherwise no clue that Rob and a Pict had been fighting to the death moments ago. Rina slumped against the wall, panting. I wondered how much energy she'd burned up creating three portals in less than a minute.

"What the hell was that?" Colleen demanded. She was standing at the bottom of the stairs, her expression somewhere between bewilderment and terror. "Does that happen all the time around here?"

"Often enough," Rina replied. She pushed off the wall and went to Rob. He folded her into his arms and pressed his forehead against her hair. I sat at the kitchen table and set the knife in front of me.

"I am not cut out for this," I said.

"You're just now realizing that?" Rina asked.

"Bah," Rob said. "Ye stood your ground. Most men would have run from those three, but ye stood firm. And, ye were quick thinking enough to call for Wyatt."

"There were three," Rina squeaked. Faith wailed, and Rob moved toward the stairs. "Don't think you're not telling me everything," Rina said, as she followed him.

"Aye, there were three," Rob said, then they disappeared into the nursery. Colleen approached the dirt Conall and Rob had ground into the carpet.

"Dirt from fairyland," she said, as she looked over the boot prints. "That's something you don't see every day."

"Like Rina said, often enough around here."

Colleen crouched down, examining a few drops of red amidst the dirt. "Blood, too. Looks like Robert got in a few licks."

Before I could speak, something heavy fell on the second floor, then Rina screamed. "Shit, that's not Conall's blood!"

Colleen and I ran upstairs and burst into the nursery. Faith was wailing in her cradle while Rina struggled with Rob's armor. Rob himself was unconscious on the floor, his skin ashen.

"Help me sit him up," Rina said. "I have to get the armor off him."

I hooked my arms under Rob's and hauled him upright. Rina and Colleen wrestled with his chain mail shirt, the back of it slick with red. They got it up and over his head, then Rina started unlacing his quilted jacket.

"There's blood everywhere," Colleen said. "When was he injured?"

"I don't know," I said. "He never said he was hit, never said ouch or even slowed down."

"He wouldn't," Rina said. "A gallowglass fights to the death."

Between the three of us, we got Rob's jacket off of him, and the thin shirt he wore beneath. After we'd peeled away that last blood-soaked layer, we found the wound. It was on his left side, just above his waist, was at least three inches long and curved toward his back. Worse, the edges of the wound were at least an inch apart.

"He needs a hospital," Colleen declared. "That cut needs stitches."

"We can't take him to a hospital," Rina said. "There'll be too many questions!" Faith howled and Rina looked toward her, torn between her baby and Rob.

"Colleen, put pressure on the wound. Rina, grab Faith." I pulled out my phone and dialed the hospital Anya had brought me to. "I know someone."

Rina nodded and went to Faith. The receptionist at the hospital picked up. "Dr. Todd, please. It's an emergency."

A moment later, Dr. Todd was on the line. "What's this about an emergency?"

"Dr. Todd, this is Chris Stewart. I need your help."

"What's happened?"

"The gallowglass is hurt."

I retrieved Dr. Todd, and thanks to Dougal's truck, we were back at the cottage in less than an hour. We found Rob in bed, still unconscious and swaddled in bandages.

"What have you done for the wound so far?" Dr. Todd asked as she stripped away the layers of gauze topped with towels.

"Only basic first aid," Rina replied. "We applied pressure until the bleeding slowed, then I washed and bandaged it."

Dr. Todd nodded. "Good. The sword that cut him, was it clean?"

"You can tell by looking at it that's a sword wound?" Colleen asked.

"Not the first such wound I've seen, not by a long shot," Dr. Todd replied. She rummaged in her bag for supplies. "The sword."

"I guess it was clean," I said. "I didn't notice anything on the blade, but I wasn't really looking either."

"All right, we'll assume it was filthy. Bring me a bowl of warm water, soap—antibiotic if you have any—and a washcloth, please."

Colleen darted out of the room. Rina paced at the foot of the bed. "Will he be all right?"

"This is a deep wound, and he's lost a good deal of blood. However, Robert's always been a hardy one. If we manage to keep infection at bay, he should recover."

"You helped Chris with the frostbite?" Rina asked.

"Aye, that I did."

"Thank you."

Dr. Todd looked up at Rina, her hands never slowing. "You're quite welcome, dear."

Colleen returned with the soap, a pan of water, and a stack of washcloths. Dr. Todd set about cleaning Rob's wound with the detached gentleness of one who'd tended many such patients. "Who cut him?" she asked.

"A Pict," I replied.

Having finished cleaning the wound, Dr. Todd picked up a tray she'd arranged with a needle, thread, and clamps. Rina set a table next to her, then grabbed a lamp and put it on the table.

"Thank you, love," Dr. Todd said. "This Pict. Was it Conall?"

"It was Conall," I said.

"He was the one downstairs?" Rina demanded, and I nodded. "Who is he?"

"Conall considers himself the leader of the Picts," Dr. Todd replied, not looking up from her work. "That one's been wanting a go at the gallowglass for years. I'm surprised he got the drop on Robert."

"Who are these Picts?" Rina asked. "Why do they hate Robert?"

"How well do you know your history?" Dr. Todd countered.

"Well enough."

"The Picts once controlled Scotland. Eventually, they merged with the Dál Riata, but not all agreed to such an alliance. When a Pictish lord called mac Fergusa sat his eldest son on the Dál Riata's throne, his second son took issue. Thought his father was an addled old fool that would lead the Picts to ruin. So he marched into Elphame and formed an alliance of his own with the Seelie King."

"Second son was not the smart one," Colleen muttered.

"No, he was not, but for all that he lacked between his ears, he made up for in ferocity. The Picts were warriors of legend in their own lifetimes, and as we ken, every legend is grounded in truth." She finished sewing the wound and clipped the thread.

"What kind of alliance was this?" I asked. "It must have benefitted Fionnlagh in some way."

"Oh, it did. Whereas Nicnevin had her spies and cutthroats, the Picts became the Seelie King's personal mercenaries."

"So they're not after Robert," Rina said. "Then why did they attack him?"

Dr. Todd fixed Rina in her gaze. "They go where the king tells them to. If they happened upon Robert and took matters into their own hands, Himself will deal with them accordingly."

"And if they were following us?" I asked, then I shook my head. "Actually, I think they've been following Anya for months. We've seen them around Glasgow."

"And why would the Seelie King have a band of mercenaries following the new Queen of Winter?" Dr. Todd wondered. When no one answered her, she continued, "The fact that none of you offered an explanation means you understand the gravity of your situation."

"We do." I looked at Rob, the strongest man I'd ever met. He lay unconscious in bed, his pale skin mottled with bruises. "We really do."

Dr. Todd declared Rob stable, so she, Colleen, and I gave him and Rina some privacy and went out to the garden.

"Tea?" I offered, as we passed the kitchen.

"Have you anything a wee bit stronger?" Dr. Todd asked. Colleen retrieved the Glenfiddich while I got three glasses. Once we were outdoors, Colleen filled the glassed and we toasted.

"To Rob's full recovery," I began. "May it be speedy and full."

"To Robert," Colleen and Dr. Todd said, and we clinked and drank.

"Do you think Robert will be okay?" Colleen asked. "He's pretty beat up."

"That he is, but the wound was a clean one," Dr. Todd replied. "Conall only got the meat of him, and missed the organs and arteries. Soon enough, Robert will be tossing that bonnie lass of his in the air again."

"Fantastic," I said. "Did you study medicine in Elphame?"

"Oh, I became a doctor before I even kent what Elphame was. Long before," she added. "I was one of the first graduates from the Edinburgh School of Medicine for Women. That made me something of a name in certain circles, and when the fae want to sway a human to their side, they always go for the ones that are names. 'Tis how Nincevin ended up with Robert in the first place."

"He was a name?" Colleen asked.

"Aye, the brilliant Dr. Kirk, the man who spoke and wrote in five languages as fluently as if each were his native tongue," she replied. "What no one realized was that his bull-headed nature was his true talent."

"That it is. Dr. Todd—"

"Call me Margaret, both of you."

I smiled. "Very well, Margaret. Why are the Picts after Rob?"

"I don't think they're after him, not exactly."

"But Conall—that's the leader's name, right?—you said he's been wanting to fight Robert for years," Colleen said.

"Every resident of Elphame what can wield a sword wants to have a go at the gallowglass," Margaret said. "With a winning streak as long as Robert's, it's your reputation that breeds enemies." She paused to empty her glass. "In Conall's case, he's never had the opportunity to challenge Robert. Even if he and his Picts were ordered to fight against Nicnevin's forces, she has mercenaries of her own. Besides, no matter how much the king and queen squabble, it wouldn't do to have the queen's assassin decimate our lord's forces," she added with a wink.

"I suppose not." I recalled a few others I'd seen in Glasgow. "Are Nicnevin's mercenaries the Romans?"

"Aye. You've seen them as well?"

"I have, right alongside the Picts. Does that mean she is following Anya, too?"

Margaret reached for the bottle and refilled our glasses. "When it comes to Herself, very little surprises me."

MY FATHER'S POWER

I cried and raged until my head pounded and my eyes ached, and eventually fell asleep. It was still dark when I woke, and for a short, blissful moment, I thought I was in bed with Christopher. But I wasn't. I remained on the sitting room's floor, our bed far out of reach.

I raised myself up from the rug I'd crumpled onto and blinked the last tears away. They fell from my lashes like snowflakes, and settled onto the drifts that had accumulated against the sofa. I brushed the snow aside, leaned against the sofa's leg, and considered things.

The man who'd raised me was not my father. I'd been lied to—by my parents, no less—since the day I was born. To say I was devastated would be an understatement. I was shocked and hurt, the betrayal burning into me like so much venom. How could they—all of them!—have kept something so important from me? Did they think I was incapable of handling the truth?

One thought overruled all the rest: Da had known I wasn't his, yet he'd never treated me as another man's child. My memories of him were of riding on his high shoulders, him taking me hunting for beehives and then streams to wash off the sticky honey, and love. More than anything, I had grown up knowing a father's love.

I blinked to Da's house in Glen Lyon and knelt before his stone.

"I learned something today," I began. "I know about Udane. I know who—what—he is to me. I want you to know that even though he is my father, you are my Da."

I touched my fingertips to the lump of granite that imprisoned him. "You knew right from the start, didn't you? Yet I was always your best lass. You never let me feel any less so." I pressed my cheek to the stone. It was warm, comforting. I liked to think that Da was embracing me the only way he could, soothing me as he'd done so many times before. "Thank you, Da."

I heard a rustle in the tall grass behind me. I stood, and I saw the Picts approaching from the west, the sunset blazing behind them. Their leader was badly hurt, and was being supported by the other two. Wounded or no, I needed to know why these men out of time kept appearing at my father's house.

"Why are you here?" I demanded. "You three have crossed my path far too often of late."

"We go where we're ordered," one replied. They stopped ten paces from me and laid their leader on the ground. "Thanks to those orders, Conall's near dead."

"What does that have to do with me?" I asked. "I did not wound him."

"You may as well have," he replied. "We heard tell of you being in the Unseelie Court. When we went to investigate, we met up with the gallowglass."

I stepped closer and peered at Conall's bloody torso. "If he has in truth tangled with Robert Kirk, he's lucky he still had a head." The Pict frowned, but didn't argue. "You say the gallowglass was in the Unseelie Court?" I asked.

"Near enough to. We met them on the road from the Unseelie stronghold into Elphame proper."

"Them?"

"Aye. A wizard was with him, and he somehow transported himself, and then the gallowglass and Conall, out of Elphame. When Conall returned a moment later, he was as you see him now."

Not only were wizards a rarity in modern Scotland, the Seelie had run them all out of Elphame long ago. "This wizard. What did he look like?"

"He was tall, but not as tall as the gallowglass. Scrawnier, too. Had straw-colored hair, and was dressed like a modern man."

My heart pounded, and I heard blood rushing in my ears. What had Christopher been doing with Robert in Unseelie territory? Gods below, I hoped the Picts hadn't hurt them. As for these Picts, I'd had enough of their sneaking about.

And if Christopher had been in Elphame, then I hadn't frozen him to death. He'd already recovered, at least enough to accompany Robert on an errand. Thank the gods, I hadn't done him irreparable harm.

I approached Conall and crouched, feigning interest in his wound. "How are you called, lad?" I asked the one who'd described Christopher.

"I am called Diarmud. This here is Niall," he added, indicating his companion.

"Diarmud, why were you in Unseelie land?"

"As I told you, we was following orders."

"Whose orders?" When Diarmud stilled, my claws sliced out. "Diarmud, lad, you have been following me. That much is obvious. Tell me who set you on my path."

Diarmud went white as sheet, his Adam's apple bobbing up and down. "Do you know who I am?" I grazed his forearm with a single claw, and left a line of ice in my wake. "Are you aware of the many ways I can make you talk?"

"The Seelie King," Conall rasped. "We follow the Seelie King."

"That wasn't so hard to admit, now was it?" I kept my voice calm as my thoughts whirled with this latest revelation. Why would Fionnlagh have me followed? Did he mean to kill me and claim the whole of the year for himself? Did he mean to complete the plan he'd once punished my father for creating?

"Why are you here, now?" I asked Conall.

Conall glared at his companions. "When we shifted from Elphame, we ended up not far from here. Diarmud thought we might take refuge in the shieling."

"Diarmud was wrong." I stood and pulled on my father's power, raising myself up into the sky until I was a giant before them. "Leave. If I find you following me again, it will mean your deaths."

I watched the quiet one, Niall, withdraw something from his cloak, then the three of them shifted away. They must be able to shift between here and Elphame, but based on what Conall said, they could only pass through the veil and not toward a specific destination. I hoped they landed square in Nicnevin's lair and she fed them to her wraiths.

Laughing, I turned to share my small victory with Da. When I saw the stones, my heart broke all over again. I hadn't called on my father's giantism to frighten the Picts into compliance. I'd inherited my abilities from a stranger.

Christopher, I need you. As soon as the words formed in my mind my mobile phone appeared in my hands. I couldn't remember the last time I'd even seen it, much less called anyone. With the ability to blink from one part of the word to the next, phone calls were more of a hindrance than anything else. But the phone was programmed with Christopher's number, and I only need touch it to be connected to him. How I yearned to hear his voice.

The phone buzzed, startling me so much I dropped it. When I picked it up and saw the screen, my breath caught in my throat. Christopher was calling me.

THE QUEEN HERSELF

Margaret, Colleen, and I sat together in the garden long after the sun set. We did some damage to that bottle of Glenfiddich, but we called it a night before we emptied it. I offered to take Margaret home, but she claimed she could make her way just fine.

"It's still dark," I argued, albeit halfheartedly. Truth be told I was beat and Rina's couch was calling me in a profound way.

"The sun will rise soon enough."

"After how you helped—"

"Don't you fret about me," Margaret said when we reached the end of the driveway. "I've been on my own longer than you've been pulling breath."

"All right, then," I conceded. "Please call if you need anything, and thank you for helping Rob."

"'Tis a small thing, but you're quite welcome," Margaret replied. "Fare well, Christopher."

I watched Margaret walk toward the village for a moment, then I returned to the cottage. Colleen was sitting at the kitchen table, but Rina was nowhere to be found.

"She's upstairs feeding the baby, and Robert is still out of it," Colleen said, before I could ask. "I checked in on them. Fresh coffee is on the counter."

I poured a mug and sat next to Colleen. "How does Rob look?"

"Battered, but the kind of battered that lives," she replied. "Can you tell me what happened to you two in the land of monsters?"

"I'm still trying to figure out where to start," I replied, then I launched into a description of the color-leached landscape, the Unseelie guards in their obsidian armor, and the Unseelie King himself, who was both the missing Summer King and Anya's true father.

"Hold up," Colleen said. "I thought Anya's father was a giant."

"So did I. So did she." I stared at the surface of the coffee, shining black like the Unseelie guards' armor. "Also, Udane was not at all receptive to helping us."

Colleen gave me a look. "What, did you think you two would team up with Udane and it would be like a buddy cop movie?"

I heard laughter from the stairs; Rina was coming down to join us. "I would pay to see that movie," Rina said.

"How's Rob?" I asked.

"He's sleeping, Faith's sleeping." Rina poured herself some coffee and leaned against the counter.

"Maybe you should sleep, too," I suggested.

"I am way too wired to sleep," she replied. "And there is clearly something big going on here. Does anyone else even know that the Unseelie King is actually the Summer King?"

"And what is Beira doing in the Unseelie Court?" Colleen added. "I don't think visiting past boyfriends is part of her exile."

"And where is Anya?" I asked. Rina sat next to me and put her hand on my forearm.

"We will find her, and we will help her," Rina said.

"How?"

"I'm working on it," Rina replied. "How big of a deal do we think it is that no one knew about Udane?"

"I imagine it's a very big deal," I replied. "Fionnlagh doesn't strike me as the sort of man who likes being kept in the dark about anything. Rob's always going on about the Seelie's network of spies."

"And that none of those spies have ever infiltrated Unseelie land," Rina added. "Fionnlagh does like to keep an eye on his rivals."

"Rivals?" Colleen repeated. "I thought the Seelie and Unseelie were two halves of a whole."

"In theory, yes, but we now know that there is more to the Unseelie than we suspected," Rina replied. "We also know that Maelgwyn-slash-Udane is not the one behind Anya's abilities going haywire."

"True. He was our only suspect."

"Maybe not." Rina tapped her chin. "Is it possible that John Damian is the sole bad guy behind all of this?"

"Is he powerful enough to affect Anya?" I countered. "Before, he had Beira on his side."

"Yeah, but that was after he wormed his way to our world from Elphame and tried recreating the Wild Court." Rina glanced toward the truck's keys, dangling from their peg next to the front door. "Think he's still where you left him?"

"Only one way to find out."

Since Rob was still sleeping, and Colleen and I had just shared a pot of coffee, she accompanied me to the warehouse in Glasgow. That's right, my backup on this quest was the head administrative assistant of Carson University's Earth Sciences Division. Her most powerful weapon was verbal evisceration, followed by the ability to resolve scheduling conflicts in under five minutes.

"What do you think will happen once we get there?" Colleen asked. Portaling would have been faster, but we'd taken the truck so Rina could focus her energy on caring for Rob and Faith. Hopefully she squeezed in a nap, too.

"Honestly? I haven't the faintest idea." I parked the truck near the center of town. Colleen followed me through the streets and toward the warehouse in question.

"This is it?" she asked when we reached the top of the alley.

"It is." We walked down the dark passage, ignoring the rats and stench of rotting garbage; as near lifelong New Yorkers, we could handle filthy streets like a couple of champs.

"What makes you so sure these two are still here?" Colleen asked. "I would have booked as soon as the coast was clear."

"Fear will keep them here." When Colleen raised an eyebrow, I elaborated, "Not of me. Rob can be pretty terrifying when he wants to be."

I pushed open the door, blinking at the harsh light. Nick was straddling a chair in the center of the room, while Damian sat on the desk.

"Back so soon?" Damian called. "And here I was hoping you'd die out there."

I ignored him and studied the pile of takeaway containers in the trash. "I see you didn't remain here as ordered," I said.

"We had to eat," Nick blustered as he got to his feet. "Only I went out, I swear it!"

And the fear of the gallowglass worked to our advantage yet again. "I believe you. Thank you, for keeping Damian here. Go."

"Really?" Nick glanced between me and Colleen. "I can just leave?"

Colleen put on her best glower, and said, "If you know what's good for you, you won't ask again."

Nick fled. I turned to Damian and said, "We assumed you were working for Maelgwyn, but we were mistaken," I began.

"I'm sure that was far from the first time you were wrong," Damian sneered.

"Your insults mean nothing to me," I said. "Tell me who you work for. Who is giving you these poisoned herbs?"

"And why should I be tellin' ye anything?" Damian countered. "Where is the gallowglass?"

"Out doing what he does best," I replied. "Would you like me to summon him?"

"And what if I don't talk to him, either? Then what?"

"Then we'll kill you," Colleen declared. "Right here, right now."

The matter-of-fact way Colleen declared she'd end Damian's life was enough to shock me. "Colleen," I began, but she shook her head.

"Rina told me everything," she said. "About how this man nearly killed her and the baby. If anyone deserves to die, it's this garbage."

I swallowed hard. I hadn't forgotten any of that, not the moment I pulled up to the cottage to find Rina missing, or when I saw Damian hand her over to Beira. While I wouldn't miss Damian if he was gone, hearing Colleen speak that way was unnerving. I hoped she was bluffing.

"See that? The boy has no stomach for this sort o' work," Damian sneered. "He is no' worthy o' the new Queen o' Winter. That one would kill me in a trice."

"You know what, that's a great idea," Colleen said. "Chris, should we call Anya and tell her exactly where this scumbag is?"

"Sure." I sat in the chair Nick had vacated, pulled out my phone and swiped at the screen. I had no idea of Anya was anywhere near her phone, but I was fairly certain Colleen just wanted to watch Damian squirm. I found her cell number and hit the call button, fully intending to leave a message.

"Hello?"

"Anya?" I stood up so fast I stumbled. "Anya, we're here in Glasgow. We may have found the one who poisoned you."

"Poison?" she repeated. "What makes you think I've been poisoned?"

"That tea you get from the coffee shop," I replied. "It's what's been making your powers act up."

Anya appeared in the room looking like winter personified, wearing a white gown and a matching cape edged in fur and rubies. Her appearance had startled Colleen and I. Damian, however, was unfazed.

"'Tis the queen herself," Damian announced. "The cold bitch with ice for a heart."

"You're well?" Anya raised her hand as if to touch my face, but held back. The last time we'd been together was when she brought my frozen body to a hospital.

"I'm fine." When she bit her lip, I added, "Promise."

She nodded, but the lines on her forehead said she didn't believe me. "Why is this one here?" she asked, nodding toward Damian.

"We think he's responsible for the poisoned tea."

"We?" Anya asked, then she focused on Colleen. "Hello again."

Collen swallowed hard. "Um, hi."

Anya rounded on Damian, and demanded, "What is your quarrel with my family? First, you engineer the humiliation of my mother, and now you try poisoning me?"

"My quarrel?" Damian repeated. "No' a quarrel so much as a vendetta. I am in the revenge business, ye ken."

"I have not wronged you," Anya said.

"No' me. My son." Damian's eyes narrowed. "Liam."

Anya clenched her fists as her nostrils flared. Liam was the boy she'd loved when she was young, and who'd rejected her when she revealed her true form. "Anya, he's lying," I said. "Wasn't Liam mortal?"

"As am I," Damian said. "We resided in Elphame at the king's pleasure, near a soft spot where the veil was thin. I thought nothing o' allowing Liam to visit this world, thinkin' he'd be safer here than amongst the fey. I was wrong."

"Liam wronged me," Anya said. "He hurt me so deeply I threw myself off of a cliff."

"Yet you are standing here, well and hale, while he died in an asylum thanks to ye." Damian spit at Anya's feet. "I'm glad your ma was dethroned, and I am glad to poison ye. My only regret is that Liam is no' alive to watch ye suffer."

"Anya." I reached for her, but she evaded me.

"You are certain he is the culprit?" Anya asked.

"The poison seems to have come from him, yes," I replied. "We don't know who else he's working with."

Anya cocked her head to the side and regarded Damian. "And he's surely working with someone. This pathetic little man could not have orchestrated all of this on his own," she murmured, then she placed her hand on his head. "Tell me what you know, and perhaps I'll let you live," she said, as frost rimed his hair and creeped down his neck.

"I've sworn an oath to beings more powerful than ye to never reveal their names," Damian said, then he went still.

Anya laughed. "I'm sure this won't be the first oath you've broken." Damian remained silent, his skin blue down to his shirt collar.

"Well?" Anya prompted. "Talk."

"I don't think he can," Colleen said. "Anya, you've frozen him solid!"

Anya snatched her hand away from Damian's head. A mere touch from her had frozen his head right down to his shoulders. He hadn't even had time to scream.

"I-I didn't mean to," she said, backing away.

"Is he still alive?" I felt Damian's hands and wrists, and found a pulse. "His heart's beating. Can you reverse this?"

"I don't know!"

"Well, try!"

Anya moved forward as I stepped to the side, giving her room to work. A rat chose that moment to scurry behind the desk, Anya glanced at it, and her hand brushed Damian's shoulder. He toppled over and his head shattered against the edge of the desk, scattering icy chunks of bone and brains across the floor.

"Gods below," she shrieked. "What have I done?"

"It was an accident." I reached for her, but Colleen held me back. "We know he was guilty, at least of obtaining the poisoned herbs, though we don't know if he was acting alone, or colluding with others—"

"Others?" Anya interjected. "What do you know of others who seek to harm me?"

"Very little," Colleen said. "It's going to be almost impossible to figure out who they are since you murdered our only suspect."

Anya drew herself up, and demanded, "You dare to accuse me of murder? You saw yourself, it was an accident!"

Colleen stood her ground. "A rather convenient accident. If there are more working against you, will they have accidents as well?"

"Tread lightly, lest something befalls you," Anya snapped.

"Does that mean I'll have an accident, too? Another one?" I placed my hand on Anya's elbow. Even through her clothing, she was cold as death. "Anya, we are trying to help you.

Two gray, pupil-less eyes fixed on me. "You can help best by staying out of my way."

With that, she was gone.

A GOOD DAUGHTER

I blinked back to my flat, proud and triumphant and only slightly aghast at what I'd done. That man—that worm!—John Damian had deserved to die, for poisoning me and a hundred other terrible things he'd done. For what he'd done to Karina and the gallowglass, he deserved to be hung, drawn, and quartered—a slow and agonizing death if there ever was one, not the quick end I'd given him. No matter that I hadn't meant to kill him. Kill him I had, and I would not regret it.

I *refused* to regret it.

With his quick death, I'd shown him mercy he did not deserve, and it was a blessing to have him removed from this earth.

Christopher hadn't thought so. Neither had Colleen—and what was she doing there, anyway? Why had she accompanied Christopher and not Robert? Surely the gallowglass would have been of far more use in a meeting with a madman than his sister's friend. And the way she looked at me after Damian's head had shattered...

No regrets.

The gallowglass, now he would have approved of my actions. Given time, Robert would have assuredly killed Damian himself, as vengeance for his bride's kidnapping. But Christopher's reaction had given me pause... Colleen's presence, more so. Their stricken faces had made me doubt myself. Made me fear I'd lost Christopher, for good.

Gods below, I killed a man.

Am... Am I losing myself?

I tore at my hair and screamed at the ceiling. I needed answers, not worries, and I needed someone who could help me. Since I couldn't blink to the Winter Palace—not yet, anyway—I returned to the Unseelie Court.

Maelgwyn's throne room was dark, not only due to early hour. A creeping fog had infiltrated the room, threatening to smother anything in its path. Since the room appeared devoid of life, I wondered if the fog had smothered all the Unseelie along with the light, and I'd blinked from an empty flat to an empty castle. I stood in the center of the room and rotated in a full circle, searching for a footman, a chamberlain, anyone.

"Hello?" I called. "Is the king in residence? I must speak with him."

"I'm here."

I followed the voice and found the Unseelie King himself seated not on his throne, but on a window ledge at the far side of the room. He was gazing at a desolate courtyard that looked as if it hadn't seen a green leaf in decades.

"Your majesty," I greeted.

"Please, we needn't have such formalities between us. Sit." He gestured to the far end of the ledge. "Why have you come?"

"I seek my mother's counsel," I replied. "Is she here?"

He nodded toward the courtyard. I followed his gaze and saw my mother strolling among the brittle hedgerows, her red gown a bloody gash against the gray landscape.

"You may join her, if you like."

"Perhaps in a moment."

"Did you not come to speak with her?"

"Yes, and I shall." I touched the cold glass, tracking my mother's slow progress across the garden. The only signs of life, aside from her, were tiny white flowers blooming near her feet. "But she looks at peace, and she's had little enough peace in her life. My worries can wait a few moments."

"You are a good daughter."

I looked at Maelgwyn—truly looked at him—for the first time since I arrived. He too seemed at peace, and I suspected Mum's presence was the reason why. "How can you ken that? You ken nearly nothing about me."

"I know enough." He leaned closer. "I've had many children, but only you have my eyes. That must be how Old Bod knew you weren't his."

I dropped my gaze to my lap. "He never treated me as anything other than his natural child."

"No, I imagine he wouldn't have. Old Bod is a lot of things, yet he was never less than honorable. Even when he was beating the bloody piss out of me, he did so with honor."

"The way Da told the story, you went mewling to your judgement," I said. Maelgwyn's jaw tightened, and I remembered that the man sitting next to me was a king twice over. Before I could beg forgiveness, he spoke.

"I had visitors after you left," he began. "The gallowglass, and a man Beira tells me you're well acquainted with."

"Christopher was here? In your court? " I asked, and he nodded. "Whatever were the two of them after?"

"Actually, they were here about you. They decided that a man had been poisoning you and requested my help in finding and eliminating him." Maelgwyn paused. "That man, this Christopher, he seeks to help you?"

"Aye." My skin warmed at the thought of Christopher not only determining who was behind my abilities going awry, but braving the Unseelie Court in order to help me. "I can't believe he took all that on for me."

"He was quite determined," Maelgwyn said, "and wearing his heart on his sleeve. That one feels strongly for you." He spoke to me, but his gaze rested on Mum as she wandered about the courtyard.

"Do you ever regret it?" I jerked my chin toward Mum, where she meandered along the garden path. As if he'd been unaware of my true meaning.

"Never," he replied. "I treasured every moment I shared with Beira, both when they were happening and later as memories. Now that I know of you, I treasure them all the more."

My throat tightened, and my eyes burned. I hadn't expected his words to affect me so.

"I killed a man today," I said softly.

"Oh?" A raised eyebrow. "Your first?"

"First human man, yes," I replied. "This man was the one Christopher mentioned to you. The one who was poisoning me."

"Then killing him was well within your rights," he said, but I hadn't come for absolution.

"Christopher said that he might have been working with someone else," I said. "Can you think of anyone who may wish to harm my mother, or me?"

Maelgwyn leaned back and regarded me. "I can think of many who wish your mother dead, or worse. I also know of one whom—if he understood your true lineage—would torture you within an inch of madness solely to make me suffer."

"Who could possibly know I'm...your..." Some things I wasn't yet ready to speak aloud. I cleared my throat and began again. "Who could know besides Mum?" I wondered. "She never told anyone, not until today."

"Aye, but we do share a single distinct trait," he said, indicating his gray eyes. The eyes that matched mine. "Anyone who has seen my face would instantly know you're my daughter."

"Then we must consider who would remember your face so clearly," I replied.

"There is one. Fionnlagh, the Seelie King."

I swallowed hard. As foes went, Fionnlagh was a powerful one. "There's something else," I said. "A group of men out of time have been following me."

Maelgwyn frowned. "Out of time? As in, they move through it?"

"I believe so," I said. "They're Picts."

Maelgwyn blew out a breath. "This is worse than I feared. The Picts are Fionnlagh's mercenaries."

"Does that mean he knows?"

"It means he suspects, and with Fionnlagh that is enough."

FAMILY TIES

Colleen and I stared at each other over what was left of John Damian. Anya hadn't meant to freeze him, just scare him a bit. Then he tipped over and his head shattered into a million tiny pieces, and now Anya was gone.

"It was an accident," I said.

"Was it?" Colleen asked. "Chris, she's dangerous. This could have been you."

She was right. The blisters and frost-damaged skin that covered my chest and abdomen were direct evidence of Anya's abilities, and what she was capable of. I'd been minutes, maybe seconds away from being frozen to death, but Anya brought me to a hospital and Dr. Todd saved me.

"It was an accident," I repeated. Colleen hadn't seen Anya's face when she realized Damian's head was frozen, the fear in her eyes over what she'd done. Then the rat startled her, and he fell. Anya hadn't meant to hurt anyone.

But she had.

Colleen frowned, but didn't argue with me. "Should we call the police?"

"And tell them what? We've got a frozen and decapitated guy, please send out CSI?" I shook my head, images of how the media had dragged my reputation through the mud after Olivia sued me for plagiarism flashing behind my eyes. If I was connected to a man who'd died under mysterious circumstances, that mud would get much, much deeper. "We can't be linked to this."

"All right, then we need to hide the body."

I nodded. I couldn't believe I was doing this. I moved to grab one of the many garbage bags lining the alley, when movement from Damian's corpse caught my eye.

"Colleen."

"What?"

"He moved."

"What?"

"Look!"

Colleen spun around and we watched Damian's body quiver. The frozen bits of head trembled, and as we watched they shriveled down to nothing. While that was happening, the rest of Damian's body liquefied. Within a few minutes, all that was left were his clothes floating in a stinking puddle.

Colleen swallowed hard. "Chris, we need to leave before I puke and they use it to trace my DNA."

"Yeah," I said, fascinated and repulsed by Damian's melting body. "Let's get out of here."

We took a minute to wipe down the door handles, then we left Damian's corpse to bubble away into oblivion. With any luck he'd be nothing but a memory long before anyone else entered that room.

"That was strange," Colleen said when we were inside the truck. "Strange, horrifying, and gross."

"Yes." I started the truck and pulled out of the parking space. "I have never seen a body do that before, and I hope to never see it again."

"You've seen others? Bodies?"

"Yeah. I've seen a few."

"Human?"

"No." We passed Glasgow Cathedral. I turned onto the A803 and headed toward Crail. "Most were not."

"I don't know how you cope with all of this."

"I'm thinking about opening a distillery. Or maybe a bar. Or maybe I'll fill a bathtub with whisky and jump in."

"That's not funny," she snapped, and I remembered all the times Colleen had gotten me home after a rough night, all the times she'd covered for me while I nursed a hangover in my office.

"Sorry," I said. "I'm trying to transition to using humor as my coping mechanism. Seems that there's a learning curve."

She leaned over and touched my hand. "I'm glad you're trying."

When we got back to the cottage, everything was quiet. We found Rina, Rob, and Faith curled up in the master bed, all of them fast asleep.

"Beautiful family," Colleen murmured.

"Yeah. I love these three."

Rob cracked an eyelid. "Really now, that love extends to me?"

Colleen laughed so loudly Faith woke with a squeak. "Funny, both of you," I said. "I see Conall didn't kill you."

"I am no' dead yet. Perhaps I'll die tomorrow, but no' today." He shifted the baby against his chest. "Might an old man trouble ye for a cup o' tea?"

"And coffee," Rina added.

"I thought you were sleeping," I said.

"Parents of infants don't sleep." Rina opened her eyes and smiled at Faith. "About that coffee."

Colleen and I made the tea and coffee, and brought it upstairs along with two kitchen chairs. By the time everyone had been served, we were gathered in a loose circle in the bedroom with Faith in the center, sprawled on the comforter. We all shared our respective stories with one another. I'd expected Rob to regret not being the one to kill Damian, but he was anything but.

"It sound like Anya was in a right terror when she left," Rob said, after I'd explained how she teleported away right after Damian's death. "'Tis no small thing to take a man's life. Like as no' she will feel it for some time, raw and red like a fresh burn."

"Why aren't you raw and red?" Colleen asked without malice. "You've been doing this for a long time."

"Aye, that I have. Perhaps my skin has thickened over the years, scars upon scars, as it were." Rob sipped his tea. "'Twould be a shame for Anya to be so scarred."

"All the more reason for us to find her and help her." Rina set her mug down on the nightstand with such force coffee sloshed up over the side. "I can hardly believe Beira had a secret affair all those years ago, and the result was Anya. And literally no one knew?"

"Apparently not," I said.

Rina shook her head. "Elphame loves gossip. They would have been all over an illegitimate winter-summer baby."

"I agree, but it seems the only people who knew that Udane was Anya's father were Beira and the Bodach," I said.

"You're telling us that Beira never told Udane or even Anya, but she told her husband all about her affair?" Colleen leaned back in her chair and shook her head. "Something doesn't seem right about that."

"You're right, and I've been thinking about that." I got up and located a pencil and notebook, then I returned to my chair and started sketching eyes. "You know how Anya's eyes are oil slick gray, and how she doesn't have any pupils?"

"Yeah," Rina said warily.

"Udane has the exact same eyes. They're identical, right down to the shade of gray." I turned the notebook around and presented my admittedly amateur sketch of two sets of eyes. "My guess is that Old Bod saw his baby daughter's eyes, and realized he wasn't her father."

"That's pretty harsh. No wonder Old Bod freaked out," Rina said as she mopped up spilled coffee with the edge of her sleeve. "How come Wyatt never mentioned their resemblance?"

"When I asked, he said all us humans look alike to him."

Rina smirked. "I guess we do. Does this mean you've ruled out Udane as the one poisoning Anya?"

"I'm ninety-nine percent certain he has nothing to do with it," I replied. "I got the impression that before today Udane didn't even know Anya existed, much less that she was his child."

"Love child, no less," Rina added.

"Makes you wonder if anyone else recently learned the same facts," Colleen muttered. Her words clicked the final pieces into place.

"Rob, did Anya ever spend time at the Seelie Court?" I asked.

"To my knowledge, she has never once set foot there," he replied. "In fact, her name was hardly spoken. When others spoke o' Beria's family 'twas always about Old Bod and the boys." Rob paused, and added, "You're going to ask if that time at Glen Lyon was the first time Fionnlagh had set eyes upon Anya."

I nodded. "It was, wasn't it?"

Rob ran a hand through his hair. "I believe so. And everyone of note in the Seelie Court is aware that Fionnlagh was once close to Udane. He would have recognized Anya's eyes instantly."

"Close?" Rina repeated. "How close are we talking? Neighbors?"

"Brothers. Which means that Anya and Fionnlagh are kin."

"Whoa whoa whoa," Rina said. "Fionnlagh is Anya's uncle?"

"More importantly, she is the heir to the Seelie throne," Rob replied.

"Fionnlagh doesn't have any other kids?" Colleen asked.

"He does, but most o' his dalliances have been with humans, and mortality breeds truer than otherworldly blood," Rob replied.

"What about Nicnevin?" I asked.

"Nicnevin can't have children," Rina said. "Whatever she did to make herself Seelie, it left her barren."

"Okay, but did Udane ever have any children?" I pressed.

"He did, but no one has heard tell o' them in ages," Rob replied. "My thought is that they're either deep in hiding in Unseelie lands, or they've all perished."

"Huh." I leaned back in my chair and took a deep breath. I didn't like the conclusion I'd reached, but it made as much sense as anything around here.

"Anya is a threat to Fionnlagh," I said. "He is the one who wants her eliminated."

We all looked toward Rob. "Do no' look to me for assurances," he said. "The king does no' share his plans with me."

"And it really wouldn't be in his best interests to tell you this, what with Chris and Anya's relationship," Rina said. "Robert, I think it's time we brought in the big gun."

He frowned. "I wish there was no need for her, but I agree. Her counsel is necessary."

"Who is this big gun?" I asked. "Persephone?"

"Worse." Rina leveled her gaze at me. "It's Nicnevin."

PROTECTION

"Nicnevin?" I repeated. My sister thought we should call on the Seelie Queen, the creature that enthralled me and made me into a sex-obsessed version of Renfield. "What makes you think she'd help us, especially against Fionnlagh?"

"She and I have an understanding," Rina replied. "She's been better, lately."

I shoved back my chair and stood. "Why are you talking about Nicnevin as if she's anything other than a monster? Have you forgotten what she did to me?"

"I haven't forgotten anything," Rina snapped. "You think I don't lie awake at night, replaying everything that happened over the last few years over and over in my head? Wondering why I never saw Olivia for what she was, why I couldn't help you? Why I never noticed you were under Nicnevin's spell?" Rina crossed her arms over her stomach. "Nicnevin may have hurt you the worst, but you weren't the only one that suffered."

"Great. You remember." Suddenly, the bedroom with everyone in it was too small for me. I stalked downstairs and paced from the living area to the kitchen, then I leaned on the dividing wall and tried to catch my breath. No matter what I did or where I went, I couldn't escape Nicnevin. Her claws were sunk deep into my flesh, ripping out whatever bits of sanity I had left.

A few minutes later, I heard footsteps; Rina was coming downstairs, followed by Colleen and Rob. Wonderful.

"Chris," Rina began, then she looked over her shoulder. "Robert, get back in bed!"

"No." Rob gingerly crossed the first floor and leaned against the kitchen counter. "A man was no' made to lie abed all the day long."

"Dr. Todd said you need to rest," Rina said.

"Any wound tended by Margaret heals in a day or so," Rob said. When Rina kept glaring at him, he added, "'Tis why her services are so valued by the Good People."

"If you keel over, I'm leaving you on the floor."

"I assumed ye would do so."

"Great. We're all here." Rina sat at the table and looked at me. "Can we talk about this?"

I faced my sister, the one person who I'd thought understood how badly Nic-nevin hurt me. Maybe I was wrong about that, too. "You still haven't explained why you brought *her* up in the first place."

"She visited me last spring, after everything with Beira. It was while you and Anya were on that road trip. We talked for a while, and she put us under her protection."

Sweat gathered between my shoulder blades as my hands started to shake. "Us?"

"You, me, Robert, and Faith," Rina replied. "It was a nice gesture, and I accepted."

"A nice gesture?" I stepped back, putting my hands on my head as the room spun around me. "A nice fricken' gesture! You told her to put me under her protection, whatever the hell that means, and you didn't even ask me? What the hell is wrong with you?"

"What the hell is wrong with you?" Rina stood and slapped her palms down onto the table. "We don't live in the normal world, not any longer. We need someone to protect us, someone powerful, so excuse fucking me if I was trying to keep anything else from happening to you!"

We stared at each other across the kitchen. Rina's shoulders were heaving, and her blue eyes were so bright I wondered if she was contemplating sending me somewhere via portal. Faith's cry broke the silence.

"I'll get her," Colleen said. "You all keep having your family drama." Colleen patted Rina's elbow and made for the stairs.

"Chris," Colleen called over her shoulder, "it's not my business, but maybe if you'd take a moment and listen to what your sister was saying, you'd realize she's only trying to help you."

With that, Collen went to see to Faith. I stared after her, speechless. When Rina told me she'd had Nicnevin cast yet another spell over me, all the pent up shame and anxiety from a year ago had bubbled to the surface. Rina never should have made such an agreement with Nincevin, not without talking to me first. But she was right. We didn't live in the normal world.

We never would again.

We needed someone to stand between us and Elphame or we all might end up enthralled to monsters.

I turned back to Rina. She had tears streaming down her cheeks. I'd yelled at my sister until she cried, all because she was trying to help me.

"I am an asshole," I said. "A complete and utter asshole."

"Sometimes." Rina came around the table and hugged me. "Usually, you're okay."

"I'm sorry," I said as I squeezed her. "It's just so much, and—"

"I know." She drew back and wiped her eyes. "I get it. Robert does too."

I glanced at Rob. He hadn't moved from her place against the counter. "Sorry for yelling."

"Karina is correct. I do understand what you're going through. The Good People have a knack for driving the best men batty." He pulled Rina against his chest and kissed her hair, then he clapped me on the shoulder, the frostbitten one. I didn't ask if he'd gotten that one on purpose. "Do no' raise your voice in me home again."

"Yes, sir."

The doorbell rang. "I'll get it," I said, since I was closest. On the other side stood a rather lovely redheaded woman. After a moment, I recognized her as Rina's friend who had brought the tiny cakes to the baby shower.

"Hello," she said. "I'm here for Karina."

"Um, sure," I said. "Come in. I'm Rina's brother, Chris."

"I remember." She slid past me into the house. "I heard my name mentioned, and thought I'd drop in."

"Nancy, right?"

She turned to me and offered the most devilish grin. Before either of us could say anything further, Rina was between us.

"You really shouldn't appear out of the blue like this," Rina hissed at Nancy. "And remember, you swore you wouldn't hurt Chris."

"Of course I remember," she said, as she shed her coat and handed it to Rina. "After all, he is under my protection."

"Protection?" I repeated, then Rina's friend Nancy transformed into Nicnevin.

Well, shit.

I held my breath, waiting for the crash of panic and cold sweat that usually accompanied hearing her name or being in her presence... But it didn't come. All I felt was a mild annoyance at being in the same room with Nicnevin. Since I understood anxiety well enough to know that it doesn't miraculously disappear, that meant either Nicnevin had been deliberately altering my reactions to her in the past, or she was doing so now.

Just when I thought she couldn't be any more despicable, she lowered the bar yet again.

"Do you often eavesdrop on my sister?" I asked. "That seems vulgar, even for you."

"I've no need for eavesdropping, but my name was mentioned three times," Nicnevin replied. "Thus was I summoned, and so I have arrived."

"And we're glad you're here," Rina said. "Would you like anything to drink?"

"Tea, please." Nicnevin and Rina sat at the table while Rob put the kettle on to boil. I remained in my spot between the entrance and the kitchen, observing the other three. Rina made some kind of small talk with Nicnevin, going on about the weather and current events in the village. Once the kettle whistled, Rob made the tea, delivered it, and returned to his post. I went to stand next to him.

"You're okay with her being her?" I whispered.

"I am, if she keeps her word."

"And if she doesn't?"

Rob grunted, his jaw tense. Nicnevin's appearance probably wasn't helping his pain levels. "She may be the Seelie Queen, but I remain the gallowglass. If I can defeat Beira, I can defeat Nicnevin."

"Even wounded?"

"Even so."

I remembered watching him take on and rout a host of giants, and go on to defeat and disempower the Queen of Winter. I'd never been more grateful to have the gallowglass on my side.

We all watched as Nicnevin slowly stirred her tea, then took a dainty sip; Rina once told me how the Seelie were sticklers for tradition, and the rules of hospitality. She hadn't mentioned how maddening these rituals were. Just when I thought I'd burst with anticipation, she spoke.

"Excellent. Thank you, Robert," Nicnevin said with a nod toward him. "Karina, please enlighten me as to why you've summoned me here today."

"We have a situation," Rina began, and she laid out everything we knew about Anya, Udane-slash-Maelgwyn, and their connection to Fionnlagh. By the time Rina was finished, Nicnevin's mouth was a slash across her face, and her previously smooth brow was creased like an accordion.

"You're certain of these facts?" Nicnevin asked.

"As certain as we can be," Rina replied.

"How can we be sure of Anya's parentage?" Nicnevin pressed. "Beira has told more than her fair share of lies."

"Have you ever been to the Unseelie Court?" I asked. "Ever seen Maelgwyn, even at a distance?"

"I have not."

"He and Anya look almost exactly alike," I said. "Same lean form, same bone structure, but mostly it's the eyes. Both Anya and he have the same oil slick gray eyes."

Nicnevin's gaze darted from me to Rob. "Is this true?"

"Aye," he replied. "I saw Maelgwyn with me own two eyes. Anya is the spittin' image of him."

Nicnevin nodded. "And you also believe this claim that the Unseelie King was once the Summer King?"

"That I do," Rob replied. "Ye ken the wights what live in me garden? As it turns out, they once tended the garden at the Summer Court. The wights recognized Maelgwyn as the Summer King straight aways, and he them. There is no doubt in my mind that when Udane disappeared after the Bodach's beating, he transformed himself into Maelgwyn."

Nicnevin took a deep breath and folded her hands together, resting them in front of her teacup. "This does complicate things, immeasurably so. If Anya is Udane's child, then she is a threat to the Seelie Throne."

"How is she a threat?" I asked.

"Because she has a claim to it," Nicnevin replied. "And a strong one, at that."

"What about Fionnlagh's children?" Rina asked. "Are they in hiding?"

"They have no need to hide. Most are dead." When Rina gasped, Nicnevin continued, "Not like that; well, mostly not. Fionnlagh has always been careful with regard to his issue, and nearly every child of his was born to a mortal woman. Mortality breeds truer than magic, which meant that he got all the joy of parenthood without the fear that he may lose his throne. He merely outlived them."

"What about the ones that weren't mortal?" Rina asked. When Nicnevin remained silent, she added, "You said nearly every child was born of a mortal. What happened to the rest?"

Nicnevin's face darkened. "He saw to it that they were born as monsters. I trust you remember the *fuath*?"

Rina's eyes widened. "You mean those water demons that hunted Robert and me were Fionnlagh's kids?"

"Why do you think they did my bidding so willingly?" Nicnevin purred. "They didn't want to disappoint their stepmother."

"I shall ne'er forget those beasts," Rob said. "Why are his children born such?"

Nicnevin shrugged. "Perhaps the parent's nature is revealed in the child. And they aren't all *fuath*."

At that, even the gallowglass stilled. "Are ye willin' to share what the rest are?"

"Oh, they take many forms," Nicnevin replied. "Some look like men, and some like horses or goats or monsters from the bottom of the sea. All are terrifying."

"They're all male?" I asked, and she nodded. "What about his daughters?"

Nicnevin's face darkened. "You... You are better off not knowing."

Rina gasped. Nicnevin placed her hand on Rina's forearm. "Now you understand why I had to bring your family under my wing. He eliminates anything that could be a threat, and he is most threatened by women."

"Why is that?" I asked.

"A female of his line could bear more children, children he would be forced to either acknowledge or hunt down and eliminate," she replied. "And a powerful female could take an equally powerful mate, and thus create a new dynasty. Who's to say that dynasty wouldn't turn against him?"

"Would he hunt down Faith?" Rina asked.

"I don't know," Nicnevin admitted. "I did not want to risk her."

Rina nodded, placed her hand on top of Nicnevin's. "I appreciate that," she said, and I finally had enough.

"You appreciate that?" I demanded. "Have you forgotten that we're only in this mess because of her? Because she sent a freaking *leanan sìth* after me?"

"Chris," Rina said. "Things are different now."

"Different enough for you to snuggle up with the enemy?" I asked. "Do you even care what she did to me?"

"Put your indignation away, Christopher," Nicnevin said. "As I recall, you came willingly into my arms."

"I thought you were a woman," I bit off, my face hot with shame, "not the fairy queen!"

"True, but once you knew my true identity, did you try to leave? Did you beg your release from my bower?"

I stared at her. It was true, I'd realized there was more to the woman I'd been seeing early on. At first I'd refused to believe that anything magical could be happening. Rina was the one who believed in magic and fairies, not me, the sensible older brother. And when I'd no longer been able to ignore the odd happenings around me...

Nicnevin was right. I would have done anything to stay with her. She'd enthralled me, yes, but I never resisted her. Not even a bit.

"You were disguised when we met," I said, but she waved my words away.

"I neither need nor require forgiveness from you," Nicnevin said. "We have more pressing concerns at hand."

"Don't shove me aside," I said.

"Would you rather debate our past intentions, or attempt to help this woman you profess to love?" she countered, rounding on me. "Save your wounded ego for another time."

I stared at her, her perfect green eyes shining like emeralds. "Another time, then."

A curt nod. "I tell you these things not to frighten you, but to prepare. While Fionnlagh has not spoken of his designs for Anya to me, I can assure you he's more likely to destroy her than seek peace."

"How do we stop him?" I asked.

"We start by making a plan."

A PLAN, AND A BOON

"How do we craft this plan?" I asked. Nicnevin gave me some side eye, proving she hadn't overlooked my sarcasm.

"First, we need to gather information," Nicnevin began. "There is much happening here, and to go in unprepared would be foolish. War in Elphame is never simple or without cost."

"Do you really think there will be a war?" Rina asked.

"It is a possibility. Fionnlagh values his position, and he's killed to keep his throne safe and uncontested more times than I can count."

Rina squared her shoulders. "All right. Preparations. What should we do?"

"I cannot work directly against my husband, but I can offer you guidance," Nicnevin said. "I will share any information with you that he also shares with his court, and the *fuath*. That which he tells me in confidence must remain so." When Rina frowned, she added, "If he tells something to me and only me, and then you have the knowledge as well, how would that appear?"

"Bad, I suppose," Rina mumbled.

"You really think he'll retaliate against you?" I asked.

"If Fionnlagh believes his hold on the Seelie Court is in peril, he will do anything to remove that threat," Nicnevin replied. "Anything."

I blew out a breath and ran a hand through my hair. Here we were talking about a possible war against Elphame, and our side consisted of me, Rina,

Colleen, an injured gallowglass, and a handful of wights. All of us would be pitted against the Seelie Court. We were doomed.

Then again, maybe we weren't. Anya would also be on our side, and I couldn't imagine Maelgwyn would let Fionnlagh wage war on his daughter without stepping in. We'd have the Unseelie at our backs, and that was something.

That something may amount to a civil war in Elphame.

"What would war in Elphame mean for this world?" I asked.

"Nothing good, of that I can assure you," Nicnevin replied. "Which is why we need to ensure that no war commences."

"Agreed," Rob said. "How shall we assist you?"

"You will assist me best by waiting," she replied. "I shall return to court, and gather information. Once I learn something of import, I shall send word." Nicnevin folded her hands before her, and looked at Rina. "Before I depart, I would ask a boon of you, one which you are free to refuse."

"What's this boon?" Rina asked.

Nicnevin dropped her gaze to her hands. "May I see her?"

"Oh. Um." Rina glanced at Rob, who nodded. "Yeah. Of course you can. I'll go get her."

Rina and Rob went together to fetch Faith. I watched Nicnevin as she waited, fiddling with the edge of her sleeve, tapping her foot. I recalled what Rina had told me, that whatever Nicnevin had done to make herself Seelie had rendered her barren. Maybe she was helping us for the all children she'd never have.

Or maybe she had another motive altogether.

"Why are you helping us?" I asked.

Nicnevin leaned back in her chair and regarded me. "You're wondering why I'm choosing to work against my husband."

"It does seem a bit odd, even for you."

"Why, Christopher, that's the nicest thing you've said about me in over a year." Her hand fluttered at her breast in mock embarrassment. When I didn't react, she continued, "You assume that Fionnlagh's and my match is one of love. It's not; well, maybe I loved him once."

"And he?"

"I don't really know. He desired me, that much was evident."

"If not love, then what brought you together?"

"Power. He had it, I wanted it, so I became," she gestured to herself, "this."

"Do you ever regret it?"

"What's to regret," she began, but was cut off by a baby's gurgling voice. We looked toward the stairs and there was Rina, with Faith in her arms and Rob right behind her.

"Here she is," Rina said when she reached the table. "Faith Elizabeth Kirk."

"Oh," Nicnevin cooed, standing to get a better view of the baby's face. "She is a sweet girl, isn't she?"

"She is," Rina agreed, then she shocked everyone by thrusting Faith into Nicnevin's arms. For a moment Nicnevin remained still as a statue and only stared at Faith, then she relaxed and held her close.

"Hello, Faith Elizabeth," Nicnevin sang. "You are a very special girl, descended from two wonderful families... And I will be here to protect you against anything that might harm you. You have my word, now and forever."

"Like a real fairy godmother," Rina said with a smirk.

"Don't expect a magic wand or singing forest creatures. I do have an image to maintain." Nicnevin passed Faith back to Rina. "Now, I will take my leave of you. If you learn of anything that may assist us, do summon me. I shall lend help as I can."

"What if the Picts rally against us?" I asked.

"I have an army of my own," she replied. "Unlike my husband's mercenaries and the *fuath*, these soldiers are sworn to me, and no one else."

"I don't need an army," Rob grumbled. "I have a score to settle with Conall."

"Are they a match for the Picts?" I asked.

"Oh, they most definitely are a match. And Robert," she added, "do let me know if you'd like me to have a look at that wound."

"We'll do that," Rina said quickly, sparing us Rob's reply.

Nicnevin turned to me. "As for you, Christopher, I have one last bit of knowledge."

"And what's that?"

"Powerful women are drawn to you—myself and Anya, for example. Even Olivia, which was why it took her so long to bring you home. She didn't want to leave you."

I bristled; I did not need a rundown of my ex-fiancée's motivations. "Where are you going with this?"

"Have you never wondered why that is? Perhaps it's because you've been surrounded by powerful women your entire life; now your sister, and before her, your mother."

"What do you know about my mother?"

"The question is, what do you know?"

With that, Nicnevin faded from view. I turned to Rina, and demanded, "What does she know about Mom?"

THE POISONED TEA

Even though I'd gone to the Unseelie Court to speak with my mother, I left without having done so. My brief conversation with Maelgwyn had revealed many things. I needed time and a bit of distance to process these facts.

The first and most unsettling of these facts was that the Seelie King and I were kin. Now I understood why Elphame had always felt off to me. It was well known that Fionnlagh went out of his way to eliminate anyone who could have a claim to his throne, and the air itself must have been warning me to stay far, far away from that madman. I also understood why Mum had never brought me to the Seelie Court. If the resemblance between myself and Maelgwyn, my natural father, was as marked as he had indicated, the whole of the court would have known of our connection, and therefore my connection to Fionnlagh. Our similarities would have also announced my mother's infidelity, thus damaging the grieving wife persona she so carefully cultivated.

That, coupled with the second fact—why the Picts kept appearing in my path—was what led me to return to my family's summer home; not the shieling in Glen Lyon, but a stone cottage on the Isle of Skye. I remembered the long, hot summer days I spent lying among the heather making pictures from the clouds, returning home to find Da and Mum sitting on the front porch sipping cool spring water...

My heart broke for Da, he who loved my mother with all of his giant's heart. But Maelgwyn also loved Mum, and even though he'd lost his kingdom and his name because of that love, it seemed that even if he could change the past, he wouldn't. He was glad to have Mum back in his life, and glad to have me as a daughter.

"Perhaps this is a good thing," I said to the empty cottage. "Perhaps having two loving and powerful fathers is a gift like none other." I plopped myself on the ground in front of Da's old porch rocker, much as I used to sit on his feet when I was wee. Then he'd laugh and scoop me onto his shoulders. Now, silence was all he could give me.

My thoughts traveled to the Picts, who apparently worked for Fionnlagh. On his orders they'd followed me to Glasgow, and appeared at least twice at the shieling. In all my days I'd never seen a real life Pict in the flesh, but since Fionnlagh had gotten a good long look at my eyes they'd been popping out of the woodwork around me. And why would they bring their wounded leader to my father's home, of all places?

Since Christopher had been traveling with Robert, he must have been present when Conall wounded the gallowglass. I hoped Christopher hadn't been hurt as well. If those Picts had touched one hair on his head...

Small bursts of coldness distracted me. In my anger I'd grown so cold it was snowing. I unclenched my fists, and the weather reverted to the sunny day it had been, and the accumulated flakes melted away. Marveling at my control, I conceded that Christopher may be right. Perhaps I had been poisoned, and there had never been anything wrong with my command over the cold. Perhaps I would be the greatest Queen of Winter in Scotland's history.

Picts still very much on my mind, I blinked to the shieling and examined the spot where their leader had lay bleeding. They hadn't left anything behind, not that I'd expected to find much. I had hoped for a clue, but as usual, reality was another matter altogether.

I turned in a slow circle, debating if I should track the approach they took through the glen, when I remembered what Christopher had said. He was certain the tea I brought home from the local shop had been what poisoned me. The next moment found me standing in the midst of our favorite coffee shop.

A quick glamour made me invisible to mortal eyes. After a few moments of invisibility with no stray gasps or stares thrown my way, I deduced that only humans were currently in the shop. I slipped behind the counted and past the hissing and spitting espresso machine, and examined the wall of teas. It was a sight to behold, with rows and rows of sparkling glass jars filled with all manner of herbs, each nestled in their designated spot on the oaken shelves. Some jars, such as the plain black and green teas, were as large as soup pots, while the rarer herbs occupied smaller and smaller containers.

A jar not on the shelves but set to the side caught my attention. It was thick, heavy glass, both old and fine enough to be a prized museum piece. Carved into the crystal lid was the image of a stag.

The Seelie King wore an antlered headdress. He also went by Fionnlagh of the White Stag.

I picked up the jar, scrutinizing the contents through the engraved glass walls. It certainly looked like the tea I'd been drinking these past months. I opened the lid and inhaled the floral scent, and nearly choked.

I grabbed the shelf for support and knocked several jars of tea onto the slate floor. People screamed and pointed toward the wreckage when they shattered, scattering glass and tea everywhere, with the baristas imploring the customers to stay calm while others shouted about ghosts and demons haunting the place. I closed the lid of the tea that had been my poison, and blinked to the Unseelie Court.

Maelgwyn remained on the window seat, but Mum had joined him, their faces close as lovers. They were lovers, I supposed. I watched them for a moment, surprised by the tenderness between them.

"I have it," I announced. "This is the tea. The poisoned tea."

Maelgwyn strode across the room and claimed the jar, scowling when he saw the stag incised onto the lid. "It's his mark," Maelgwyn said. "Fionnlagh did seek to harm our Anya."

"And how will we respond?" Mum asked.

The Unseelie King closed his hands around the jar. When he opened his hands, a shiny gray lump was all that remained. "We stand our ground, and return every one of his actions tenfold. My little brother shall learn his place."

DIARIES AND CANES

Rina stared at the empty spot Nicnevin disappeared from, then at Rob and me. "How could Nicnevin possibly know anything about our mother?" she demanded.

"That one kens all sorts of things she shouldn't." Rob made his way to the couch and sat, clutching his side the entire way. "I will say this. If she believes there was something interesting about your ma, best you learn it as well."

"I don't suppose Nicnevin would just tell us whatever she's hinting at?" I asked.

Rob's gaze slid toward me. "And when has she ever been helpful?"

"She's helping us against Fionnlagh," I said, but Rob shook his head.

"All we did was discuss perhaps obtainin' her assistance. No help has yet been lent." Rob patted the cushion beside him. Rina sat and passed him the baby, and I took the chair opposite them. Colleen hovered near the television, ready to intercede if things got too heavy. "Now, Karina love, tell me. What do ye remember about your mother?"

Rina blinked. "Anxiety. Kindness. Borderline agoraphobia."

"More like xenophobia," I added. "Mom didn't trust anyone she didn't already know. It made school functions awkward."

"It wasn't trust so much as fear," Rina said. "She was constantly terrified that something might happen to one of us, but only when we weren't home."

"True," I said. "While we were on our property, we could set the barn on fire, electrocute ourselves, or jump off the roof. She would laugh, patch us up, and send us on our way. But if we came home with a scratch or bruise, she was convinced people were out to deliberately harm us."

"Wait, so you two did burn barns and jump off roofs?" Colleen asked.

"I did," Rina said. "I wanted to see if I had superpowers. Chris electrocuted himself trying to make a grilled cheese in the toaster."

"That is not how you make grilled cheese," Colleen said.

"It was Rina's recipe," I said. "My point is, maybe Mom was someone of otherworldly importance. Why else would she be so worried about the outside world?"

Rina shrugged. "Anxiety disorder? Borderline depression? PTSD?"

"How did your father react to her idiosyncrasies?" Rob asked.

"Like water off a duck's back," I replied. "Nothing fazed Dad. He was also the only one who could calm her down." My gaze dropped to my hands. "I tried using some of his tactics with Anya. I didn't do half as well as him."

"Dad had years to perfect his technique," Rina said. "He also wasn't wrangling the Queen of Winter."

"Okay, so we've established that your father was awesome," Colleen said. "Who was your mother?"

Rina and I looked at each other. "She was Elizabeth Jane Stewart," I replied.

"But what else was she?" Colleen pressed. "She was more than a wife and mother. Who was she before you were born? What was her maiden name?"

"Lund," I replied. "When Dad met her in Iceland, her name was Elisabét Lund. She Anglicized her name to Elizabeth after they got married," I added.

"That's something," Colleen said. "What else do you know about her?"

"Not much," I replied. "She never talked about herself."

"Almost like she didn't want to burden us," Rina added. "I always felt like she thought not telling us about her past was for the best."

"Okay, then how do we learn more about her?" Colleen asked. "Are there relatives we can call, genealogy databases we can search?"

"There's not much of our family left," I said. "My father was an only child, and his parents are gone. He's got some cousins in Queens, but we don't see them often. As far as we know, Mom didn't have any living relatives."

Rina tapped her chin. "Maybe the cornucopia can help."

"Can you use it to contact Persephone?" I asked.

Rina gave me a look. "That is easily the hundredth time you've conveniently thought of Persephone as our only hope," she said. "I meant, maybe we can ask the cornucopia for help."

Rob shook his head. "I do adore the way ye mind works, *mo chroi*, but a cornucopia brings forth sustenance, no' knowledge," he said. "However, I do believe we have the perfect item to bring about that which ye seek."

"And what's that?" Rina asked.

"Dougal's toolbox."

"Do we really think this is a good idea?" Colleen asked. After Rina quashed my attempts to bring Persephone into the mix, I'd gone out to the truck and retrieved the toolbox. Now, the shiny red case sat in the middle of the floor with Colleen and me sitting on either side of it.

"A better question is, do we think this will work," I said. "It's one thing to ask the box for something generic like a hammer. How could it produce a specific person's possession?"

"I do not know," Colleen said. "How does this thing operate, again?"

I rubbed the back of my neck. "According to Rina and Rob, they ask the box for items they need, and then those items appear."

"Like magic?"

"Ah, yeah. It's all magic, all the time around here." I rubbed the back of my neck. "I used to be the skeptical one. Now I'm conjuring memories from a toolbox."

"We do what we need to do." Colleen leaned over and peered into the box. "We should probably do a test run."

"You don't want to wait for them?" I asked, since Rina and Rob were upstairs with the baby.

"Nah, let's go for it." Colleen stretched her arms and cracked her knuckles. "Box, I would like you to produce the notebook I used in the eighth grade."

"Whoa, Captain Specific."

"It is a test," she began, then a creaking sound came from the box. A moment later, a pink notebook with frayed edges rose up on a metal tray.

"Ohmygod." Colleen snatched the notebook and flipped through its pages. "Chris, this is my notebook! It's my actual notebook!"

"Guess it works." I lifted the toolbox and ran my hand across the bottom. It was a solid sheet of metal. "Maybe it has some kind of built-in portal, or it somehow feeds off Rina's—"

"Chris."

I set down the box. "What?"

"This notebook doesn't exist. I burned it on the last day of school."

I looked at the very real, very not burnt notebook in Colleen's hands. The cover was so battered it was barely attached, and the interior pages were dog-eared and covered in cursive writing and stickers. It definitely wasn't a new notebook, and I'd seen Collen's handwriting often enough to recognize the writing on the pages as hers. "Are you certain this is the one you burned?"

Colleen extended her left arm and indicated a scar near her wrist. "See that? I burned myself, too." Her gaze fell to the notebook in her lap. "The last time I saw this notebook, it was ashes."

"So the box can get...anything? From anywhere or any time?"

She turned the pages, her eyes wide as saucers. "I'm going to say yes."

"Huh." I went to the bottom of the stairs and yelled, "Rina, what do you remember most about Mom's things?"

"Her weird cane," Rina yelled back.

"Cane it is," I muttered as I returned to the box. "Mr. Box, could you please send up my mother's cane?" The box shuddered, and I heard gears moving in the depths. Maybe this box backed up to a pocket dimension.

"Was your mother disabled?" Colleen asked.

"What? Oh, no. In fact, I never saw her use the cane, but she always kept it nearby." The noises emanating from the box grew louder. "If anyone asked her about it, she said it was something she'd kept from a long time ago and left it at that."

"I wonder how long," Colleen said, then she was cut short by the cane's appearance. It was exactly as I remembered it, dark wood polished to a soft sheen and decorated with ribbons and baubles. I pulled it up and out of the box, all four feet of it.

"Chris, that is not a cane," Colleen said. "That is a staff. In other words, it's a giant-sized magic wand."

I looked at the cane in my hands, and realized Colleen was right. The wood itself had symbols burned into it, and the ribbons were braided into ropes that crisscrossed the length of it. The top of the staff was bound with lengths of silk and lace, and was decorated with strung beads and feathers. This was not an item to help someone walk. No, this was something used to focus one's intent.

"Rina," I yelled, "you need to see this. Bring Rob."

"I need to see what?" she asked as she and Rob descended the stairs. "Oh, you got her cane."

"Not a cane," Colleen muttered.

"Was your mother a sorceress?" Rob asked. "What do these runes mean?"

"Runes?" I asked, but he was referring to the symbols. "I thought they were just decoration."

Rob frowned, then he addressed the box. "I do require a book focused on translatin' Icelandic runes to English."

"You're going to translate the symbols on the cane?" I asked.

The box produced the book. Rob grabbed it and went to sit at the kitchen table. "That I am. Bring the staff here, would ye? And some paper and a pencil or two, if ye please. This may take a bit o' time."

Almost an hour later, Rob announced, "The short version is that yes, your mother was indeed a sorceress."

I glanced at Rina. She shrugged. "My mother was a what, now?"

"A sorceress," Rob repeated. He pushed his notebook toward me. On it was his translation of the symbols that wound around Mom's cane. Every one of them was a type of protection spell. "Specifically, she was a sort o' Norse witch called a volva."

I swallowed hard. "And what are volvas known for?"

"Foresight." Rob closed the book he'd been using and set his hand on top of Rina's. "Ye have often spoken o' your mother's anxiety, especially o' her fear that harm may come to you or Christopher. Was it possible she was worried about things yet to come?"

"Maybe." Rina chewed her lower lip. "She was surrounded by fear, wore it like a hat."

"Do ye remember what the fear centered on?" Rob asked.

"Yeah." Rina faced me. "Chris."

"Me?" I asked. "How was I scaring her?"

"Honestly? I have no idea," Rina replied. "But she wasn't just scared, she was terrified. When you started driving, she became obsessed with crash reports, and pressured Dad to find the safest car for you. The first time you went on spring break she took out travel insurance, cleared all her credit cards in case she needed to book you a new flight home, and was so worried you'd get alcohol poisoning she stocked up on homemade cures. No matter what you did, she was convinced it would hurt you."

I wanted to argue with Rina, but I couldn't. She was right, and I remembered endless conversations with my mother about staying safe, being cautious, and not trusting anyone. More than anything, Mom had warned me to stay away from strangers.

I ran a hand through my hair and stared at the ceiling. "Mom, what were you so worked up about?"

Rina slumped in her chair. "If only we could ask her."

Maybe we can. "There's only one way to learn what she was thinking." I approached the toolbox, and said, "I need my mother's diary from when I was a kid."

"You can't read her diary," Rina said.

"What else am I supposed to do?" I countered. "Like you said, I can't ask her these things myself."

The box whirred to life. I swallowed the lump in my throat and watched as a nondescript book bound in blue fabric rose up from the depths of the box. Mom had always chosen bound books with unlined pages for her diaries, I'd thought so she could draw as well as write. Now that I knew she was a volva, I wasn't so sure.

I grabbed the book, set it on the kitchen table and sat opposite Rina. She nodded, then she turned the book so we could both read it and we opened it together. The first page was an account of one of her first dates with Dad.

"I can't do this," Rina said as she shoved the book away. "It's an invasion of privacy."

"Give it here, love." Rob flipped through the pages, glancing through the contents with a scholar's practiced eye. He was halfway through the book when he announced, "She was in a state over ye, Christopher."

"She was?" I leaned forward. "Does she say why?"

"No' specifically." He found a particular page, and pointed to a line of writing. It said, "*He is doomed and I won't be there to help him.*"

"You're sure she meant me?" I asked.

"I am," he replied. "This diary starts out as a lass recountin' her courtship and marriage. As soon as she was carryin' ye, she was overtaken by visions about your future."

"I guess that explains her anxiety." I turned the page and lost my breath. Scrawled across both pages was, *She will kill him*.

"What?" Rina asked. I shoved the book at her, watched her eyes widen. "She who? Nicnevin? Beira? Anya?"

"Not Anya," I said. "Anya would not hurt me."

Rina frowned. "Chris, she already has."

I got up from the table and walked toward the sink. I leaned on the edge and stared out at the garden. The wights were flitting about, preparing it for winter. It seemed that everyone and everything knew how to handle winter, except me.

"What am I supposed to do?"

LINEAGE

"I'll not stand for it, not this time," Maelgwyn said as he paced across the room. We—Maelgwyn, Mum, and I—had retreated to his private chambers. There, I'd told my parents everything about my varying ability to control the cold, beginning with the day Fionnlagh had bestowed them on me at Glen Lyon to my freezing half of Glasgow in August. All the while Maelgwyn paced, the gray blob of glass that was recently the jar of poisoned tea clutched in his hand.

I also told Mum that I'd killed John Damian, but she was an unconcerned with her daughter committing murder as Maelgwyn had been.

"And how were you expecting me to react?" Mum demanded.

"I expected you to be shocked, or at least concerned," I said. "One of you, at least."

"As I said, killing him was within your rights," Maelgwyn said. "I only wish I'd gotten the chance to question him myself."

I imagined the Unseelie King stalking through the streets of Glasgow, searching for suspects. It was not a pleasant thought. "What would you have asked?"

"How he became entangled with the Seelie, for one." Maelgwyn tightened his grip on the glass blob. "Of all the fell acts Fionnlagh has committed, this is one of the lowest."

"He's already taken so much from you," Mum said to Maelgwyn, ever ready to fan the flames of someone else's anger. "You can't let him take our daughter, too."

"You think he wants to take me?" I asked. Surely they couldn't mean John Damian. For one, he was dead, and I assumed he would stay that way.

"I am certain of it." Maelgwyn stopped pacing and faced me. "Forgive me. I forget that you are largely ignorant of your heritage, and thus our history."

I tamped down all the smart remarks fighting for release. This situation was not Maelgwyn's fault, and I refused to punish him for that which was out of his control. "No matter. You can tell me of my lineage now."

"You'd best sit." When I remained standing, he continued. "Firstly, few ken that Fionnlagh is my brother."

"Why is that?"

"There are precious few still alive who remember that the Summer King's upstart younger brother went on to make a name for himself," Mum said. "After Fionnlagh blazed to power, most forgot he had any relations at all. Soon enough, your father was the only relation left that still breathed."

"What happened to the rest?" I asked.

"He killed them," Maelgwyn said bluntly. "He hunted down and destroyed anyone with the barest claim to his throne. He wishes to rule his court unchallenged."

"What about your family?" I asked. "Surely there were more than just you and he." Maelgwyn's mouth worked. Mum laid her hand on his arm, whispered something too low for me to hear.

"It's fine," he said, caressing Mum's cheek. "Anya has a right to know, and the right to hear it from me."

Maelgwyn sat in one of the large chairs before the hearth, and indicated that I take the one opposite. After I did, he began, "Your brothers in stone aren't your only siblings."

It took me a moment to gather his meaning. "You have children," I deduced, and he nodded. "Had you a wife, once?"

"No, never. The woman I loved was spoken for." Maelgwyn's gaze never left me, giving no clues as to who this unattainable partner was. Even Mum was silent. "But yes, I had children. Many, many children, and I adored them all."

"That's lovely," I said, imagining being introduced to many more brothers, and perhaps a few sisters. "Are they here?"

"There is nothing left of them but ashes and bone."

For a moment, I didn't understand. Then I gasped, covering my mouth. "All of them?" I asked, and he nodded. "Was it him?"

"Aye. It was my brother. After Bod beat me near to death, it took me years to recover. In that time, my brother stole my crown, murdered my children, and began a court of his own."

"Nicnevin went along with this?" I asked.

"Nicnevin wasn't around to protest," Mum replied. "He decimated Udane's family long before she came along. Why do you think she's barren? The only way he'd allow her to be queen was if he was certain she wouldn't bear children that might one day turn on him."

"I had no idea she was barren," I murmured, then I met Maelgwyn's gaze. "I am so, so sorry for your loss."

"As am I," Mum said, as she sat on the arm of Maelgwyn's chair. "Bod would be too, if he knew." He took her hand and kissed her knuckles.

"You bear no blame," he said. "Neither does Bod. He only meant for me to stay away from you. Bod would never harm a child, of that I'm certain. Only Fionn is to blame." Maelgwyn leaned forward, and continued, "Now you understand how dangerous my brother can be. I refuse to let him take you from me before I have the chance to properly know you. Daughter, will you allow me to defend you against the Seelie host?"

He shocked me when he called me daughter. I suppose it was his right; more, it was the truth. I wondered what my real Da, the sweet gruff man who was trapped in stone, would say about all this.

Actually, I kent exactly what he'd say. He'd say having the truth on your side was always best, no matter what pain you bore to get it. He'd say that fighting for the truth was what made good men into great men.

"Father, I will allow it," I said. "What shall we do?"

"We shall marshal our forces, and we will strike first."

FAIRY POST

After learning that my mother had foreseen my demise by an unknown woman's hand, I grabbed what was left of the Scotch and went out to the garden. How could Mom have known something so terrible would happen to me, and not warn me? Why didn't she leave me any clues, or a hint as to who this murderess might be?

Then again, she might not have had a choice. My parents died in a car wreck when I was twenty, and Rina was only thirteen. Maybe whatever or whoever was supposed to happen to me had still been far off in the future, and Mom thought she had time to alter my fate. The fact that I was still alive was a strong indicator that I had yet to meet this deadly woman.

Unless, I already had. Within the past few years I've been engaged to a *leanan sìth*, spent time with the Seelie Queen, and had disagreements with the former Queen of Winter. Any one of those three could have killed me as easily as batting an eyelash, but I'm still standing. Was it luck that let me move on from all of them relatively unscathed, or something more?

I thought about the protection runes on Mom's cane, and remembered her paintings. She was always embroiled in one art project or another, her sleeves rolled up, and paint or varnish splattered around the room and on her smock in artful disarray. Her subjects were never realistic, and I used to consider her an abstract artist. Now, I wondered if she'd been painting protection spells on every available surface.

I shifted, trying to relieve the dull ache in my shoulder. I'd run across four very powerful women, and the most powerful of all had nearly frozen me solid. After seeing what Anya had done to Damian's head, I couldn't ignore the fact that she could be the one that kills me.

My love life is a disaster.

After she'd let me stew and drink for a while, Rina joined me in the garden.

"So, mom was a volva," she began. "Bet you didn't see that coming."

"No, I did not." I offered her the bottle, but she waved it away.

"Can't. Breastfeeding."

"More for me." I took a swig. "Has Rob found anything else, like the name of whoever's going to kill me?"

She shook her head. "I guess Mom didn't know her name. Or maybe she was seeing something else. Maybe she thought Nicnevin would kill you, but you survived. Maybe she saw Anya freezing you, but not your recovery."

"You have a point, but there's still time for all of that to change." I lifted the bottle and drank again. When I lowered it, I saw a chicken standing in front of me.

"Do you see that chicken?" I asked, wondering how strong this Scotch really was.

"Yes, I see the chicken," Rina replied, then she addressed the bird. "Do you have a message for me?"

Before I could speak, the chicken hopped up on the bench and dropped a scroll onto Rina's lap. "What."

"Fairy post." Rina unrolled and read the scroll. "Come on," she said as she stood.

"Why?"

She handed me the message. The first line read, "Mistress Nicnevin has been imprisoned by the Seelie King."

"Fionnlagh imprisoned his wife," Colleen said. "That sounds—actually, that sounds right up his alley."

"Wait, there's more." Rina flattened the scroll out on the counter, and read, "'When the time comes, summon help with this.'" She held up a small rod topped with an eagle. "Is this a pencil?"

"It's a Roman standard," I said. "In miniature, of course."

Rina handed the standard to me, and the pole lengthened from four inches to five feet in the blink of an eye. The eagle's wings were outstretched, and its top-heavy weight made me wonder if the raptor was solid gold.

"Okay, not a miniature," I said.

"'Tis an *aquila*, to be sure," Rob said, using the standard's Latin term. "If Nicnevin has given us command of her legion, she must truly be in dire straits."

"Wait." I leaned the standard against the wall. "Nicnevin has a legion? A *Roman* legion?"

"Aye, that she does," Rob replied. "They marched north from England, oh, nearly two millennia ago, and got a bit waylaid in Scotland, though the land wasn't called Scotland then. The legion ended up crossing into Elphame, and after a time were employed by Herself."

"You are referring to the Ninth Legion?" I pressed. "The one that went missing north of Hadrian's Wall around the beginning of the second century? The legion that was sent to Britain by Imperial Rome?"

"O' course," Rob said, as if he hadn't just shared the most amazing bit of news in history. "Where else would this legion have originated from?"

I remembered the day Anya froze an entire antique market. "If that's so, then the Romans we saw in Glasgow last August must have been the Ninth."

"Ye saw Romans last summer?" Rob demanded. "Legionnaires in public, on the street?"

"Um, yeah."

"Why didn't you mention Romans before now?" Rina squeaked.

"I was hoping they weren't relevant."

"What happened to all magic, all the time around here?" Colleen asked. "Can't assume any of this hocus pocus is unrelated."

I pinched the bridge of my nose. "All right. We saw some Romans. More importantly, if Fionnlagh has imprisoned Nicnevin, it probably means he knows she tried helping us. Being that he gave you this house, it's not safe here. We need to go."

"But go where?" Rina asked.

"You can all come to my place," Colleen said. "Rina can portal us there in a hot second." When no one spoke, she continued, "Listen, this is our best option. Not only does this fairy man not know where I live, I don't think he's going to look for us in New York."

"He's been to the city before," Rina said.

"Then we'll go to my dad's place in Philly," Colleen said. "We cannot get caught with a baby in the middle of a fairy war."

Rina and Rob stared at each other for a moment, then Rob nodded. "I'll pack up Faith's things," Rina said. "Chris, do you need to stop by your flat?"

"I'm staying," I said. "I can't leave Anya."

"Even though she might be the one Mom was worried about?"

"Even though."

Rina nodded, then she said to Rob, "I take it you're staying too?"

"Aye," he said. "I can no' run from a fight that is mine, even if only partly so."

"Honorable old fool." Rina squeezed his hand. "Come on, Col. The suitcases are upstairs." Rina paused, and asked, "You're sure, Chris?"

"About this imminent war? No. But I am sure about Anya."

It didn't take long to get Faith ready for her first trip overseas, or for Rina and Colleen to pack a few things for themselves. What was taking forever was Rob and Rina saying their goodbyes.

"You can't really blame them," I said when Colleen rolled her eyes. "The last time they were apart for more than a day, Rob was sent to a hell dimension. And they have a baby now."

"I know, I know. All this mushiness just reminds me of my perpetually single status." Colleen walked out the front door, and, since the other two could use a bit of privacy, I followed. Standing in the middle of the driveway was Margaret Todd.

"Ah, hello," I said. "Did you come by to check on Rob?"

"I've come to warn you." She ran toward us, and I noticed how her hair—which had always been held back in a sleek bun—was loose and disheveled, and the way she wrung her hands. "Himself, he kens where you've gone, what you've done."

"How much does he know?" I demanded.

"Enough," Margaret replied, then she looked over her shoulder and cringed. "He's here!"

I looked past Margaret and felt my stomach drop. Rising out of the meadow behind her was the Seelie King. When I'd encountered Fionnlagh in the past, he'd looked like a man in his mid-thirties, tall and lean, with sharp eyes and a confident demeanor. Now he was so tall his antlered crown scraped the sky, his eyes were blood red, and his body billowed outward like so much black smoke.

Gone was any semblance of humanity. The creature bearing down on us was a monster.

"Margaret, come on," I yelled, then I grabbed Colleen's hand and ran inside. As I passed through the doorway, I grabbed the *aquila*. "Rina, we need to go now!"

She stepped back from Rob and wiped her cheeks. "Why?"

Fionnlagh crashed into the cottage, his form now solid as a bull's. The walls buckled under his weight as the solid oak door was smashed to kindling. The sharp points of his antlers ripped apart the ceiling and the roof above. Faith wailed as plaster and splinters rained down around us.

Rob was in his armor, sword out as he faced down the Seelie. "No' another step!"

"Traitors," Fionnlagh boomed. "You swore an oath!"

"Everyone on me," Rina yelled.

I lunged toward Rina. Colleen tripped, and her hand slid out of mine. "Go! Don't wait for me," she shrieked.

Fionnlagh loomed over Colleen, his dark shadow covering her. Rob threw a dagger, striking the Seelie in his shoulder. Fionnlagh recoiled, and Rob lunged for Colleen.

"We do no' leave people behind," he said as he grabbed the back of Colleen's sweater and hauled her to the rest of us.

"Chris, think about Anya," Rina said.

I closed my eyes and imagined Anya's face. "Wait, what about Margaret?"

"Margaret?" Rob's head whipped toward the door. Margaret was slumped across the threshold, blood from her gored abdomen soaking into the floor.

"She's gone," Rob said. "Now, love."

"Everyone think about Anya," Rina shrieked, and a moment later we were in a bedroom fit for a king. Staring at us were Anya, Beira, and Maelgwyn.

I waved. "Um, hello."

YOU ALWAYS FIGHT FOR FAMILY

One moment, Maelgwyn, Mum, and I were alone in his chamber.

In the next four people appeared in the center of the room without any sort of warning. They looked like refugees from a bombing, huddled together and covered with dust and debris. A bairn cried out, and I realized that Karina had transported her entire family from wherever they'd been to the Unseelie Court.

"What is happening?" Maelgwyn demanded. "Who are these people?"

"It's the gallowglass," Beira said. Faith cried out again, and Mum added, "Gods below, they've brought the bairn."

"Christopher!" I rushed to his side but didn't touch him. Gods only knew if I'd freeze him again. "What happened? Why have you all come here?"

"Fionnlagh knows we tried to help you, and he is not pleased," he replied.

"Unpleased," Karina muttered. "He is definitely unpleased." Faith squealed, and Karina bounced the bairn as she whispered in her ear.

"You are the walker," Maelgwyn said.

Robert murmured something to Karina, no doubt telling her Maelgwyn's identity. Karina didn't show a drop of fear as she faced the Unseelie King, rocking her bairn all the while. "I am the walker. I take it you're the king around here?"

"I am." Maelgwyn approached Karina and looked her over. The gallowglass's hand moved toward his sword. "Why are you a walker, I wonder?"

"Probably the same reason you're the Unseelie King."

"And why is that?"

"Because we are."

Maelgwyn threw back his head and laughed. "I like you. Are you the one that upset my brother?"

"We all upset him," Karina replied, then she turned her attention to Faith. Maelgwyn glanced at Robert.

"The Seelie King has truly run amok," Robert began. "In addition to poisoning our Anya, he has set Conall's band after us, imprisoned his wife, and destroyed my home. He also murdered Margaret Todd, the midwife, for darin' to warn us o' his rampage."

"Why is he doing this?" I asked. "I am no threat to him! I can barely wield the cold. He could kill me in a trice."

"You were pretty fierce when you took care of Damian," Colleen said. Mum moved to chastise her, but I stayed Mum's hand.

"What she said is fair," I said. "What happened to John Damian is further proof of my weakness."

"Your control is weak only because Fionnlagh made it so," Mum said. "Once Samhain comes, your power will wax and his will wane. He needs to remove you before that happens."

"Remove me," I repeated. "You mean he must kill me."

"He means to remove you by any means necessary, but I will not allow it," Maelgwyn said. "You have the Unseelie behind you."

"War it is, then?" I asked.

Maelgwyn nodded. "My brother has forced my hand."

"And mine," Robert said. "My sword is yours, if you'll have me."

"Truly, gallowglass?" I said. "You're sworn to serve the Seelie."

"Aye, that I am," Robert replied. "But Fionnlagh also swore an oath to me, one that included keepin' Karina and our bairn safe. He broke that oath when he crashed into my home, and afore than when he colluded with Damian. He is the one that broke his oath to me, and I owe him nothing."

"I'm with Robert," Karina said. "And I can help, too. I know you can teleport, but I can send people anywhere in Elphame or the mundane world."

"Can you?" Maelgwyn asked, clearly delighted. I must caution Karina against revealing too much around fae ears.

"And you have me," Colleen said. "I'm here for the non-magical stuff."

I nodded at the three of them, my heart swelling. I'd gone from a girl with most of her family in stone to one surrounded by love. But Christopher, he hadn't said a word.

"Any you?" I asked. "I'd understand if you were done with this."

"Done with you? Never." He took my hands, and I didn't freeze him. He didn't even shiver. "I am going to be right here, by your side, for as long as you'll put up with me."

"Christopher, you could be hurt," I whispered.

He shrugged. "I've been hurt before. I've always gotten better. Oh, and I have this." He brought forward a staff topped with a golden eagle. "I'm not one hundred percent sure, but I believe this gives me command of a Roman legion."

With the addition of the gallowglass's sword and Christopher's legion, we went from a formidable force to one that was nearly unstoppable. While Christopher and the others worked out how to summon the legion, I approached Karina.

She'd retreated to Maelgwyn's bedchamber, and found a quiet corner to nurse her bairn.

"I should begin by apologizing," I said, but she waved away my words.

"No apologies are needed," Karina said. "Elphame's nuts. You just got swept up in it."

"That is kind of you, but still. I must say it. I am sorry for what happened. For everything that has happened."

"Well then, I accept your most gracious apology." Karina smiled, and looked to her bairn.

"How is she doing?"

"Faith's tough, like her father," Karina replied.

"And her mum," I added. "Karina, while I do appreciate your presence, I must caution you. We are going into battle, perhaps the first of many."

"I know. The original plan was for me to take Faith and Colleen to New York and hide out until the dust had settled."

"What changed?"

"Fionnlagh. He changed." She paused to adjust the bairn against her breast. "He'd always been so kind to me and Robert, but he turned on us in a hot second. He was more interested in staying in power than protecting his family. He did the same with you. He didn't even bother to find out if you cared about his throne, he just went after you."

"True. If he hadn't poisoned me in the first place, our connection may never have come to light."

"And now everything's out." She lifted Faith against her shoulder and patted her back. "I may be new to the way things are done in Elphame, but I know one thing. You always fight for family."

"Aye. Both of the men I've kent as fathers have said much the same."

Karina leaned closer to me. "How are you taking all of this? How is he?"

"It is all very new," I replied. "But Maelgwyn has been kind to me, and patient. I believe him to be a good man."

"I'm glad you found him."

"Me, too." I paused, and added, "What I've always yearned for is a sister."

Karina grinned. "Me, too."

Karina wasn't harboring a shred of animosity toward me over my erratic behavior, and neither were Colleen or the gallowglass. Still, my belly was in knots when I finally got up the nerve to speak with Christopher, alone. He was studying the eagle standard, concentrating so intently I thought I'd approached him unawares. Before I had the chance to speak, he looked up at me and smiled.

"Hey, beautiful," he said. "You okay?"

"I meant to ask you the very same thing." I touched his forearm. "I am so deeply sorry for what happened."

Christopher leaned the standard against the wall and cupped my face with his hands. "It's okay. I'm okay." He closed his eyes and pressed his forehead against mine. "I was so scared I'd never see you again."

"As was I." We stood that way for a moment, then Christopher leaned back and searched my face.

"I have to tell you something about my mother."

I began to say it was an odd time to discuss a woman long since dead, but recent events within my own family made me hold my tongue. "Go on."

"We recently discovered she was a volva."

"Was she?" I placed my hand on Christopher's cheek, wondering how I'd never seen it before. "A Nordic seeress?"

He blinked. "You've heard of them?"

"Of course I have. Her being one explains so much."

"It does?"

"Oh, yes, about both you and Karina. Your brilliance, your beauty… You and your sister are rare beings. It stands to reason you were born of magic."

I'd expected him to be flattered, perhaps blush a bit. Instead, he took my hands in his, and said, "Mom had foresight—"

"As all volvas do."

"And she saw a woman who would kill me."

"Did she?" I regarded Christopher, my fragile human who wasn't so breakable after all. If his mother was in truth a volva he was as resilient as I. "But who could really harm you?"

"I don't know. She wrote all of this in a diary, but didn't leave the woman's name." He moved closer, and said. "After this is over, I need to learn more. About her, and about whoever this woman is."

I nodded. "I will help you. Christopher, I won't let anyone harm you."

He kissed my knuckles. "I won't let anyone hurt you, either."

What a ludicrous thought, him keeping me safe. I was the Queen of Winter, heir to an ancient and terrible power, and yet I believed him. Christopher had already proven how he cared for me many times over, and once we learned more about his mother, who knew? Perhaps he was the true force to be reckoned with.

"Then we have an accord." I wound my arms around him, felt him wince. "What is it?"

"Nothing, really," he said against my neck. "The frostbite made my skin tender and my joints a little stiff. It's getting better, though."

"Did you ken," I said as I slid my hand underneath the hem of his shirt, "that as Queen of Winter, I can heal wounds caused by the cold?"

"Really." He drew back, and looked from the lump my hand made beneath his shirt to my face. "Or this is an excuse to feel me up?"

I laughed, the sound foreign in my throat. When had I last laughed, last been happy? Yes, Christopher would care for my body and my heart. I was certain of it. "You've found me out. You always were a sharp one."

He tugged my hand free, then flexed his shoulder. "My joints do feel better. Thank you." He kissed my knuckles. "Are you powers better now that you're not drinking the tea?"

"Much better. They're settling down nicely."

"Good. I'm looking forward to an excellent winter with you."

PREPARATIONS FOR BATTLE

Anya smiled the slow, knowing smile I hadn't seen her wear since we were first together. "Are you, now? And how will we pass this winter?"

A hundred images passed behind my eyes, each one more inviting that the last. "However you want. You're the queen around here."

A shadow passed over her face. "You're truly all right with this? With me being what I am?"

I slid my hand behind her neck. "When have I ever not loved you for exactly what you are? Well, there was that time you went fifty feet tall without warning me first." We'd been tracking giants that day, and Anya had needed to become giant sized, too. "That was a little stressful."

"I was nowhere near fifty feet. Perhaps thirty, but not fifty." She affected a pout, and I was about ten seconds away from forgetting we were in her father's house. Someone cleared their throat behind us, thus saving us all from embarrassment. Anya and I turned as one, and saw one of Maelgwyn's servants waiting for our attention.

"My lady," he began. "Our spies have returned. The Seelie host is advancing toward us."

"Are they," Anya said as she unwound herself from me. "What a foolish move on Fionnlagh's part. Where is Maelgwyn?"

"This way." The servant spun on his heel, and we followed him to the throne room. There we found Maelgwyn pacing in front of the dais while Beira lounged on his throne. Rina, Robb, and Colleen were also there, and the area behind the throne was packed with an assortment of generals, servants, and soldiers.

"Anya," Maelgwyn said when he saw us, his eyes lighting up. It seemed that the Unseelie King enjoyed having his daughter at his side. "Have you heard?"

"I have," Anya replied. "Do we know when the Seelie will reach us?"

"Unsure. Within the day, I presume," Maelgwyn replied. "Fionn's actions have forced us to change our plans. But is this change for the better? Robert!"

Rob stepped forward. He was wearing his armor again, his helmet tucked under one arm and his sword strapped across his back. "My lord?"

"You understand the Seelie better than anyone here," Maelgwyn continued. "What do you make of Fionnlagh's march toward my home?"

"Is speaks to his worst qualities," Rob replied. "Begging your pardon for my opinion, the Seelie King is both proud and arrogant."

Maelgwyn stilled. "You don't see those qualities in me?"

"If I did, I certainly wouldn't mention it within your hearing."

Maelgwyn laughed, and us mortals let out a collective breath. "Go on."

"Fionnlagh believes himself to be the smartest, strongest, and best being that has ever lived," Rob continued. "He craves victory, but not to quell his enemies or protect his people. His only aim is for whatever glory he can bring to his name. He wishes for songs to be sung about him, and stories told about his bravery for generations to come. He is the proudest among us, and in his pride, he has overlooked a few key facts."

"And those facts are?"

"In the centuries I served Nicnevin, never once did she or Fionnlagh set foot in Unseelie land," Rob replied. "Nor have the Seelie spies ever breached your borders. What fool would march thousands of soldiers across Elphame into unknown territory? It is both foolhardy and reckless. We can turn his recklessness against him."

"Thousands of soldiers?" I whispered. "That's a lot."

"We have thousands, too," Anya whispered back.

"My brother can be foolish," Maelgwyn said. "The challenge for me will be to not match his mistakes with my own. Christopher?"

My back straightened. "Yes, sir!"

"How many soldiers can we count on in your legion?"

"A standard legion has anywhere from three to six thousand fighters," I replied. "Historically, the Ninth Legion was comprised of over five thousand men. I anticipate the majority will be available to us."

I left out that I still had no idea how to summon the legion. I'd examined the *aquila*, poked and prodded its various designs, yet no legion appeared. There wasn't an inscription on the standard telling me how to find this legion, either. If this was another of Nicnevin's tricks and I wasn't able to produce the legion, I would lose whatever credibility I had with Anya's father.

My response must have satisfied Maelgwyn, because he nodded and moved on to speak with his generals. I slumped against the standard, my heart hammering against my ribs.

"Don't be so nervous," Anya said. "You answered him well and truthfully."

"I left out the part about how I have no idea how to work this thing."

Anya shrugged. "Magical items can be fickle, as can their owners. I have no doubt you'll solve the *aquila's* mysteries before long."

I stared at the golden eagle's face. It stared back, silent as a tomb. "I hope you're right."

Thanks to Maelgwyn's incredibly competent and resourceful staff, within a few hours we were as ready as we'd ever be to face the Seelie King. The servants moved quickly throughout the castle, boarding up windows and transferring valuables to the more secure inner rooms. They even relocated Maelgwyn's throne and rolled up the carpets and tapestries from the public areas on the first floor.

"Do we really expect the fighting to get past the gates?" I asked as three servants hoisted the last of the carpets onto their shoulders and disappeared into the bowels of the castle. Based on the massive stone walls and the myriad of Unseelie soldiers positioned in front of them, all of this last-minute redecoration this seemed like misdirected energy.

"Expect? No," Rob replied. "But if even a single warrior were to breach the walls, that one could set the place alight, and carpets and drapes burn a fair sight faster than stone."

"I hadn't thought of that."

Rob clapped me on the shoulder. "O' course not, bein' as this is your first siege. After this battle's won, and perhaps a handful more, ye shall be an expert in castle defense."

I adjusted my grip on the *aquila*. How many times would I be wading into battle alongside Anya? While no one knew the answer to that, I knew more battles were coming, sooner rather than later. War and chaos were the way of things in Elphame. "I guess I will be."

Rob and I exited the castle and surveyed the plain below. The Unseelie soldiers had organized themselves into ordered battalions on the meadow below, hundreds if not thousands of fairy warriors garbed in shining black. From our vantage point at the castle's main entrance, their obsidian armor made them resemble a company of well-behaved beetles.

As for the rest of us, Maelgwyn and Anya would jointly lead the charge; the hope was that the sight of the Unseelie King and Queen of Winter standing together would cause many of the Seelie forces to turn tail and run. Rina was tasked with standing in front of the main gates and portaling away any Seelie forces that breached our defenses, all while Rob defended her and the gate from anyone who got too close. Being that Rob had served the Seelie for over three hundred years, I was betting most of them had enough sense to steer clear of an angry gallowglass.

Rob looked over the assembled Unseelie and grunted. "Here is a spot I never thought to find meself in."

"How so?" I asked. "At war with the Seelie, or on the side of the Unseelie?"

"Both," he replied. "All me life, as gallowglass and before, I never thought of the Seelie and Unseelie as good and evil. 'Tis no' so simple, ye ken?"

I considered Nicnevin, the Seelie Queen who had enthralled me and then sent me the means to fight against her husband; and Beira, the former Queen of Winter who'd almost killed my sister and unborn niece, yet here we were on the same side. "Yeah, I get it. If these fae abide by any kind of ethics or moral code, it's not one I recognize. They're all in it for themselves."

Rob clapped my shoulder. "At last, a man who thinks as I do. Perhaps once this is done and dusted, we shall have that philosophical debate we've been putting off."

I adjusted my grip on the *aquila*. "We sure will."

We reentered the castle and checked on our most breakable companions, Colleen and Faith. The two of them were to be sequestered in Maelgwyn's own chamber, protected by magical wards and no less than forty armed guards. That abundance of caution didn't stop Rina and Rob from personally examining the room.

"T'will have to do," Rob declared at last. "Though I would feel much calmer if I were protectin' her meself."

"I do have six younger brothers, and dozens of cousins," Colleen huffed. "Taking care of a baby is nothing new for me."

"We have no doubt she'll be fine with you," Rina said, as she gave Faith her tenth goodbye kiss. "You'll be good for Auntie Colleen, won't you, sweetheart?"

"Auntie Colleen," I said, and Col jabbed me in the ribs. I saw a servant lead in a goat, followed by another dragging a bale of hay. "Why are they putting a goat in here?"

"To feed Faith," Colleen replied.

"Oh." Images of Colleen milking the goat flitted behind my eyelids, and I made a conscious effort not to laugh. "They really have thought of everything."

"They sure did," she replied, then she embraced me.

"Be careful, okay?" Colleen whispered. "This is an actual battle. I know we've seen some shit, but we've never seen anything like this."

"I know. I'll be careful." I gave her a final squeeze. "Besides, if I don't make it, who will harass you at Carson next semester?" My voice caught at the end; neither of us knew when or if Carson would ever be rebuilt, or if we'd ever see the campus again. Colleen swatted my arm, but I saw her eyes shining. Rina and Rob approached us, and Rina handed off Faith to Colleen.

"All right," Rina said as she fussed with Faith's bonnet. "We're as ready as we can be. Let's go beat these Seelie bastards."

I gripped the *aquila* a bit harder. "Let's do it."

COUSINS

A calm yet vigilant air had settled over the Unseelie palace. I'd gone to into battle often enough to recognize the feeling; the warriors were armed and ready, their swords long since sharpened and their quivers full, and there was nothing more to do but wait for the enemy to arrive. For all that the sensation was familiar, I didn't welcome it. I wanted this business dealt with and behind me, the sooner the better.

Those who didn't fight yet supported the battle, the porters and chamberlains and even the sculleries, they all felt it, too; they crept around corners and down staircases, wary of the tiniest sound. We held our collective breath as we waited for the first hint of our adversaries. And so we waited, and watched.

A horn sounded in the distance. *Finally, something happens.* I turned to Maelgwyn, intending to ask what the sound signified, but he was speaking with a messenger.

"Fionnlagh approaches," Maelgwyn said. Mum came to stand beside him, frowning toward the distance. "It is as we suspected. He has the whole of the Seelie host behind him."

I raised my hand and brandished a dagger of ice. The ice shone clear, and not a single crack dulled its surface. Mum had been right all along; as the poison left my body, my innate command of the cold grew stronger and more precise. "Let's meet them, shall we?" I asked.

Maelgwyn grinned. "Aye, we shall."

Maelgwyn took Mum's hand, and I strode out to the battlefield alongside my parents. By bringing his forces to Unseelie land, Fionnlagh had committed a grave error. The land may be new to me, but Maelgwyn had crafted every rock and tree and blade of grass, and littered the countryside with tricks aplenty. As for Mum, trickery may as well be her middle name.

In less time than I'd have thought possible, the Seelie's forces were assembled in front of us. Their armor was bright silver in contrast to the Unseelie black, the two halves of Elphame at last together. The Seelie and Unseelie forces were both vast, which meant that Fionnlagh himself remained leagues away from the castle proper. Our first and most important directive was to keep him there.

"Little brother." Maelgwyn's magically enhanced voice boomed across the fields, the first of his ploys. Now all were aware of the fae kings' relationship to one another. "How thoughtful of you to visit me."

"How thoughtful of you to reveal your deceit to all and sundry," Fionnlagh retorted. "My people, behold the Summer King! Udane himself has masqueraded as the Unseelie Lord lo these past years! Tell me, how should we punish such treachery?"

Maelgwyn's eyes narrowed. "Watch yourself, little Fionn. Most of the people on this field are mine."

"Let's change things, Udane." Fionnlagh spat Maelgwyn's first name as if it were a curse, but I had no time to think about those implications. Creeping up around the edges of the Unseelie horde were monsters of flesh and fin, hoof and claw.

"What are these beasts?" I demanded.

"They are the *fuath*," Mum said, her hands a blur as she wove protection spells around the three of us.

"What are the bloody *fuath* doing here?"

"Did you not know? They're Fionnlagh's children," Maelgwyn replied. "Your cousins."

"She has other cousins," Mum said, then she withdrew a pouch from her sleeve and threw it as far as she could. It exploded above the center of the Seelie forces, sending sparks and burning ashes over the company. When the smoke cleared, the warriors nearest to the blast backed away, their faces writ with fear. Standing among our foes were the thirteen giants Christopher and I had freed from the churchyard in Cumbria, led by Long Meg herself.

Long Meg cracked her knuckles. "Onward toward the king," she bellowed, and the giants waded into Seelie host, whacking aside and stomping on those too terrified or foolish to get out of their way.

"Full of surprises you are, my love," Maelgwyn said. "Come, daughter, we cannot let others have all the fun."

I grinned, and followed my father into battle.

REINFORCEMENTS

Colleen was right. We'd seen some shit, but this battle was a whole new batch of crazy.

I was standing on a ridge to the side of the palace gates, watching the battle spread out below me; I still hadn't wrapped my head around how to summon the Ninth Legion, and figured I could do the most good by staying out of the way. This position also meant I could keep watch over Rina, and Anya.

At first the contrast between the black-armored Unseelie and silvered Seelie soldiers was sharp, like a living yin-yang symbol. The Unseelie steadily gained ground, and the image morphed from a yin-yang into that of a checkered flag, then the colors were further scrambled until the plain was an undulating gray sea. Splashes of red appeared, and black threatened to overwhelm silver.

"We're winning," I said, to no one in particular. "We are actually going to win!"

Then the monsters appeared.

Billowing upward from the ground were hundreds, if not thousands, of monsters.

They began as smoke, much like how Fionnlagh had appeared when he destroyed Rina's house and murdered Margaret Todd. The smoke quickly coalesced into terrifyingly misshapen bodies, covered in scales and claws. Some had two legs, others had three or five. They all had fangs, and uttered the most blood-curdling cries I'd ever heard. If I'd encountered one of these beasts a year ago, I would have had a fear-induced heart attack, but I recognized these monsters. They were the *fuath*.

I remembered the first monster I'd ever seen. Monsters aren't something you forget, no matter if you encounter them dead or alive. It was the morning after Rina had picked up a guy at a historical site in Aberfoyle and brought him back to the bed and breakfast we were staying at. I'd thought it a bit reckless and out of character for her, but trusted she knew what she was doing. She was an adult, after all. Oh, and I was drunk. So, so drunk.

The guy was still around the next morning and he tagged along with my sister and me to the next stop on our itinerary, which was a visit to the priory at Lake Menteith. We hadn't been there an hour when Rina's freeloader whipped out a sword and decapitated an elderly woman. Upon closer inspection that woman had at least a hundred needle-like teeth crammed in her maw, claws that would have rivalled an eagle's, and the stump of her neck was discharging black, stinking blood that rotted everything it came in contact with. In short, Rina's freeloader was none other than Robert Kirk, the gallowglass, and that woman had been one of the *fuath*.

I've encountered a few more monsters since that day at the priory, but none had made my blood run cold like the *fuath* had. And now I stood watching as hundreds of them swarmed across the battle, destroying Unseelie and Seelie warriors alike.

"He cares nothing for his own people." The evidence of Fionnlagh's indifference was plain before me. He'd ordered his creatures to kill, but didn't specify which side. In his mind, all deaths were fair game as long as he retained his throne.

"Did ye ever think differently?" Beira asked as she came to stand beside me.

"Once, I thought Fionnlagh was the better ruler."

"Aye. Times past, we all thought as such."

"Even Maelgwyn?"

"Yes. 'Twas some time ago, but yes, him too."

I wondered what had happened to change Fionnlagh from an admired leader to a bloodthirsty madman. Perhaps he'd always been a madman, and had been able to hide his true nature for a time. As the saying goes, what's done in the dark will eventually come into the light.

I glanced at Beira. I disliked her only slightly less than Nicnevin, and the few points she had in her favor existed only because she was Anya's mother. I had many questions for Beira—did she know anything about volvas; why hadn't she just asked Rina to help her go to the Winter Palace instead of hiring John Damian to kidnap her; why was she still so powerful even after her exile? However, those and all my other inquiries would have to wait, at least until after this battle ended.

"I'm glad you and Anya are together again," I said. "She's really needed you these past few months."

"I needed her as well," Beira said. "I need all my children with me."

"We will get them back."

Beira nodded. "Of that, I have no doubt. I told Maelgwyn that Anya made a good choice in you. Honor and intelligence don't usually go hand in hand, but in you, and your sister, they have."

My jaw gaped open as I struggled to respond to Beira's unexpected compliments. Thanking her was certainly out of the question. "It was good of you to say that," I said at last.

"I'm not fae, so thanking me won't make you beholden to me," Beira said, then she nodded toward the melee. "They could use some reinforcements."

Near the center of the field, Unseelie and Seelie warriors had melded together until the field was awash in dust and blood. The only differentiation was the Picts, whirling like dervishes as they tried to catch Rob off guard. The few Rob hadn't dispatched had been sent elsewhere by Rina, but the more Rob focused on the Picts, the less attention he paid to the *fuath*.

The *fuath* were getting dangerously close to my sister.

"They could," I agreed. Beira looked pointedly at my standard. "I haven't figured out how to turn it on."

"'Tis a standard," Beira said. "Thrust it into the ground, and the company it is beholden to shall appear."

Her tone relayed that everyone else had learned how to use enchanted standards in grade school. Of the two of us, she was the expert on magical items, so I did as she suggested and thrust the *aquila* into the earth at my feet.

Thousands of legionnaires appeared behind me.

"Holy shit," I said, much to Beira's amusement. The legionnaires were outfitted for battle, wearing the traditional Roman breastplates and helmets, and each soldier was armed with a spear, shield, and sword. I'd never been good at judging crowd sizes, but this looked to be a full cohort, which translated to five thousand men who'd been trained by one of the greatest military empires in history.

In other words, reinforcements.

The legionnaires stared at the battle on the plain below, understandably confused. I strode to the man in front, and asked, "Are you the *legatus*?"

He looked down his nose at me as if I were a bug, letting me know I'd assumed correctly. "What is this place?" he demanded. "How have you come by our standard? Where is Domina?"

"Domina," I repeated, then I remembered that these were Nicnevin's men.

"Nicnevin has been betrayed by her husband," I said. "She sent me your standard so I might summon you, and turn the battle against Fionnlagh."

The *legatus's* sharp gaze surveyed the battle. "Where is Domina?" he asked again.

"I don't know," I replied. "Fionnlagh has imprisoned her. Will you and your men help me capture him, and rescue Nicnevin?"

His eyes narrowed. "You presume to refer to the Domina by her name?"

"I always have."

He was taken aback by my response, and I realized that to these men, Nicnevin wasn't the seductive Seelie Queen. She was the leader of their army, and had long ago earned their loyalty and respect.

"Very well." The *legatus* issued a few commands to his officers, then he regarded me. "As you are Domina's confidant, you shall act as my *aquilifer*."

I blinked. Beira leaned close and whispered, "That means you get to carry the standard."

"I know what it means," I snapped. I also knew that the standard bearer was a coveted and prestigious position within the legion, and that Nicnevin had arranged for me to fill it. That, and the fact that she'd sent the Ninth Legion to fight on our side against Fionnlagh, made me understand why Rina had accepted her offer of protection.

We needed it.

The Ninth Legion forced its way through the battle in a blur of javelins and short swords. I kept pace with the *legatus*, holding the standard aloft so all could see the eagle. If only my sophomore Latin instructor could see me now.

It wasn't long before the legion hacked its way through to where the Picts were holding ground—bit of history repeating itself there, I feared—and I saw Rina and Rob. They were in the midst of what was left of the Picts and the *fuath*.

"Oh, you figured it out," Rina said, jerking her chin toward the standard. She waved her hand and a group of the *fuath* disappeared.

"Where are you sending them?" I asked.

"The middle of the ocean."

"Can they swim?"

"Not my number one concern at the moment," Rina said as she disappeared a few more.

A wave of *fuath* rolled up behind Rina and paused. I pushed Rina behind me as Rob spun around with his sword raised, but the *fuath* didn't strike. They weren't even looking at Rob, or Rina. They were staring at my standard.

Black smoke coalesced into a vaguely anthropomorphic form a few feet in front of me. "That is hers," it hissed.

"Hers?" I asked. "Oh, you mean Nicnevin?" The monsters growled in agreement.

"Wait," Rina said. "These are Fionnlagh's children, but Nicnevin's their stepmother. She's the one that takes care of them. They've always followed her, done whatever she asked."

"Really." I held the standard aloft, and shouted, "Nicnevin has been imprisoned! She sent me this standard so the legion might free her! Will you join us and save our mistress?"

The *fuath's* hooves and talons tore at the ground, and they gnashed their teeth. "Who has imprisoned her?" asked the smoke monster.

Here goes nothing. "Fionnlagh."

The *fuath* roared, and I feared I'd made a terrible mistake. Then they swept up and away, skimming over the battle and toward where Fionnlagh sat astride his horse. Their dark, smoky forms swarmed so densely around him I couldn't see what happened next.

But I did hear him scream.

AN ICY DEFEAT

"**W**hat is happening?" I demanded. One moment the battle was pure chaos, and the next saw Fionnlagh beset by demons. "What are those smoke monsters?"

"Not monsters. More of your cousins, the *fuath*," Maelgwyn replied. "My brother took great pains to make them as nightmarish as possible." He rubbed his chin. "But why have they turned on their father?"

"It's because of Nicnevin," Christopher yelled, from behind me. I turned, and saw Christopher approaching us whilst carrying his Roman staff. He was followed by Karina and the gallowglass. The legionaries shifted toward us as well, guided by the *aquila*. Mum appeared out of the ether and took her place next to Maelgwyn.

"Did Nicnevin order them to capture him?" I asked.

Christopher shook his head. "She didn't order them to do anything. I told them that Fionnlagh imprisoned her." He looked at the swarm of monsters and frowned. "I guess we know who their favorite parent is."

"Indeed." I glanced at Karina. "Would you mind moving some of the *fuath* to the side? Don't hurt them," I added. If the *fuath* were also against Fionnlagh, we may need them.

"No problem." Karina waved her hand, and cleared a path to what was left of the Seelie King. I strode up to him, and regarded the crumpled being before me. He lay on his side, covered in blood and mud, the points of his antlered crown broken off and lost. Any other creature I'd have pitied, but not him. He was not worth one single drop of emotion.

"Why do you hate me?" I demanded. "Why do you hate my family? You've done nothing but work against us for centuries. You profited from your brother's humiliation, you sent my father and brothers into stone, stripped my mother of her rightful crown, and then you tried poisoning me. Why?" When he didn't respond, I kicked him in the side. "Why?"

"Touch me again—" he roared.

"And what?" Maelgwyn roared back. "The only thing keeping you on this side of the veil is Anya's good will. Lose it, and lose everything."

Fionnlagh glared at Maelgwyn until his eyes glowed red. Maelgwyn countered by having his own eyes glow green.

"Enough with the cursed lights," I said, and they ceased tormenting each other. "Am I right in assuming that you, Fionnlagh, sought to rule all the year just as my da did, but you made sure he was the one caught and punished? That you perhaps framed him, and my brothers? That you have been working against every creature in Elphame, even your own wife and children, only to hoard power for yourself?"

"And what of it?" he countered. "I am the strongest! It is my right to rule!"

"Actually, it's not." Maelgwyn crouched before Fionnlagh and removed what was left of his crown. "This crown belonged to our grandfather. It was meant to be passed down from one firstborn son to the next, but you must have stolen it from our father's deathbed. No one knew where the headdress had gone; Mama assumed it had been lost in Papa's last skirmish."

Maelgwyn stood, crown in hand. As he rose, the antlers grew and reshaped themselves until the crown shone like new. "This never belonged to you, nor did your throne. Your resentment at not being firstborn has caused you to destroy everyone around you. For this, you must be punished."

"You cannot punish me," Fionnlagh said. "The laws are clear! A council of equals may pass judgement, not a single man!"

"No one is your equal," I said. "No one is your equal in deceit, in lies, or in betrayals. Where is Nicnevin?"

He bared his bloody teeth. "You'll never find her without me."

The *fuath* wailed around us. "Fear not, we shall find her," I said to the beasts. "We don't need him or his lies to do so."

"You can—" Fionnlagh began, then was silent.

"Gods, I was sick of that noise," Mum said, her fist clenched. She'd grabbed his voice out of the air and was holding it captive in the palm of her hand. "Are we in agreement with the charges laid before Fionnlagh, and that he must be punished?"

"Aye, I believe we are," Robert said. He drew his sword. "Am I to do it, then?"

"He does not deserve the peace of death," I said. "He deserves to suffer, as Da and my brothers have suffered. As we all have."

I reached out my hand. Christopher grasped it and squeezed. "Fionnlagh of the White Stag, former King of the Seelie, I pronounce you guilty of crimes against Elphame. For that you shall be imprisoned for half a millennia, the same sentence you wrongly passed on my father and brothers."

"You're going to put him in stone?" Christopher asked.

"No. Ice." I tugged on his hand. "Let me know if you get cold."

"I will."

I raised my other hand, and frost formed on the ground beneath Fionnlagh. Icy tendrils twined around his legs, then his torso. He twisted and fretted as he tried to escape, but in less than a minute he was frozen fast to the earth. His mouth was open, and he reached toward me, I assume to curse my life and that of my kin. I hoped the words rotted in his gullet.

"We can't leave him here," Karina said. "No matter how cold that ice is, he'll melt way before five hundred years passes."

"Aye, you've a point there," I said. "If I think of a location, can you put him there for me?"

"Of course." Karina stepped forward and grasped my other hand. "Just say when."

"When."

And with that, he was gone.

"Where did you send him?" Christopher asked.

"The Winter Palace is carved from the oldest glacier in existence," I replied. "Fionnlagh is now resting beneath it. I am certain that ice won't be melting anytime soon."

Aftermath

The chaos that followed the battle almost outshone the battle itself.

Maelgwyn's warriors and the Ninth Legion swarmed across the battlefield, spreading word of Fionnlagh's defeat, and subduing those few Seelie that refused to accept the truth about their king. As for the *fuath*, they dissipated as quickly and creepily as they'd arrived, but not before promising Anya their support. I wasn't sure if her associating with the *fuath* was a good idea, but it had pleased Anya. The only faction still causing trouble were the Picts.

"By God Almighty, Conall, stand down," Rob demanded. Conall had seized his opportunity for a rematch against the gallowglass, and he wasn't going down easy.

"Can't you just *whoosh* Conall out of here?" I asked Rina. We were standing at a safe distance, watching the two of them spar.

"I could, but Robert's enjoying himself," she replied.

"Are you sure?" I asked.

"I'll never stand down, ye fecking *blaigeard*," Conall retorted.

"*Blaigeard*," Rob roared as his claymore crashed into Conall's shield. "I'll no' have ye insult me mam, ye *cacan*! *Falbh a ghabhail do ghnuis airsun cac*!"

"See that," Rina said, smiling. "He's having fun."

The Picts and Unseelie watching the bout cheered. Whatever Gaelic insult Rob had lobbed toward Conall, it met with their approval. I shook my head, and went to find my girlfriend.

Anya was standing with Beira and Maelgwyn, listening to reports from both the Seelie and Unseelie commanders. I knew without asking what they were inquiring about. Signs of Nicnevin.

"Any luck?" I asked.

"Unfortunately no," Anya replied. "The last anyone saw of Nicnevin was when she returned from Crail. She retrieved the legion's standard and sent it off with a messenger, and then she was gone. Even her own ladies have no idea where she is."

"Maybe Fionnlagh didn't imprison her," I said. "Maybe she went into hiding to avoid the battle, and he took credit for her abscence."

"That's certainly Fionnlagh's way," Beira said. "To appropriate someone else's hard work and declare it his own invention."

"No matter how or why her person is missing, locate her we must," Maelgwyn said. "The Seelie throne cannot remain vacant for long."

"Can't you oversee the Seelie?" I asked.

Maelgwyn glanced at me, the corner of his mouth curled up. "Oversee it I could, but I have my own kingdom to rule."

"Then maybe it doesn't need to be Seelie and Unseelie any longer," I mused. "Maybe it can return to the things were, with a Summer King and a Winter Queen." When the others only stared at me, I continued, "You two could rule the year together, father and daughter. And you would have to fight each other at the change of seasons."

"They weren't fighting," Anya said, tossing a glare at her mother.

Beira smirked. I ignored her, and continued, "Still, maybe that's a solution. Even if it's not a forever solution, it could work until we find Nicnevin."

"You're all right with searching for her?" Anya asked. She took my hand, and rubbed her thumb across my knuckles.

"I am." When she raised her brows, I continued, "No, really, I am. What she did to me was horrible, but this is about more than just me. I don't forgive her—I don't know if I'll ever do that—but Elphame needs her."

Anya smiled. "That is very noble of you."

"Speaking of nobility, there is also the matter of Bod and the boys," Maelgwyn said. "Since we now suspect Fionnlagh of manipulating the events leading up to their punishment, by rights we should set them free as soon as possible."

"Agreed," Beira said. "I do miss my lads."

"What will you tell Da?" Anya asked.

Beira touched Maelgwyn's forearm. "The truth."

Maelgwyn wrapped his arm around Beira's shoulders, and they went to speak with the Useelie commanders. "What do you think will happen with them?" I asked.

"I couldn't say," Anya replied. "Fancy Mum as the Summer Queen?"

We laughed together, and I fell in love with Anya all over again. "Anything's possible. Look at me. I command a legion," I said, indicating the standard.

Anya leaned close, and asked, "Does that mean you'll be my Winter King? Will you serve me well and true, and perform whatever tasks I set before you?"

"I will," I said. "Anything you need from me, consider it done."

She smiled. "Good. I am looking forward to an excellent winter."

FAR TO GO

While the battle had been won and the evil king deposed, there remained quite a bit of work to do. First and foremost we needed to set to rights all the harm Fionnlagh had caused. As soon as things quieted down in Elphame, Rina portaled us to her and Rob's home in Crail so we could assess the damage.

"It is absolutely as bad as I remembered," Rina said. Fionnlagh had taken out the entire front wall of the cottage, and the damage extended through the second floor and to the roof. A shingle picked that moment to detach itself from the roof and land at Rina's feet. "Maybe worse."

"I will go inside first and ensure the cottage's stability," Anya said. "Falling debris won't hurt me overmuch."

I watched Anya cross the threshold where the front door had once stood. "I hope it's safe in there."

"Where is Margaret?" Rob demanded. The spot where she'd fallen was soaked in blood, but her body was gone.

"Would Fionnlagh have taken her body?" I asked, hoping the authorities hadn't been by and opened a murder investigation. Wyatt arrived from the garden with the answer.

"Forgive us, Master Kirk, but we took care of the doctor." Wyatt gestured for us to follow him. In the center of the wights' prized rosebushes was a mound of freshly turned earth. "We understood what the doctor meant to you and all of

Elphame, and we couldn't leave her unattended," Wyatt said. "I apologize for not inquiring as to your intentions before we acted."

"No apology is necessary." Rob sank to his knees before the mound. Rina passed Faith to Colleen and knelt beside him. "Ye did well, Wyatt. All of ye did. Ye have created an honorable grave for an honorable woman."

Faith squeaked, and Colleen and I walked a few paces away. The damage to the cottage looked just as bad from the garden as it did from the front of the house.

"We're going to need a supply run," I said. "Tarps, plywood, all of that. I can take the truck to the hardware store if you guys want to see if anything is salvageable inside."

"Let me repair your home," Anya said as she emerged. "It's the least I can do after all that's happened to you."

"How would you repair it?" Rina asked. "With ice?"

Anya gave her a look, but honestly I was wondering the same thing. "I would have it repaired by workmen," she said. "Carpenters, tilers, and the like. Elphame's resources are vast. I imagine the work can be done in a few weeks, perhaps less. In the meantime, you are all welcome to stay in my flat in Glasgow." Anya faced Colleen. "There is room for you, as well. Or if you'd prefer, I can send you home. The choice is yours."

"Glasgow would be great," Colleen said. "Is there really room for all of us?"

"There is," I replied. "The flat has four bedrooms and a huge common room. Faith could have her own nursery."

Rina leaned against Rob. "What do you think? Should we stay in Glasgow for a bit?"

Rob frowned. "'Tis a generous offer, and I do appreciate it," he began. "What I'm wonderin' is if we shouldn't relocate permanently. This cottage was fair given to us by Fionnlagh, and I'm of a mind to move on from that part of my life."

"But, this is your home," Anya said.

Rob wrapped an arm around Rina's shoulders. "Home is where me family is."

Anya nodded. "Then it's settled. You shall have use of my flat for as long as you need it. I will have the cottage repaired, and whilst doing so I will try to remove Fionnlagh's influence from the grounds, assuming any of it is left."

"You can do that?" I asked.

"I can try," Anya said. "If I cannot accomplish it, perhaps Maelgwyn can. Once all of that is complete, you can decide what you'd like to do with the cottage."

I nodded. I'd barely gotten used to the idea of Anya being a giant's daughter, and now she was the Unseelie King's heir. "Thank you, for looking after my family. Now we need to see to yours."

Rob, Rina and Colleen entered the cottage to pack up what they needed to bring to Glasgow. While they did so Anya wove glamours and spells around the cottage, both to keep others from noticing its ruined state and to mitigate the damage. I sat in the garden with Faith on my lap and watched Anya work. She was amazing as she wielded her power, her hands drawing runes in the air while the wind lifted her long, yellow hair like a crown of sunbeams around her head.

"That's your Auntie Anya," I said to Faith. "She's going to make sure your house stays safe and warm. Isn't that nice of her?"

"You are a natural with her," Anya said. She'd finished her spellwork and sat beside me. Faith grabbed a length of Anya's sunny hair and gurgled approvingly.

"She's just like Rina was as a baby," I said. "Happy, and curious, and you can see how intelligent she is."

"You speak as though she's already writing and doing complex arithmetic."

"She will. Just you wait."

"Chris," Rina yelled from the kitchen window. "Look what I found!" She held up a gray lump in the window. I squinted, and saw it was the ammonite fossil I'd given her for her thirteenth birthday.

"I can't believe it survived," I said.

"Well, it is four hundred million years old," Rina said. "It's pretty solid. Oh, and we found Mom's cane, and the toolbox, too."

"That's awesome," I said. Rina ducked back inside. I tipped my head back and felt the sun on my face. A lifetime's worth of experiences had happened to us over the last few days, and we still had far to go; Rina and I needed to learn more about our mother's side of the family, we needed to repair the cottage and the pathways from this world to the Winter Palace, and Anya needed to commence her reign as Queen of Winter.

"Why are you smiling?" Anya asked.

"Just thinking about how great our life is."

She kissed my cheek. "It certainly is, and it will only get better. Just you wait."

Anya and Chris's story continues in **Giant's Daughter**, available now. Keep reading for a preview!

GIANT'S DAUGHTER

Chapter One

It was the second day of winter, and Christopher and I were standing before the shieling in Glen Lyon. Today was the day we'd free Da and my brothers from their stone prisons. Hopefully.

We'd waited until after Samhain to allow my new abilities to fully manifest. Mum's theory was that since it had taken the full might of the Seelie King to imprison Da and the boys, it would likely take all of the Winter Queen's power to undo the curse. Never mind that when Mum had attempted to free them in the past, nothing had happened, not even when she threw every spell and trick she knew at the boulders. Still, even though my mother had reigned as Queen of Winter for thousands of years, and my reign had lasted mere days, I had an advantage she'd never have: my father's blood.

No one, least of all myself, had suspected I'd been fathered by Udane, once Elphame's Summer King, and now known as Maelgwyn, the Unseelie King. These odd branches on my family tree meant I had inherited a portion of my father's power, which, along with what I'd gotten from Mum, meant I might actually be able to do this.

And what if I could free them, and live among Da and my brothers as a complete family again? I'd wanted this for so long I could feel it. Needed it so much I could taste it.

Don't worry, Da. I've almost got you.

I reached not toward the stones, but to my right. Christopher, there as he always was, grasped my hand and squeezed.

"Are you ready?" he asked.

"Yes. You have your phone?"

"I do."

Christopher held up his phone, revealing his sister Karina's information queued up on the screen. We probably wouldn't need her assistance, but Maelgwyn had pointed out that the stones may be portals, thus meaning Da and the rest were actually imprisoned elsewhere. If portals were involved, best to have the walker on hand to deal with them.

"I doubt they're portals," Christopher said. "We retrieved Long Meg and her crew directly from their stones. I imagine it's the same here."

I nodded, and refocused my attention on the stones. When we freed Long Meg, we'd walked widdershins around the stone that held her, thus undoing the knot of spells around her boulder. I didn't sense the same type of spell around the *shieling*. Whatever was holding my family fast, it wasn't with knots.

"If not knots, then what?"

"What was that?" Christopher asked.

"Just thinking out loud."

I squinted at the stones, wondering if I could see evidence of whatever magic had been used. I'd never seen such things before, but then again, I'd never been the Queen of Winter, either. What this magic would look like, I couldn't guess. Sparkles, maybe? Just as I was about to ask Christopher to call his sister and ask if she had any ideas, I spied something near the largest stone's base.

"Could this be it?" I wondered, crouching down to have a closer look. Around the base of Da's stone weren't any sparkles or other obvious signs of spellcraft, but the area looked different. The colors of the grasses were more vibrant, and the air smelled of lightning.

"The spell is in the base," I said. "Whatever's holding them in the stone, it's where the stones meet the ground."

Christopher crouched beside me. I wondered what he saw, this brilliant mortal who'd been touched by Elphame. "Does that mean if we tip them over, your family will be free?"

I blinked. It couldn't be that easy, could it?

"Only one way to find out." I stood and heaved at Da's stone. I've always been strong; I used to think it was on account of being a giant's daughter. Now I know my strength comes from elsewhere, but it was my Da's memory I pulled on. Still, the stone didn't budge.

"Maybe we need to rock it back and forth," Christopher suggested. "It's been here a while, right? Maybe it's just stuck."

"All right, then." We positioned ourselves on either side of the stone. "Toward me."

Christopher pushed, then I heaved it back toward him. After we did this a few times, the stone moved. It was the barest movement, but it was there.

"It's working," Christopher said. "Harder, now."

We kept rocking the stone back and forth, it loosening ever so slightly. Then the stone moved of its own accord, trembled like a leaf in a gale, and flopped to the side. Underneath the stone was a deep, dark hole. I peered inside, and called, "Da?"

"Anya?"

"Da!"

I went flat on my belly and thrust my hand as far into the hole as it would go. "Da, grab on!"

I felt a set of fingers, gritty from years in the ground, wrap around my wrist. Christopher latched onto my waist and together we hauled my Da, the legendary Bodach himself, up and out of his dark prison.

"Och, it's bright," Da said, blinking in the sunlight.

"Have you really been down there in the dark this whole time?" I asked.

"Aye, that I have. Let me look at you."

I drew back, and got a good, full look at my father for the first time in more than two hundred years. He was the same as always—tall and broad, with hands the size of hams and feet so big it took a full cowhide to make him a single pair of boots—if a bit dirtier. More than my glimpse of him, he got a look at me.

"You're grown," Da said; I'd still been a girl hurtling barefoot over the fields when he'd gone away. "Anya, you are no longer my wee lass."

"Da," I said as sobs choked me. "I'm still her."

He ran his hand over my hair, cupped my chin. "Bonnie like your mum, that you are." Da glanced around the shieling. "Where is she? And who is this?" he asked, his gaze landing on Christopher.

"Christopher Stewart." He stepped forward and stuck out his hand. Da looked down at him like he was a bug. "I am with Anya."

"I recognize your voice," Da said. "You've been here before. You spoke to us through the stones."

"Yes, sir, that's true."

"That was good of you." Da faced me. "And now you will tell me where my wife is."

"She couldn't be here," I began. "Oh, Da, so very much has changed. For starters, Mum's no longer the Queen of Winter. I am."

Da nodded, his brows low over his eyes. "Well, then. I supposed we'd best set about freeing the boys, and you can share the news with all of us at once. Christopher!"

"Here, sir."

"First of all, you can dispense with calling me sir. It's Bod, or Old Man, or whatever other names we devise while in our cups. Understand?"

"I do, Bod."

Da smiled. For all that he was a bruiser, he valued a quick mind. "Good. Now, I have a great deal of sons trapped under these rocks, and my back is weak and may give out at any time. Can I count on you to help me with these boulders?"

"Absolutely." Christopher pushed up his sleeves. "Which one should we start with?"

Giant's Daughter is available wherever books are sold.

GLOSSARY

Glossary

Alchemy – a form of chemistry and speculative philosophy concerned with discovering methods for transmuting baser metals into gold, finding a universal solvent, and an elixir of life.

Anya Darach – Queen of Winter. Daughter of Cailleach Bheur/Beira and the Bodach. Partner to Christopher.

Beinn na Caillich – a hill west of Broadford on the Isle of Skye. Its name is translated into English as Hill of the Old Woman.

Bodach [BOD-ack] – a trickster or bogeyman figure in Gaelic folklore and mythology. Husband of Beira.

Cailleach Bheur/Beira [kall-EE burr/BEE-ruh] – Celtic weather deity. Personification of winter. Mother of Anya.

Carson University – an institution of higher learning in Manhattan that studies sciences, liberal arts, and theoretical magic.

Christopher Stewart – an Elizabethan scholar and bestselling author, and older brother of Karina. Partner to Anya.

Colleen Worley – administrative assistant for the earth sciences division at Carson University. Karina Stewart's best friend.

Cornucopia [kôrn(y)əˈkōpēə] – a symbol of plenty consisting of a goat's horn overflowing with flowers, fruit, and corn.

Daedalus – the father of Icarus.

Demeter [dɪ-MEE-tər] — in Greek mythology, Demeter is the goddess of the harvest and agriculture, who presided over grains and the fertility of the earth.

Dob's Linn – a site near Moffat, Scotland. It is the location of the Global Boundary Stratotype Section and Point which marks the boundary between the Ordovician and Silurian periods.

Doon Hill – a hill near Aberfoyle, Scotland that some believe to be a gateway to Elphame. Some believe that Robert Kirk is still imprisoned in the Minister's Pine at the crest of the hill.

Drakaina [dra-KAY-na] — a female serpent or dragon, sometimes with human-like features.

Elphame [el-faym] – Fairlyand; abode of the fairies.

Fairy ointment – an ointment applied to a mortal's eyes that allows them to see fairies in their true form.

Fash – to worry, trouble, or bother.

Fath-fidh [fath fee] – a spell to keep things close, yet hidden.

Fionnlagh [fin-lay] – the Seelie King.

Fuath [fuə] – malevolent water spirits. Their name literally means "hate" in Gaelic.

Gail Berkley — head of the earth sciences division at Carson University. Karina Stewart's mentor.

Gallowglass [gal-oh-glas] – a heavily armed mercenary soldier. In Elphame, the gallowglass is the Seelie Queen's personal assassin.

Geas [geSH] – (in Irish folklore) an obligation or prohibition magically imposed on a person.

Glamour [glam-er] – an illusion that conceals flaws or distractions.

Good People – a euphemism for fairies.

Habetrot [hay-*beh*-trot] – an imp concerned with household chores.

Hades [hay-DEEZ] — the ancient Greek chthonic god of the underworld, which eventually took his name.

Haver [hey-ver] – to equivocate; vacillate.

Heracles [HERR-ə-kleez] — Gatekeeper of Olympus. God of strength, heroes, sports, athletes, health, agriculture, fertility, trade, oracles and divine protector of mankind.

Icarus – son of Daedalus. He died when he flew too close to the sun and the wax portions of his wings—constructed by his father in an escape attempt—melted.

Jared St. Lawrence — student at Carson University.

Karina Stewart – an American geology studying at Carson University and the only living walker. Younger sister of Chris, partner to Robert, mother of Faith.

Ken [ken] – knowledge, understanding, or cognizance.

Kirk [kurk] – a church.

Leannan sìth [leh-nan shee] – a fairy woman who acts as a muse and offers inspiration to an artist in exchange for love and devotion. In time, she siphons off all of the artist's creativity.

Leprechaun [lep-*ruh*-kawn, -kon] – an Irish dwarf or sprite employed in making or mending shoes.

Loch [lok] – a lake.

Mares of Diomedes — also called the Mares of Thrace, were man-eating horses in Greek mythology.

Maelgwyn [MAIL gwyn] – the Unseelie King.

Nemeton [neh-*meh*-ton] – places sacred to the old Celtic religion, primarily trees but also including temples and shrines.

Nessus — a centaur who was killed by Heracles, and whose tainted blood in turn killed Heracles.

Nicnevin [nik-*neh*-van] – the Seelie Queen.

Persephone [per-SEH-fə-nee] — goddess of the underworld, springtime, flowers, and vegetation.

Phooka [poo-KA] – considered to be bringers both of good and bad fortune, they could either help or hinder rural and marine communities.

<u>Robert Kirk</u> – currently the gallowglass. Before that, he was a minister, Gaelic scholar, and folklorist, best known for writing *The Secret Commonwealth of Elves, Fauns, and Fairies*. Partner to Karina, father of Faith.

<u>Seelie Court</u> – the home of the light or good fairies.

<u>Sgian dubh</u> [skeen doov] – a small, single-edged blade.

<u>Sorcha</u> – a woman Chris meets in a pub, and proceeds to have a relationship with.

<u>Tantallon Castle</u> – a semi-ruined mid-14th-century fortress in East Lothian, Scotland. It sits atop a promontory opposite the Bass Rock, looking out onto the Firth of Forth.

<u>Teind</u> [tend] – a tribute due to be paid by the fairies to the devil every seven years.

<u>Transmutation Regulations</u> – regulation passed during the Industrial Revolution limiting the practice of alchemy in the US.

<u>Udane</u> – the Summer King. He was dethroned by the Bodach.

<u>Wight</u> [wahyt] – a small, winged fairy commonly found in gardens.

<u>William Hargill</u> – dean of the English department at Carson University.

ABOUT THE AUTHOR

Jennifer Allis Provost is a native New Englander who lives in a sprawling colonial along with her beautiful and precocious twins, a dog that thinks she's a kangaroo, a parrot, a junkyard cat, and a wonderful husband who never forgets to buy ice cream. As a child, she read anything and everything she could get her hands on, including a set of encyclopedias, but fantasy was always her favorite. She spends her days drinking vast amounts of coffee, arguing with her computer, and avoiding any and all domestic behavior.

Find Jenn on the web here: http://authorjenniferallisprovost.com/

For up to the minute sale notifications, follow her on Bookbub here: https://www.bookbub.com/profile/jennifer-allis-provost

For exclusive content, follow her on Patreon: https://www.patreon.com/jenniferallisprovost/

Friend her on Facebook: http://www.facebook.com/jennallis

Follow her on Instagram: @jenniferaprovost

Happy reading!

ALSO BY JENNIFER ALLIS PROVOST

The Chronicles of Parthalan, a six volume epic fantasy (and one short story collection)

Heir to the Sun

The Virgin Queen

Rise of the Deva'shi

Pieces of Parthalan: Six All-New Stories From The Land Of Parthalan

Golem

Elfsong

Sunfall

The Copper Legacy, a four book urban fantasy:

Copper Girl

Copper Ravens

Copper Veins

Copper Princess

A duology based in the Copper world:

Redemption

Salvation

Poison Garden, an urban fantasy filled with seers, witches, and one seriously hot detective:

Belladonna

Oleander

Bleeding Hearts

Thornapple

Wolfsbane

Mistletoe

Mandrake

Gallowglass, an urban fantasy set in Scotland and New York:

Gallowglass

Walker

Homecoming

Winter's Queen, an urban fantasy set in Scotland and Elphame:

Touch of Frost

Giant's Daughter

Elphame's Queen

Merrowkin, an urban fantasy set in Ireland above and below

Merrowkin

Death's Door

Manannán's Pearl

Changes, a contemporary romance:

Changing Teams

Changing Scenes

Changing Fate

Changing Dates